MAIRELON
THE
MAGICIAN

Patricia C. Wrede

A TOM DOHERTY ASSOCIATES BOOK
NEW YORK

NOTE: If you purchased this book without a cover you should be aware that this book is stolen property. It was reported as "unsold and destroyed" to the publisher, and neither the author nor the publisher has received any payment for this "stripped book."

This is a work of fiction. All the characters and events portrayed in this book are either products of the author's imagination or are used fictitiously.

MAIRELON THE MAGICIAN

Copyright © 1991 by Patricia C. Wrede

All rights reserved, including the right to reproduce this book, or portions thereof, in any form.

A Starscape Book
Published by Tom Doherty Associates, LLC
175 Fifth Avenue
New York, NY 10010

www.starscapebooks.com

ISBN: 0-765-34232-4

Originally published in hardcover by Tor Books, 1991

First Starscape edition: April 2002

Printed in the United States of America

0 9 8 7 6 5 4 3 2 1

There was a violent, soundless explosion and Kim was flung backward against the cupboards on the other side of the wagon. Through a haze of violet light, she saw the lid of the trunk slowly close itself. Purple spots danced before her eyes, then spread out to cover her entire field of vision. Her last coherent thought, as the purple deepened into black unconsciousness, was an angry curse directed at the toff waiting for her in the public house. Five pounds wasn't anywhere near enough pay for snooping on a *real* magician.

Don't get left behind!

STARSCAPE

Let the journey begin . . .

From the Two Rivers
The Eye of the World: Part One
by Robert Jordan

To the Blight
The Eye of the World: Part Two
by Robert Jordan

Ender's Game
by Orson Scott Card

Jumper
by Steven Gould

Briar Rose
by Jane Yolen

The Cockatrice Boys
by Joan Aiken

Dogland
by Will Shetterly

And look for . . .

Ender's Shadow (5/02)
by Orson Scott Card

Wildside (9/02)
by Steven Gould

The Whispering Mountain (5/02)
by Joan Aiken

The One-Armed Queen (9/02)
by Jane Yolen

Orvis (6/02)
by H. M. Hoover

Jumping Off the Planet (10/02)
by David Gerrold

The Garden Behind the Moon (6/02)
by Howard Pyle

The College of Magics (10/02)
by Caroline Stevermer

Deep Secret (11/02)
by Diana Wynne Jones

The Dark Side of Nowhere (7/02)
by Neal Shusterman

City of Darkness (11/02)
by Ben Bova

Sister Light, Sister Dark (7/02)
by Jane Yolen

Prince Ombra (8/02)
by Roderick MacLeish

The Magician's Ward (12/02)
by Patricia C. Wrede

White Jenna (8/02)
by Jane Yolen

Another Heaven, Another Earth (12/02)
by H. M. Hoover

MAIRELON
THE
MAGICIAN

SHATFORD LIBRARY

FEB   2004

PASADENA CITY COLLEGE
1570 E. COLORADO BLVD
PASADENA, CA 91106

ONE

Kim walked slowly through the crowd, slipping in and out of the traffic almost without thinking. She enjoyed the noise and bustle common to all the London markets, but Hungerford was her favorite. Though it was small by comparison to Covent Garden or Leadenhall, it was very busy. Carts stood hub-to-hub along the sides of the street, leaving only narrow aisles for the customers. The more fortunate among the sellers had permanent stalls; others displayed their shoes or brooms or baskets on bare strips of pavement. Still others walked through the crowd with baskets of turnips, apples, parsnips, onions, or cress, crying their wares in unmusical voices.

Kim let the flow of traffic carry her closer to the market's most recent addition, eyeing it with a mingling of curiosity and professional appraisal. It was a wagon painted in sunbleached yellow and gold, its tall red wheels half hidden by the stalls on either side. Two large doors made up the end of the wagon that faced the street, and they were fastened with a rusty padlock. The doors carried a rough painting of a man in a black top hat, with a string of incomprehensible but decorative letters just below him.

The wagoneer had bagged one of the best spots in the market, right between Jamie the Tailor and Red Sal's fish stand. Kim frowned. Sal was a good sort, but she wouldn't take kindly to having Kim lighten a wagon next to her. Even if "lightening" wasn't exactly what Kim planned to do. Jamie was more irritable but not so noticing. Kim's frown deepened. She wondered, not for the first time, whether she'd been wise to take this job. Toffs were trouble, no two ways, and a toff knowing enough to find Kim in the back streets of London . . .

Firmly Kim brought her mind back to the business at hand. The wagon was close enough to Red Sal's to have scraped the paint off the side of the stall, had there been any paint to scrape. Small as she was, Kim would never be able to squeeze through. She'd have to go in past Jamie's, then, and time things so he was busy with a customer. She looked at the wagon with misgiving.

A man came around the corner of the wagon and began undoing the latches at the rear. He was tall and thin and everything about him seemed to droop, from his baggy trousers to his sloping shoulders to the brim of his slouch hat. Even his mustache drooped, and as he worked he chewed absently first on one end and then the other.

The doors swung open, and Kim blinked in surprise. The entire rear end of the wagon was occupied by a tiny stage. A faded red curtain separated the back of the stage from the wagon's interior. Kim forgot her eventual goal and slid closer, fascinated. The droopy man swung a small ladder down at the right side of the stage and latched it in place, then climbed onto the stage itself. He vanished behind the curtain, only to reappear a moment later carrying a table, which he set carefully in the middle of the stage. Then he began hanging lanterns on either side.

A crowd began to collect around the end of the wagon, drawn by the curious spectacle of something being set up in the market in complete silence. Some of the bystanders offered comments as the lanterns were hung and lit—"Waste o' good oil, that," and "Bit crooked, ain't she?" The droopy man chewed on his mustache, but gave no sign that he had heard.

He finished his work and disappeared once more behind the curtain. For a long moment there was no further activity, and the small crowd murmured in disappointment. Before they could begin to drift away, there was a loud crash, and a thick cloud of white smoke enveloped the stage.

"Come one, come all!" called a ringing voice from the center of the smoke. "Prepare to be amazed and astonished by the one, the only—Mairelon the Magician!"

With the last words, the smoke dissipated. In the center of the stage stood a man. His hair was dark above a rounded face, and he had a small, neat mustache but no beard. He wore a black opera cape and a top hat, which made it difficult to assess his height; Kim judged him middling tall. His right hand held a silver-headed walking stick. "Another toff!" Kim thought with disgust. She did not for a moment believe that he was a real magician; if he were, he would never waste his time working the market. Still, she felt a twinge of uneasiness.

The man held his pose for a moment, then threw back

his cape. "I am Mairelon the Magician!" he announced. "Lend me your attention and I will show you wonders. The knowledge of the East and the West is mine, and the secrets of the mysterious cults of Africa and India! Behold!"

Mairelon pulled a silk handkerchief from his pocket and displayed both sides. "A perfectly ordinary handkerchief— as ordinary, that is, as the finest silk may be. Stuff of such worth should be kept close." The crowd chuckled as he stuffed it into his closed fist and it vanished.

"Dear me, I seem to have lost it in spite of my efforts," the magician went on, opening his fist. "Now, where . . . ah!"

He reached down toward a pretty muffin-maid standing in front of the stage and pulled the handkerchief out of her bonnet. A string of colored scarves came with it, knotted end-to-end. Mairelon frowned. "Now, what am I to do with all of these?" he mused. Carefully he folded them into a compact ball and wrapped the ball in the white handkerchief. When he shook it out, the scarves were gone.

The flow of chatter continued as Mairelon borrowed a penny from a man in the crowd and made it pass through his handkerchief, then vanish and reappear. He pulled an egg from behind another man's ear, broke it into his hat, then reached into the hat and removed a live dove. He covered it briefly with his cloak, then drew the cloak aside to reveal a large wicker cage with the dove inside. He placed cage and dove on the floor of the stage and gestured with his walking stick, and they vanished in a puff of smoke and flame. He showed the crowd a shallow bowl and had one of the barrow boys fill it with water, then dropped a sheet of paper in and pulled out ten tiny Chinese lanterns made of folded paper.

Kim watched the show with unabashed enjoyment. Near the end, the droopy man reappeared, carrying an ancient tambourine. As Mairelon finished his performance, his companion circulated among the crowd, collecting pennies and shillings from the onlookers.

Reluctantly Kim pulled her mind away from the fascinating sight of Mairelon the Magician juggling eggs that, as they passed between his agile fingers, changed from white to red to blue to yellow in rapid succession. This was the first time both men had been outside at once, and she had to know how long the wagon would be empty.

She started singing "Darlin' Jenny" in her head to mark the time, and scowled in irritation. Her dislike for this job was growing stronger every minute. Nicking a purse or pocket watch from the swells in the High Street had never bothered her, but she'd always hated working the markets. Hungerford was the nearest she'd had to a home since old Mother Tibb dangled from the nubbing cheat, and even if all she had to do this time was a bit of snooping, it felt the same as nabbing a haddock from Red Sal's stand when her back was turned. Kim contemplated conveniently forgetting to return to the public house where the toff had arranged to meet her, but the memory of the pound notes the stranger had offered held her like an iron chain.

Five pounds was a fortune by Kim's standards; she could eat well and sleep dry for months and still have enough left to replace the ragged jacket and boy's breeches she wore. If she played her cards right, she might even get out of the streets for good. It was time and past that she did so; she was, she thought, nearing seventeen, and her long-delayed growth was finally arriving. She wouldn't be able to play the boy much longer. A chill ran down her spine, and she pushed the thought, and the darker knowledge of the inevitable consequences that would follow the end of her masquerade, resolutely from her mind. Mairelon the Magician was, for the moment at least, of far greater importance than her own uncertain future.

Mairelon finished his show in a flurry of flashing knives and whirling scarves, and bowed deeply "Thank you for your attention—and for your gracious contributions." He waved at the tambourine his dour assistant carried, and the crowd chuckled. "That concludes this performance, but soon Mairelon the Magician will return to perform even more wondrous feats for your delight and astonishment! Until then, my friends!" In a second puff of smoke and flame, the magician vanished.

Kim stopped midway through the eighth verse of "Darlin' Jenny" and slipped away as the crowd began to disperse. She did not want Sal or Jamie spotting her and remembering it later. Once she was safely away from Mairelon's wagon, she breathed more easily. She couldn't do anything about the magician until the end of his next show. She had time, now, to enjoy the market.

She stopped an ancient woman in a faded kerchief and exchanged one of her carefully hoarded pennies for a bag of roasted chestnuts. She ate them slowly as she walked, savoring the taste. The unaccustomed warmth in her stomach made her feel more cheerful, though she still wasn't too keen on the idea of mucking about in Mairelon's wagon. For one thing, she didn't like the look of the skinny toff who'd hired her.

Unconsciously she flexed her fingers, making the bag rustle. Five pounds would buy a lot more than chestnuts. The skinny toff hadn't asked her to nick anything, she reminded herself, just to look around and tell him what she saw and whether the magician kept a particular bowl in his wagon. The toff had claimed it was a bet. He might even be telling the truth; swells'd bet on anything.

She stepped aside to let an oyster-seller push his barrow past. It didn't feel right. The gentry cove had been too keen on her finding that bowl. He'd gotten positively excited when he started describing it—silver, he'd said, with a lot of carvings and patterns whose details Kim had seen no reason to bother remembering.

Kim frowned. Curiosity was her besetting weakness. And five pounds was five pounds. It wasn't as if she'd be doing any harm. She finished the last of the chestnuts and stuffed the bag into one of her many pockets, in case she found a use for it later. She'd do it just the way the toff had asked: go in, look around, and slip out. Mairelon would never know anyone had been there.

And if she did happen to find that bowl, maybe she'd see what was so special about it. But she wouldn't mention it to the skinny toff. She'd collect her money and leave. She might even come back and warn Mairelon about the swell that was showing so much interest. Market folk should stick together, after all. She smiled to herself; that'd serve the skinny toff a bit of his own soup! Whistling cheerfully, she strolled off to see if the puppet show was still stopping at the far end of the market.

*　　*　　*

Evening found her lurking near Mairelon's wagon once more. This time she stood in the shadows next to Jamie's stall, leaning on one of its support posts. As the crowd grew larger, she let herself be pushed back until the open rear door of the wagon, which formed one side of Mairelon's stage, all but hid the performance from her sight.

Mairelon was as good as his word. He did not, as far as Kim could tell, repeat any of the tricks he had used in his earlier performance. This time, he made three unbroken silver rings pass through each other, locking and interlocking them in intricate patterns. He bought an apple from a passing vendor and cut it open to reveal a shilling at its core. The apple seller was promptly surrounded by hopeful customers, but his remaining wares proved disappointingly ordinary.

Meanwhile, the magician went smoothly on with his act. He borrowed a hat from one of the men in the crowd, boiled an egg in it, and returned the hat to its owner unharmed. Then he brought out a pack of playing cards and ran through a series of increasingly elaborate tricks.

Kim was so enthralled by the show that she almost missed seeing a small door open near the front of the wagon. The jingling noise of the tambourine caught her attention at last. Hastily she mashed herself flat against the side of Jamie's stall, holding one ragged sleeve up to obscure her face. Mairelon's droopy henchman glanced in her direction as he passed, but his eyes moved on once her dirty and impecunious appearance sank in.

As soon as the man had been absorbed into the audience, Kim darted for the wagon door, hoping Mairelon's show and the growing shadows would keep her from being noticed. Her luck held; no shouts followed her down the narrow aisle, and when she reached it, the door was unlocked. Kim pushed it open and half jumped, half fell into the wagon's interior, the first chorus of "Darlin' Jenny" echoing through her mind.

She paused briefly to get her breath back and look around. Once again, she found herself staring in surprise. The wagon's interior was paneled in dark wood, polished to a high gloss. Rows of cupboards ran down one side, topped by a shelf of smooth grey tile. A long chest was built into the other wall; from the neat roll of blankets at one end, Kim guessed that it doubled as a bed. Presumably the droopy man slept on the floor, or perhaps under the wagon, for she saw no sign of a second bed.

A small lamp, which Kim decided had to be pewter because it could not possibly be silver, hung near the door. Its light threw back rich highlights from the walls and cupboard doors. A wool carpet, deep red with strange designs in black and cream, covered the floor. Kim had never been anywhere half so elegant in her entire life; even the back room of Gentleman Jerry's was nothing to it.

The faded curtain at the far end of the wagon swayed as Mairelon crossed his little stage. Kim came out of her daze as she realized that the curtain was all that separated her from discovery. She could hear the magician's patter quite clearly. He would be able to hear her just as easily, should she be clumsy or careless.

Kim glanced around the wagon again, painfully aware of the need for haste. She had wasted nearly a whole verse in her musing. The cupboards were the most likely place to start. She stepped forward, like a cat stalking a particularly suspicious mouse, and opened the first door.

The cupboard was filled with dishes. Three mismatched plates and a shallow ceramic soup bowl occupied the lowest shelf; a row of china teacups hung from hooks on the bottom of the shelf above. The upper part of the cupboard contained a neat stack of copper pans, iron pots, and assorted lids. Kim took long enough to make sure there was nothing hidden in or behind any of them, then went on. Her hasty search revealed nothing of any interest in the remaining cupboards, and she turned to the long chest.

The lid did not respond to her careful tug. Closer inspection revealed a hidden lock. Kim hesitated. She had nearly three full verses of "Darlin' Jenny" left, even if she allowed herself all of the last one as a safety margin. And the skinny toff would hardly be pleased if all she had to tell him was that Mairelon the Magician kept pots in his cupboards and his chest locked. Her lips tightened, and she reached into her pocket for the stiff bit of wire she always carried.

The lock was a good one, and the overhanging wood that concealed it made her work more difficult. Two more verses of "Darlin' Jenny" went by while she twisted the wire back and forth, coaxing the tumblers into position. She was about to abandon her efforts when she heard a faint click and the lid of the chest popped up a quarter of an inch.

Kim straightened in relief and pocketed the wire. She took hold of the chest's lid and lifted, forcing herself to move slowly in case the hinges squealed. Then she held it in position with one hand and bent over to peer inside.

Piles of brightly colored silks met her eyes. Beside them were slotted wooden boxes, a bundle of tiny Chinese lanterns, several mirrors, a glass tube with a painted paper cover, a top hat, and several decks of playing cards, all arranged neatly and precisely according to some order Kim could not fathom. A few she recognized as props from Mairelon's first show, none of them looked at all like the bowl the gentry cove had gone on about. As she started to close the lid, she saw a swatch of black velvet sticking out from under a stack of neatly folded silk handkerchiefs. One last try, she thought, and brushed the silks aside.

Her hand closed on something hard and heavy, wrapped in velvet. Then there was a violent, soundless explosion and Kim was flung backward against the cupboards on the other side of the wagon. Through a haze of violet light, she saw the lid of the trunk slowly close itself. Purple spots danced before her eyes, then spread out to cover her entire field of vision. Her last coherent thought, as the purple deepened into black unconsciousness, was an angry curse directed at the toff waiting for her in the public house. Five pounds wasn't anywhere near enough pay for snooping on a *real* magician.

TWO

Kim awoke all at once. She was propped against something hard, in a semi-sitting position, and she could feel cord around her wrists and ankles. She heard voices above her and forced herself to be still, feigning unconsciousness. This was not, apparently, expected; after a moment, she heard a worried voice say, " 'Adn't 'e oughter be waking?"

"He *is* awake," said the voice of Mairelon the Magician. "He's just pretending. Come on, child, you might as well admit it. You'll have to open your eyes sooner or later."

Kim sighed and capitulated. She gave a hasty look around as she opened her eyes, in the faint hope of discovering a way out of her predicament. She was propped against the row of cupboards; one of the doors was open, presumably jarred free when she had been thrown against them. The cord that tied her looked regrettably sturdy, and the knots were unfamiliar tangles. After one glance, she abandoned any thought of slipping free while her captors' attention was elsewhere.

"Quite so," said Mairelon.

Kim looked up. Mairelon was standing next to the chest, on the opposite side of the wagon. He had removed his cloak and hat; without them, he seemed both shorter and younger than he had appeared on stage. His expression held none of the anger and annoyance Kim expected; instead, there was a gleam of something very like interest or amusement. She began to hope she would come around from this, after all.

Beside Mairelon stood the droopy man. He, too, had removed his hat, and his grey and black hair was plastered flat against his head. He alternated sour glares at Kim with nervous looks directed at Mairelon, and he was chewing continuously on one end of his mustache.

Kim looked back at Mairelon. "Proper knowin' one, ain't you?" she said in her best boyish tone.

"As far as you are concerned, not nearly so knowing as I would like to be," Mairelon replied affably.

"You going to call the nabbing culls?"

"That depends on how much you are willing to tell me."

"I got no reason to keep quiet," Kim said frankly. If the toff who'd hired her had been more open, she might have felt some obligation to keep her mouth shut, but not even an out-and-outer would expect her to protect an employer who'd withheld crucial knowledge about a job. Especially when she hadn't been too keen on it in the first place.

"Then perhaps you would explain just what you were doing in my wagon," Mairelon said.

"Lookin' about," Kim said promptly.

The droopy man snorted through the damp ends of his mustache. "Stealing, more likely."

"Quiet, Hunch," Mairelon said. He looked from Kim to the open cupboard with a speculative gleam. "Just looking?"

"That's right," Kim said firmly. "Just lookin' about."

The magician's eyes narrowed, and Kim wondered whether her reply had been too forceful for the boy she was pretending to be. It was too late to change it now, though.

"That accounts for the cupboards, I think," Mairelon said after a moment. "How did you—"

"You don't never believe 'im, do you?" the droopy man demanded.

"Hunch! Refrain from interrupting, if you please."

"And let you get yourself in a mort o' trouble from believing things you 'adn't ought to?" Hunch said indignantly. "I won't never!"

Mairelon gave his henchman an exasperated look. "Then you can go outside until I'm done."

Hunch's face took on a grim expression. "Nay."

"It's that or be silent."

The two men's eyes locked briefly; Hunch's fell. "Aye, then, I'll 'old my peace."

"Good." Mairelon turned back to Kim, who had been watching this exchange with great interest. "As I was saying, I think you've explained the cupboards. The chest is another matter. How did you open it?"

"Picked the lock."

"I find that a little difficult to believe. It's not a simple mechanism."

"Didn't have to be," Kim said, allowing herself to bristle at the implied reflection on her skill.

Mairelon raised an eyebrow. "Well, we'll leave that for the moment. Just *why* were you, er, looking about in my wagon?"

"A gentry cove at the Dog and Bull said he'd pay five pounds to know what you had in here. Said he had a bet on it."

"Did he." Mairelon and Hunch exchanged glances.

"He thought he'd gammoned me proper," Kim said. She took a perverse pleasure in betraying the toff who'd gotten her into this. "But if it was just a bet, why'd he let me talk him up to five pounds? And why was he so nattered over that wicher-bubber?"

"Wicher-bubber?" Mairelon said, looking startled, and not altogether pleased. "You mean a silver bowl?"

"That's what I said. The toff wanted me to look for it."

"Did he ask you to steal it?" Mairelon demanded, his expression tense.

"No, but I ain't saying he wouldn't of been right pleased if I'd a nicked it for him."

"There!" Hunch said. "What was I telling you? 'E's a thief."

"Look, cully, if I was a sharper, would I be telling you straight out?" Kim said, exasperated. "All I said was, I'd keep an eye out for it, and that's truth!"

"So all you agreed to do was come in, look around, and let him know whether you saw this bowl?" Mairelon said.

"That's it," Kim said. Hunch snorted, and she glared at him. "There wouldn't be no harm done, after all; just lookin' about. But he ought to of said somethin' about you being a real magician with fancy locks and exploding chests."

"What did this toff of yours look like?"

"A real swell. Top hat, and gloves better'n the ones Jamie sells, and a silk cravat." Kim shook her head in wonder that was only partly simulated. "A top hat, at the Dog and Bull."

"What color was his hair?"

"Muddy. Thin, too."

"His hair or himself?"

"Both."

Mairelon nodded, as if he had expected that answer. "And did he give you something to make it easier for you to get in here? And into my chest?"

"No, and I wouldn't of took it if he'd offered. I ain't no flat."

"Then suppose you show me how you managed it," Mairelon said.

Kim nodded, and the magician reached for the rope that bound her hands. Hunch made a strangling noise. Mairelon paused and looked at him with an expression of innocent inquiry.

"You're never letting 'im go?" Hunch said, plainly appalled by the idea. "You got no idea what 'e's up to!"

"I think the two of us can handle her."

Hunch bit down hard on the right side of his mustache. " *'Er?*"

"Oh, you didn't realize?" Mairelon said. He turned back to Kim while Hunch was still gaping mutely, and gave one of the loops of cord a sharp tug. The knot slid apart as though someone had greased the rope, leaving Kim's hands free. She blinked, then darted a hand forward and yanked on the cord that held her ankles.

Nothing happened. "There's a trick to it, of course," Mairelon said blandly. "I'll show you, if you like, when you've finished your own demonstration."

Kim looked up in disbelief. Mairelon was smiling in what appeared to be genuine amusement. "You will?"

"Yes. When you're finished," he added pointedly. Hunch scowled ferociously at his master's back, but did not dare voice any more criticism.

"All right, all right," Kim said. She reached into her pocket, pulled out the bit of wire, and set to work. She was fairly sure by this time that the magician would not turn her over to the constables, but instead of reassuring her, the knowledge made her even more uneasy. Why did he hesitate?

She watched Mairelon surreptitiously as she wiggled the wire. He didn't look particularly impressive, but he was no flat, that was certain. He was no ordinary street magician, either, not with the inside of his wagon done up like a gentry ken. Not to mention that thing in the chest that had blown Kim halfway across the room.

The memory slowed her fingers. True, she'd actually been poking around in the chest when the spell or whatever it was had gone off, but Mairelon could easily have changed it while she was unconscious. She had no desire to repeat the performance.

Hunch shifted impatiently. "She ain't going to get it, not with just that bit o' wire."

"Give over," Kim snarled, and twisted her wrist. Again she heard the faint click, and the lid of the chest rose fractionally. Kim lifted it open and looked triumphantly at Hunch.

"Impressive," Mairelon said. He looked at Kim thoughtfully, and the gleam of interest was back. "I didn't think anyone but old Schapp-Mussener himself could open that chest without the key."

"It's a knack," Kim said modestly.

"It's a talent, and a very impressive talent, too." The gleam became more pronounced. "I don't suppose—"

"Master Richard!" Hunch interrupted.

"Mmmm?"

"You ain't a-going to do nothing dreadful now, are you?" Hunch said in a severe tone.

"No, no, of course not," Mairelon said absently, still looking at Kim.

"Good," Hunch said, much relieved.

"I was just going to ask our guest here—what is your name, by the way?"

"Kim."

"Kim. I was just going to ask Kim here if she would like to come with us when we leave London."

Hunch bit both ends of his mustache at once. "You ain't never going to bring her along!"

"Why not?" Mairelon said in a reasonable tone. "It might be useful to have someone along who's familiar with . . . things. A lot has happened in the past four years."

"You want me to come with you, after I snuck in here and blew things around?" Kim said incredulously. "You're bosky!"

Hunch started to nod agreement, then caught himself and

glared at Kim. "You can't do it, Master Richard! She's a thief!"

"I ain't!"

"Stop it, both of you." Mairelon's voice was firm. He looked at Hunch. "I don't think Kim is a thief, though it's plain that she's had some of the training. Not that it matters."

"It do too matter! What are you going to do with 'er?"

"She could help with the act," Mairelon said. "She seems a handy sort of person."

Hunch snorted. "Ain't that what you said about that Frog 'oo sherried off with ten guineas and your best coat?"

"Yes, well, he was a little too handy. I think Kim will do much better."

"At what?"

"She could make a very useful assistant eventually. Provided, of course, that she would be willing to come along?" Mairelon looked questioningly at Kim.

"You ain't gammoning me?" Kim said suspiciously.

"No."

The single word was more convincing than Mairelon's speeches had been, but Kim still hesitated. What did he expect to get out of hauling her along with him? From the luxurious interior of the wagon, it was plain that Mairelon could afford the company of the best of the fashionable impures, if what he wanted was a doxy. He had no reason to pick a grubby imitation boy out of the market instead. And he wasn't the sort who *preferred* boys, Kim had learned long ago to spot and avoid them. So what *did* he want?

"You ain't unfastened me yet," she pointed out at last.

"An oversight." Mairelon bent and tugged at the cord that fastened Kim's ankles. Again the rope slid apart, and Mairelon straightened with a flourish. "Now, what do you say?"

"You'd really show me how to do that?" Kim asked, her mind whirling. If she could learn a few of Mairelon's tricks, she might be able to get steady work at one of the Covent Garden theaters—real work, the sort that required more than a low-cut dress and a willingness to do whatever might be asked. She could earn enough to eat regular and sleep warm without looking over her shoulder for watchmen or constables or Bow Street Runners; she could stop being afraid of Dan Laverham and his like, she could—she forced herself to cut that train of thought short, before the hope grew too strong, and waited for Mairelon's answer.

"That and quite a bit more," Mairelon said. "How else could you be any help in the act?"

"She don't look like she'll be much 'elp anyways," Hunch muttered. "Nobody's a-going to pay to watch a grimy little thief."

"Call me that once more, cully, and—"

"Enough." Mairelon's voice was quiet, but Kim found herself swallowing her words faster than she ever had for Mother Tibb's angry screeching. "Stop provoking her, Hunch."

"If you can't see what's under your nose—"

"Oh, she doesn't look like much now, but I think you'll be surprised at how well she cleans up."

"I ain't said I'm coming with you yet!" Kim said crossly.

"And you haven't said you're not, either," Mairelon replied. "Come, now; make your decision. I have things to do if you aren't."

"Huh." Kim was unimpressed. "I ain't wishful to get into no trouble with the nabbing culls. What's your lay?"

Mairelon smiled. "I'm a traveling magician. I play the markets and fairs."

"Give over! I told you, I ain't no flat. Folks that can do real magic don't waste time flashing tricks at the markets. And you ain't got yourself no wagon done up like a gentry ken that way, neither."

"That's my affair. I'll give you my word that we're doing nothing illegal; if you've other questions, you'll have to wait for answers. After all, we don't know you very well yet."

"No, nor want to," Hunch said under his breath.

Kim frowned at him automatically, but her mind was busy elsewhere. She'd never get a chance like this again, she was certain. Risking Mairelon's unknown objectives was a small price to pay for the promise of a few days' worth of regular meals and a safe place to sleep, even without the promise of tutoring. Add in the possibility of learning something that would free her from the perilous hand-to-mouth world of the London slums and Mairelon's proposal was well-nigh irresistible, especially since she'd probably never find out what the magician was really doing or what was so important about that bowl if she didn't go along. And if she didn't like it, she could always tip them the double and come back to London. She'd be no worse off than she was now.

"Well?" Mairelon asked.

"All right, then," Kim said. "I'll do it."

Hunch groaned.

"Good!" Mairelon said, ignoring Hunch. "We'll see the tailor tomorrow about getting you some clothes. We won't be long in London, so I'm afraid there won't be many of them."

"Sounds bang-up to me," Kim said. It took most of her will to sound moderately pleased instead of all but stunned speechless. Clothes from a tailor? For her?

"She'll run off as soon as she's got everything she can off you," Hunch prophesied gloomily.

Kim started to protest, but Mairelon's voice overrode her "Hunch, if you don't stop trying to pick out a quarrel with Kim, I shall be forced to leave you in London."

"You wouldn't never!" Hunch said.

"No?"

Hunch muttered something under his breath and stomped to the far end of the wagon. Mairelon looked after him and shook his head. "He'll come around, never fear. You've nothing to worry about."

"Ain't you forgetting something?" Kim said.

"What?"

"That skinny toff down at the Dog and Bull, that sent me in here lookin'. What're you going to do about *him*?"

"I think he ought to get what he's paying for," Mairelon said after due consideration. "Don't you agree?"

Kim thought of the underhanded way the skinny toff had held back information to keep the price down. "No."

"Yes, he certainly should," Mairelon said, as though he hadn't heard Kim. "I think you should go back to that place you mentioned—what was the name again?"

"The Dog and Bull."

"Of course. I think you should go back and collect your five pounds." He paused and smiled at Kim. "What do you say?"

THREE

Kim darted across a street directly in front of a hackney, causing the horses to shy. The driver's curses followed her as she slipped into the pedestrian traffic on the other side, but she paid no attention. She was late for her appointment, and she didn't know how long the skinny toff would wait.

Not that she was particularly anxious to see him again, five pounds or not. She still wasn't sure how she'd been talked into this. Maybe it was because Hunch had been so set against it; knowing how much he disliked the idea, she couldn't resist going ahead with it. Or maybe it was Mairelon's persuasiveness. The man made it all sound so *reasonable*, and he knew just how to appeal to Kim's curiosity.

That, of course, was the root of the problem. Kim dodged a lamplighter, ducking under the end of his ladder. Someday she was going to get into real trouble if she didn't stop poking her nose into things just to find out what they looked like.

Still castigating herself, Kim turned down the crooked lane that led to the Dog and Bull. Here the traffic was less, and she made better time. When she saw the cracked sign with its garish painting, she broke into a run, and a moment later she was inside. She stepped to one side of the door and paused, panting, to survey the room.

It was a moment before her eyes adjusted to the gloom. Though the single window was large, half or more of its panes had been broken and stuffed with paper, and those that remained were dark with dirt. What light there was came from the fire in the huge, blackened hearth, and it did not penetrate far into the smoke and steam that filled the air.

Three long, bare tables occupied the center of the room. The backless benches on either side were half full of large men in well-worn clothes. Most were hunched over mugs of beer; some were eating with single-minded intensity from an assortment of battered bowls. There was no sign of the toff anywhere.

Kim frowned. Had she missed him, then? There was no way of telling. She decided to take the chance that he, too, was late, and made her way to one of the tables. She squeezed herself into a corner where she could watch the door, ordered a half-pint of ale, and settled in to wait.

The procession of customers entering the room was not exactly encouraging. Most were working-class men identifiable by their clothes—carters, bricklayers, a butcher, one or two costermongers, a swayer. A nondescript man in a shabby coat slouched in and crept to the far corner of the table as if he expected to be thrown out. Kim sipped at her ale, wondering unhappily whether she should risk attracting attention by asking questions.

The door opened again, and another collection of solid men in rough-spun wool and grimy linen entered. In their wake came a tall man made even taller by his top hat. He wore a voluminous cape that made it impossible to tell whether he was fat or slim, but the white-gloved hand pressing a handkerchief to his lips was impossible to mistake. Famble-cheats and a top hat, Kim thought disgustedly, in a place like this. He was the one she was waiting for, all right. She straightened, trying to look taller so that he would see her.

The toff surveyed the room disdainfully, then made his way among the tables and stopped beside Kim. "I trust your presence means you have succeeded, boy," he said.

"I done what you asked," Kim said.

"Good. I suggest we conduct the remainder of our business in one of the private rooms in back."

"You want everyone here knowin' you got business with me?" Kim asked without moving.

The toff's face darkened in anger, but after a moment he shook his head. "No, I suppose not."

"Then you'd better set down afore everyone here ends up lookin' at you," Kim advised.

The man's lips pressed together, but he recognized the wisdom of Kim's statement. He seated himself on the bench across from her, setting his hat carefully on the table. The publican, a fat man in a dirty apron, came over at once, and the toff accepted, with some reluctance, a mug of beer. As the publican left, the toff leaned forward. "You said you'd done as I asked. You found the bowl, then? You have a list of what is in Mairelon's wagon?"

"What would the likes of me be doing makin' lists?" Kim said sarcastically.

The man looked startled. "I had anticipated—"

"You wanted a list, you should of hired a schoolmaster," Kim informed him. "I can tell you what I saw in that magic-cove's wagon, but that's all."

The man's eyes narrowed. "In that case, perhaps five pounds is more than the information is worth to me."

"In that case, you ain't getting no information at all," Kim said, mimicking his tone.

"Come, now, I think you are unreasonable. Shall we say, three pounds?"

Kim spat. "I done what you said, and you never said nothing about no list. Five pounds and that's flat."

"Oh, very well. Did you find the bowl?"

"I ain't saying nothin' until I get what you promised."

The toff argued, but Kim remained firm. Eventually he agreed, and unwillingly counted out the five pounds in notes and coin. Kim made a show of re-counting it, her fingers lingering over each coin in spite of herself. She had never had so much money at once in all her life, and every silver shilling and half crown meant another day or week of food and possible safety. She stowed the money safely in the inner pockets of her jacket, feeling highly pleased with both herself and Mairelon. If it hadn't been for the magician's urging, she might have passed up an easy mark.

"Satisfied?" the man said angrily. "All right, then, tell me what you found."

Kim smiled inwardly and launched into a detailed and exhaustive description of the interior of the magician's wagon. She noticed the anticipation on her listener's face when she talked of the pots and pans in Mairelon's cupboard, and carefully saved the information that they were all made of iron for the end of the sentence. She got a perverse satisfaction out of seeing the flash of disappointment on the toff's face.

The man got more and more impatient as she went along. Finally she mentioned the locked chest. The toff sat up. "Locked?"

"Yes." Kim paused. "But I got in."

The man leaned forward eagerly. "And?"

"It looked like that's where the cove kept his magics. There were a whole bunch of little paper lanterns, and a couple of them little wooden boxes, and a stack of silk—"

"Yes, yes, boy, but the bowl!"

"Bowl?" Kim said, feigning innocence.

"The silver bowl I described to you! Did you find it?"

"I didn't see nothin' like that in Mairelon's wagon," Kim said with perfect truth.

"What!" The toff's voice was loud enough to make heads turn all along the table. He controlled himself with effort, and when the other customers had turned away, he glared at Kim. "You said you'd do as I asked!"

"And so I have," Kim retorted, unperturbed. "Ain't nobody could of found somethin' that ain't never been there."

"Not there?" The man sounded stupefied.

"Use your head, cully," Kim advised. "If this Mairelon swell had something like that, I would of seen it, wouldn't I? And I ain't. So it ain't there."

"You're certain?"

Kim nodded.

The toff glared as though it were her fault. "Not there," he muttered. "All this time, wasted on the wrong man. Amelia will never let me hear the end of it. Merrill could be anywhere in England by now, anywhere!"

"That ain't my lookout," Kim pointed out. "You want to hear what else he had, or not?"

"And you," the toff went on in a venomous whisper, "you knew. That's why you made me give you your money in advance, isn't it? You little cheat!"

On the last word, he lunged across the table. The sudden movement took Kim completely by surprise. He would have had his hands at her throat if a grimy, disreputable-looking man had not half lurched, half fallen against the toff's back at that moment.

The unexpected shove knocked the toff heavily into the edge of the table; Kim heard his grunt of pain plainly. She stood and backed away a little, watching with interest. She recognized the grimy man now, he had come into the public house just before the toff's arrival.

The grimy man was the first to recover. "Sh-shorry, very shorry," he said. "The floor jusht, jusht shook me over, thash all." He waved a hand to demonstrate, and lost his balance again.

"Get away from me, you idiot!" the toff snarled.

"Right. Very shorry." The drunk made ineffectual apologetic motions in the toff's direction. Since he was still draped halfway over the toff's shoulder, this succeeded only in knocking over the almost untouched mug of beer in front of them. A wave of brown foam surged across the table, picking up dirt and grease as it went.

The toff made a valiant effort to spring back out of the way, but with the drunk still leaning helpfully across his shoulder, he didn't have a chance. The pool of cool, dirty beer swished into his lap, thoroughly drenching his previously immaculate attire. The taproom exploded in laughter.

The drunk began a tearful apology, which was more a lament for the wasted beer than anything else. Cursing, the toff shoved him aside. He began wiping vainly at his clothes with a pocket handkerchief while the publican escorted the drunk firmly to the door. Kim judged it a good moment for her own departure and slipped quietly out in the drunk's wake. Her last sight was of the toff, gingerly picking his dripping top hat out of the pool of beer.

Still chuckling, Kim paused in the lane outside. It was now fully dark, and a yellow fog was rising. Not the best time for running about the London streets, even for as ragged a waif as Kim looked. Still, she hadn't much choice. She swallowed hard, thinking of the coins in her pockets. If she lost them, she'd have nothing to fall back on if her arrangement with Mairelon fell apart. She started off, hugging the edge of the lane.

As she passed the corner of the Dog and Bull, a pair of dirty, beer-scented hands grabbed her. One clamped itself over her mouth, the other pinned her arms. Kim threw herself forward, but the man was too strong. She was dragged quickly and quietly into a filthy alley beside the public house.

She kicked backward, hard, and connected. The man made no sound, but his grip loosened, and Kim wrenched one arm free. She bit down on the hand covering her mouth and felt her captor jerk. Then she heard a whisper almost directly in her ear. "Kim! Stop it! It's Mairelon."

Without thinking, Kim struck at the voice with her free hand. Then the words penetrated, and she hesitated. She couldn't imagine what Mairelon might be doing in this part of town, but magicians were a queer lot, and she'd already decided that Mairelon was one of the queerest of them all. And who else would expect that name to have any weight with her?

"It really is me, unlikely as it seems," the whisper said. "If I let go, you won't make a sound until you're sure, will you? Nod if you agree."

Kim nodded, and the hands released their hold. She turned and found herself confronting the drunk who had caused so much trouble a few minutes before. He no longer seemed drunk in the least, though he still looked and smelled thoroughly unpleasant.

Kim took a step backward. The man raised a warning hand and she stopped, peering at him. He was the right height for Mairelon, but he had no mustache and his face was half hidden by a layer of greasy dirt. Then he grinned, and Kim's doubts vanished. Impossible as it seemed, this *was* Mairelon.

She smiled back and he doffed his grimy cap and bowed with a stage magician's flourish. She opened her mouth to ask what he was doing, and at once he held up a warning finger. She stepped closer, wondering even more what was behind his strange behavior.

The creak of the public house door swinging open filtered into the alley. Mairelon flattened himself into a niche along one wall and motioned to Kim to do the same. She complied, still puzzled. Then she heard the skinny toff's unmistakable whine.

"—don't expect such treatment! You haven't heard the end of this!"

"Mebbe," the gravelly voice of the publican said. "And mebbe not. Evenin'."

Kim heard the door shut, then the toff muttering curses under his breath. A moment later came the incongruous sound of a small silver bell, ringing.

A large shadow passed the mouth of the alley. "There you are, Stuggs!" the toff said pettishly. "Did you catch the boy?"

"I ain't seen 'im," said a deep, slow voice.

"Not seen him? But he left just a few minutes ago."

"I ain't seen 'im," the second voice reiterated patiently.

"You fool! He must have gone the other way."

"Couldn't 'ave. Street's blocked."

"Then he slipped by you in the dark. Idiot! Nothing has gone right tonight, simply nothing! We've spent five days tracing the wrong man, my clothes are ruined, and on top of everything else you let the boy escape!"

"I never seen 'im. If I'd seen 'im, I'd a catched 'im."

"Oh, well. Under the circumstances, it hardly matters. But if it *bad* been Merrill's wagon, we would have needed the boy. You're lucky."

Something in the man's voice made Kim shrink back against the wall of the building, trying to become one with the bricks and half-timbering. Why were they so interested in her? Surely five pounds wasn't worth such trouble to a swell!

"You want I should look for 'im?" Stuggs's deep voice said, and Kim held her breath.

"Weren't you listening? There's no need; he didn't find anything. And I'm not going to stand here smelling like a brewery while you blunder about. Come on."

Footsteps clicked against the cobblestones, passing the end of the alley. Gradually they died away, but Kim did not move until she heard the distant rattle of carriage wheels. Then she looked across at Mairelon.

The magician motioned to her and started off, but instead of heading back out to the lane, he went farther into the alley. Kim followed with some trepidation. The cramped maze of garbage-strewn alleys that twisted through the spaces between the main streets was no place for anyone who didn't know where he was going.

Mairelon, however, chose his course without hesitation, and in a few minutes they emerged on a side street two blocks from the Dog and Bull. "You can talk now," he said.

FOUR

im was silent for a moment, trying to decide what to ask first. "Why was that skinny toff so wishful to get his dabbers on me?" she said finally, starting with the question which was of the greatest personal interest.

"I rather think he was afraid you might come and tell me what he'd been doing," Mairelon replied.

Kim did a quick review of the conversation they'd overheard. "He thinks you're this Merrill cove?"

"Not any more," Mairelon said cheerfully. He tipped his cap to a heavily rouged, overblown woman in an exceedingly low-cut gown. She eyed his shabby raiment and wrinkled her nose, then hurried past in search of more promising customers.

"So that's why you was so set on me gammoning the cull I'd done what he wanted," Kim said. She looked at Mairelon thoughtfully. "Are you?"

"Am I what?"

"Are you Merrill?"

" 'What's in a name? that which we call a rose by any other name would smell as sweet.' "

"Huh?" Kim said, thoroughly confused.

"Not literary, I take it? No, of course not, you wouldn't be. We shall have to do something about that."

"About what?"

"Teaching you to read."

"Read?" Kim's eyes widened, and she stopped short. "Me?"

"Why not? It's bound to be useful. Come along; you don't want to spend the night standing in the street, do you?"

Kim nodded and started walking again. It was a moment before the novelty of the idea wore off and she realized that she had been very neatly distracted from her original question. She scowled and kicked a pebble. It skittered over the cobblestones and disappeared into the damp and foggy darkness in the middle of the street.

Mairelon looked across at her and raised an eyebrow. Kim's scowl deepened. "You knew all that was going to happen!" she said accusingly.

"Hardly. I was suspicious, that's all."

"Then what were you doin' down at the Dog and Bull?"

"I was looking out for you," Mairelon said promptly.

"I don't need no lookin' out for," Kim retorted. She was suddenly tired of all these swells talking her into things without telling her enough about them first. Of course, her own curiosity was at least as much to blame as Mairelon, but that only made her more irritable.

"I'm inclined to agree," Mairelon said. He raised his

hand and touched his right eye gingerly. "I believe you blacked my eye with that last swing."

"Too bad," Kim said callously. "It wouldn't of happened if you'd of told me you'd be there."

"If I'd told you I was planning to follow you, you would have told me to be off about my own business," Mairelon pointed out. "Which, as things turned out, wouldn't have been at all wise, now, would it?"

"Huh." Kim couldn't contradict him, but she wasn't willing to admit it.

"Besides, it wouldn't have been at all the thing to have sent you off into trouble without warning you *and* without sending along anyone to help in case there was trouble."

"Then why didn't you warn me?"

"About what? I wasn't *sure* anything was going to happen. And would you have listened?"

"If you would of explained—" Kim started with some heat, then stopped, her brain working rapidly. Mairelon had caught her rifling his wagon; he would have had to be very stupid to give her any explanations without learning more about her first. And however careless he might seem, he was not stupid. The thought crossed her mind that he had been watching to see whether she would tell the skinny toff the whole truth about what she had found in his wagon.

Curiously, the idea that he had been testing her drained away most of her anger. Caution was a thing she understood; if she wanted Mairelon's trust, she would have to earn it. She wasn't about to admit she knew it, though. "You shouldn't of gone," she said grumpily.

Mairelon gave her a quizzical look. "I couldn't let you

go alone, and there was no other choice. I simply couldn't send Hunch."

Kim stared at Mairelon. Then her mind brought up a picture of Hunch, drooping over the skinny toff's shoulder and chewing on his mustache while he tried to tip over a beer mug. It was too much for her sense of humor, she burst into laughter. "No, I guess you couldn't. I bet he didn't want you goin' off in them flash togs, neither."

"You're right about that," Mairelon replied cheerfully. He raised his hand to touch his eye again, and winced. "He's going to be simply delighted about this, I'm sure."

"Not hardly he won't."

"He'll say it's what I deserve for going off without him. He may, just possibly, be right," the magician added thoughtfully.

"You goin' to tell him how you got it?" Kim said.

Mairelon looked at her and blinked; then he grinned. "Oh, I see. I hadn't thought of that." The grin widened, giving him a strong resemblance to a mischievous small boy. "Well, such things happen quite frequently in taverns, particularly the less respectable ones. I don't think there'll be any need to go into details, do you?"

Kim shrugged, sternly suppressing a flicker of relief. "It don't matter to me."

"Quite so," Mairelon said gravely. They walked a block in silence, watching the heavy, wide-wheeled drays clatter by over the cobblestones. Then they turned a corner and the sights and sounds of the Hungerford market washed up to greet them.

To Kim's surprise, Mairelon did not go directly to his wagon. Instead, he led Kim around the fringe of the market

to a cramped alley. He paused in the shadows, watching
the lamplit shops. Though the twists of the buildings hid
them from sight, Kim could hear the calls of the costermongers clearly. It was a good place to hide; Kim had used
it herself a couple of times. She was surprised that Mairelon
knew it.

Kim heard a scratching sound behind her and tensed.
Mairelon smiled and turned, his shoulders brushing flakes
of paint off the building on his right. A moment later,
Hunch appeared from an even skinnier opening near the
back of the alley.

"Well timed, Hunch!" Mairelon said in a low voice.
"You brought everything?"

"Right 'ere," Hunch said, lifting a large canvas bag in
one hand and scowling as if he wished he could disasso-
ciate himself from such undignified proceedings.

"Good!" Mairelon stripped off his cap and dropped it,
then pulled off his tattered jacket. He wiped his face and
hands on the shreds of lining, which seemed relatively
clean, then dropped the jacket on top of the cap and begin
pulling off his heavy workman's boots.

"Master Richard!" Hunch's voice was not loud, but it
expressed volumes of scandalized disapproval.

Mairelon paused and looked up. "What is it?"

"You ain't never going to just—" Hunch stopped and
looked at Kim. "Not with 'er standing there!"

"Oh, is that all that's bothering you?" Mairelon looked
at Kim and grinned. "Turn your back, child; you're offending Hunch's proprieties."

Kim flushed, as much from surprise as embarrassment,

and turned away. "I ain't no child," she muttered under her breath.

"Under the circumstances, that's so much the worse," Mairelon replied cheerfully.

Kim snorted. She could hear various scraping and rustling noises behind her, and Hunch muttering through his mustache. She frowned, certain that at least some of the mutterings were derogatory comments directed at her. She couldn't quite hear them, and after a moment she was glad. If she knew what Hunch was saying, she would have had to answer in kind, and she couldn't see arguing with someone while her back was turned. It was too much of a disadvantage.

The rustlings stopped, and Mairelon said, "There, that's better. You can turn around now."

Kim did, and blinked. Mairelon still smelled faintly of beer, but otherwise he was once more the well-dressed stage magician she had first seen. Top hat, cape, mustache—mustache? "How'd you do that?" Kim demanded.

"The mustache?" Mairelon said. "Spirit gum and horsehair. It isn't crooked, is it?"

"Not as I can see," Kim replied.

"Good! I was wondering; it's a bit tricky to do without a mirror. Still, it only has to last until we get back to the wagon."

"What about them things you was wearing?" Hunch demanded. "You 'adn't ought to be leaving them 'ere."

"No, I suppose not," Mairelon said, nudging the little pile of dirty, beer-scented clothing he had been wearing. He glanced at Hunch's face and turned to Kim. "Can you get rid of them?"

"I could pitch them in the river," Kim offered, eyeing the clothes almost as dubiously as Hunch.

"No, no, sell them somewhere or give them away. Preferably not in this market."

"Huh. You don't expect much," Kim muttered, but she picked up the clothes and wadded them into a compact bundle. The boots were in fairly good shape; she might actually be able to turn a few shillings on them.

"We'll see you at the wagon in an hour or so, then," Mairelon said. He smiled as he followed Hunch out the back of the alley.

Kim whistled softly through her teeth as she finished making up the bundle. The secondhand clothes dealers on Petticoat Lane ought to fit Mairelon's requirements. Tom Correy would be the best; he was sure to take the clothes in order to get the boots. He'd think Kim had stolen them, so he wouldn't pay much, but he wouldn't ask questions, either. It evened out.

She swung the bundle to her back and hesitated. Mairelon had sounded casual enough, but he'd nonetheless been taking fairly extreme precautions against being seen. Maybe she should do the same. She slipped easily through the crack at the back of the alley and worked her way among the courtyards to the street.

She was turning to head for Petticoat Lane when she remembered the money she'd collected in the Dog and Bull. Tom was a good fellow, but some of his customers weren't. She didn't want to lose her five pounds before she'd even gotten used to the idea of having them.

Changing direction, she circled the market until she came to the hidey-hole where she spent most of her nights. It was little more than a few rotting boards leaning against a tenement, but it provided privacy and a minimum of shelter. Kim wormed her way inside, then set about redistributing her newfound wealth. She buried a few shillings in the corner of the hidey-hole and slipped a few more into her shoes.

After some consideration, she tore a strip of cloth from the bottom of the shirt Mairelon had been wearing and bound the rest of the coins tightly around her bare waist. She pulled her own shirt down over the resulting lumpy wrap and belted her breeches. She studied the effect, then smiled and patted her belt with a sense of satisfaction. In the dark, and with her jacket over the top of everything, even old Mother Tibb would have been hard put to notice anything unusual.

She rebundled the clothes and set off. Near Holborn Hill she swung herself onto the rear end of a farmer's wagon that was heading in the right direction. She hunched down behind the hay, clinging to the backboard and hoping she would not be noticed. Her luck held; not only did the wagon continue east, but the driver did not see her until she jumped off. She darted into the gloom, pursued by his angry cries. He'd settle down once he realized that all she'd stolen was a ride.

Petticoat Lane was only a few minutes' walk. Tom's shop was closed, but Kim had expected as much. She slid around to the rear of the building and rapped at the weathered oak door. She had to repeat her knock before a stocky, grizzled man opened the door and peered out at her. " 'Oo's that?"

"Kim. I got somethin' for Tom."

"Ah. Inside, then." The man stepped back and Kim lifted her bundle and followed him in.

The back room of Tom's secondhand shop was a mess, as usual. Clothes were piled carelessly in every corner and stacked on top of the single chair. Kim saw everything from a laborer's homespun smock to a tattered but undeniably silk cravat.

Four men were seated on crates around the rickety table in the center of the room. The tin cups and the reek of gin made it clear what they had been doing before Kim's arrival; just at the moment they were staring at her. Two of them were as unknown to Kim as the doorkeeper. The third was Tom's brother-in-law Jack Stower, a dirty dish if Kim had ever seen one. He'd never had much use for her, either.

The last person at the table was a grey-haired man with squinty eyes, wearing a dark grey coat and a linen cravat. Kim stiffened. "Dan Laverham!" she blurted. What was that flash cull doing in Tom's back room? For all he carried himself like Quality, he could call up half the canting crew from Covent Garden to the Tower of London if he had a need for them.

"Kim, dear boy, how good to see you," the grey-haired man replied. His eyes raked her apparel, and she was suddenly very, very glad she had hidden her money so carefully before setting out. Dan would think nothing of ordering his men to strip her of her hard-won gains, if he knew of them.

"Been a long time," Kim offered, keeping her tone noncommittal. Dan was a bad one to offend. He was smart and smooth, and he'd hold on to a grudge until the moon turned blue. She suspected that he was the one who'd turned stag and peached on Mother Tibb to the constables, though he was too clever to have acted openly.

"That it has," Dan said, leaning back on his crate as though he sat in a tall, straight-backed chair. "And to what do I owe the good fortune of your arrival?"

"Say 'e's got sommat for Tom," the doorkeeper said.

"Then, my dear, go and fetch him," Dan replied. The doorkeeper grunted and clumped up the stairs. Dan looked at Kim. "Do join us," he said, and waved at the table.

Kim shook her head. "I ain't got time," she lied.

Jack Stower shifted so that his crate creaked alarmingly. "Think you're too good to have a drop of Blue Ruin with your friends, eh?" he mumbled.

It was on the tip of Kim's tongue to retort that he, at least, was no friend of hers, but caution restrained her. Gin made Jack's uncertain temper positively explosive, and she doubted that the other men would intervene if Jack started something. She tried to make her voice placating as she said, "It ain't that. I got to meet a man down by the docks in less'n an hour, and I ain't going to finish with Tom in time as it is."

Jack started to reply angrily, but Dan put a hand on his arm and he subsided at once. "An appointment on the docks?" Dan said. "That's a bit out of your usual way, isn't it?"

Kim shrugged, wishing the doorkeeper would come back with Tom. "I go where the pay is."

"Not always, my dear, or you would have accepted my generous offer," Dan said, watching her with bright, penetrating eyes.

"I like bein' on my own," Kim said shortly. And she

strongly disliked the idea of falling into Dan's clutches. He'd have her forking purses off the market crowds during the day without regard for her scruples, and once he discovered her sex she'd spend her nights in the stews. Kim had no illusions about that sort of life. Let alone she had no taste for it, she'd be lucky not to end swinging from the nubbing cheat as Mother Tibb had.

"Well, let it pass," Dan said, waving a hand. "But tell me, what has lured you to Tom Correy's establishment tonight?"

"Bilking old Tom out of a tog and kicks, I'd say," Jack muttered.

"Quietly, my dear." Dan's voice was velvet-smooth. Jack shot him a glance of mingled fear and resentment, but he did not speak again. Dan gave Kim a look of polite inquiry.

"I got business with Tom," Kim told him.

"Really." Dan's eyes shifted to the bundled clothes dangling from Kim's right hand, then back to her face. "Not back on the sharping lay by any chance, are you, dear boy?"

"No, nor I ain't goin' to be, neither."

"I can give you a better price than Tom, if you've any trinkets to dispose of," the man persisted.

Kim suppressed a scowl. Dan had been trying to get a handle on her for a long time. He was obviously hoping that greed would get the better of her sense. She shook her head. "I ain't got nothin' in your line, Dan."

"Pity. You're quite sure—"

The creaking of the stairs interrupted as Tom Correy came down them, followed closely by the doorkeeper. Tom scowled at the gin drinkers, but his face lit up when he saw

Kim. "Kim, lad! Where've you been keeping yourself?"

"Around," Kim said with deliberate vagueness. She didn't grudge Tom the knowledge, but there were too many interested and not entirely friendly ears present to overhear.

"You come for another coat?"

"What'd I say?" Jack muttered.

"Quiet, you," Tom said without looking. "It's my shop and I'll run it my way, see? And the boy looks like he could do with a jacket."

"I ain't after one," Kim said hastily.

Jack snorted and gulped at his cup. Tom looked at her. "What, then?"

"I got some stuff for you to look at. Here." Kim crouched and undid the bundle.

"Where'd you come by this?" Tom said, studying the untidy pile with disfavor.

"Got it off a bingo-boy up by Spitalfields," Kim said glibly. "What'll you give me for 'em?"

Tom knelt and examined the clothes more closely. "They ain't much."

"Those're good boots," Kim pointed out quickly. "Some people would give three shillings just for the boots."

"Three shillings? You must think I'm as lushy as that lot," Tom said, waving towards the table. "I'll give you a bender for the whole pile."

"Sixpence ain't enough," Kim said stubbornly. "Two shillings ninepence."

Dan and his cohorts soon lost interest in the bargaining and began a muttered conversation of their own, punctuated by frequent passage of the gin bottle. Kim watched them warily from the corner of her eye while she dickered. Jack was thoroughly castaway, and one or two of the others looked at least a little lushy. Dan, however, was being careful not to get the malt above water; though he passed the bottle and refilled cups with a comradely air, he himself drank little. And several times, Kim saw him watching her.

By the time she had finished her bargaining and collected one-and-sixpence from Tom, Kim was worried. She bade Tom a cordial goodbye and the drinkers a polite one, then stepped out into the cool, damp night. As the door closed behind her, she took a deep breath to clear the gin fumes from her head. The fog had thickened; the streetlamp by the shopfront was a dim smear of yellow light, blurred by the veil of moisture in the air.

Whistling softly, Kim started down Petticoat Lane. Half a block from Tom's, she cut sharply to the left. She hunted along the backs of the shops until she found one with a drainpipe she could climb, then shinnied up it. She crept to the front of the building and lay flat, peering down at the street.

A moment later a man came skulking down the street from the direction of Tom's shop. She couldn't make out his face in the foggy darkness, but his silhouette was stocky and he moved like the man who had been keeping the door for Dan and his friends. He hurried by, heading toward the docks.

Kim stayed where she was for a while, considering. Dan had sent the doorkeeper after her, but why? She could think of no answer. Finally she slid down the drainpipe and started back toward the City. Her mood was thoughtful, and she made sure she took a circuitous route. Whatever the reason for Dan's renewed interest in her, she was sure she wouldn't like it when she found out what it was. She was glad she'd accepted Mairelon's offer. With any luck at all, she'd be out of London long before Dan could find her.

FIVE

It was near midnight when Kim arrived back at Mairelon's wagon and rapped softly at the door. To her surprise, it swung open instantly. Mairelon stood just inside, dressed in evening clothes fine enough for gentry. His right eye seemed puffy, but showed no signs of discoloration. Kim looked more closely and saw streaks of stage makeup, all but invisible in the dim light. "It's me," she said to cover her sudden, irrational feeling of guilt.

"Ah, Kim," Mairelon said with no perceptible change in his worried expression. "I'm glad you're back."

"Not so's you'd notice," Kim muttered as she entered the wagon. "I got rid of them flash togs, right enough."

"Good," Mairelon said absently, still frowning at the door.

Kim looked around for some hint as to the cause of Mairelon's abstraction. She saw no sign of the droopy assistant, and on impulse asked, "Where's Hunch?"

Mairelon picked up a top hat from the grey tile that

topped the row of cabinets by the door. "I was just going to find that out."

"You mean he's run missing?"

"I sent him on an . . . errand. He should have been back an hour ago."

Kim sighed. "It's your lay. Where do we start lookin'?"

"*We* don't start anywhere. You're going to stay here and keep an eye on things, in case he gets back before I do."

"I ain't fond of sittin' and waitin'," Kim objected. "And if you're that nattered about it, maybe you ought to take along some help."

"I'm afraid you'd be rather out of place where I'm—" Mairelon broke off in mid-sentence, and his head turned toward the door. A moment later it swung open and Hunch climbed into the wagon. He looked at Mairelon, and a disapproving frown settled over his face. Mairelon grinned like a schoolboy caught in a prank and tossed his top hat back onto the shelf.

Hunch snorted. "You ain't queering me none, Master Richard. You was a-going to go looking for me."

"It seemed like a good idea."

"You 'adn't ought to of done it," Hunch said severely.

"Yes, well, I didn't. What took so long?"

Hunch looked at Mairelon sharply, but allowed himself to be drawn away from his scolding. "Couple of sharpers tried to follow me, and I 'ad to lose 'em afore I come back."

"What?" Mairelon looked up in the act of seating himself on top of the chest that had caused Kim so much trouble. "How many?"

"Two as I noticed."

"Anyone we know?"

Hunch shook his head. "I 'adn't seen neither of 'em afore."

"Mmm-hm. I suppose they could have been some of Shoreham's."

"That's as may be," Hunch said. He sounded both skeptical and disapproving. Mairelon looked up. Hunch gave a warning jerk of his head in Kim's direction.

"What? Oh, yes, of course," Mairelon said. "Did you get what you went for?"

"Aye."

"Well, let's have it, man!"

Hunch shot another look in Kim's direction, then reached stiffly into one of his pockets. He pulled out a folded paper sealed with a great blob of crimson wax and handed it to Mairelon.

Mairelon held it up to the light, edgewise. "The seal hasn't been tampered—oh, Lord."

"What is it?" Hunch said anxiously.

"Shoreham's done it again," Mairelon replied in annoyance. He turned slightly, so that his back was to Kim, and muttered something under his breath.

There was a bright flash of blue-white light that left Kim's eyes momentarily dazzled. When her sight cleared, Mairelon was squinting at a fine dust of ashes that drifted from the folded paper. "I do wish he'd stop using that Egyptian Light-Lock," he complained. "I never manage to get my eyes shut in time."

Hunch grunted. Kim realized that he had turned his head away before Mairelon broke the seal, and so escaped the temporary blindness. She glared first at him and then at

Mairelon. One of them might have warned her what to expect.

Mairelon shook the letter open and began to read. A moment later he straightened with an exclamation. "Tomorrow!"

"What's that?" Hunch said.

"Shoreham wants us to meet him tomorrow evening." Mairelon looked up. "How long was this waiting?" he demanded, waving the note.

"Since yesterday. Where's 'e looking to be? Same place as last time?"

"Yes." Mairelon shook his head. "He's in a rush again. Blast the man!"

Hunch considered. "We'll 'ave to leave early," he said at last.

"I know," Mairelon said irritably.

"What about 'er?" Hunch said, jerking his head in Kim's direction.

"What?" Mairelon looked up from rereading the note. "Oh. You wouldn't mind leaving London a little earlier than we'd planned, would you?" he asked Kim.

"No," Kim said, remembering Dan Laverham and his unpleasant crew. She thought of mentioning them to Mairelon, but caution made her hold her tongue. If he knew about Dan, he might change his mind about letting Kim accompany him.

"That's settled, then," Mairelon said. He folded the note and tucked it in an inner pocket, then picked up his top hat. "I'll be back in an hour or so."

"You ain't never just leaving without telling me where you're off to!" Hunch sounded outraged.

Mairelon looked back over his shoulder and smiled angelically at Hunch. "Exactly," he said, and the door closed behind him.

Hunch glared at the door. After a moment, he transferred the glare to Kim. "And what's 'e want me to do with you?" he muttered.

"I'll just go doss under the wagon," Kim offered, sidling toward the door. She wanted to think about what she'd overheard, and she wanted to get away from Hunch. She also wanted to retrieve the shillings she'd left in her hidey-hole; she might need them once she left London.

"No, you ain't," Hunch said, leaning against the door. " '*E* may be willing to let you go jauntering about, but I ain't 'aving you blabbing things all over London."

"What things?" Kim asked scornfully. "You ain't told me nothin', neither one of you."

"Hah." Hunch squinted at her, and his mustache seemed to droop even more. "You 'eard enough to make trouble. And don't gammon me you don't know it, neither."

"Maybe." Kim studied Hunch. She was rapidly acquiring a good deal of respect for him; despite his appearance, he was no fool. "But I ain't no troublemaker."

" 'Ow do I know that?"

"You've had time enough to ask questions about me all round Hungerford," Kim said shrewdly. "And if you ain't done it, I don't know a sharp from a Robin Redbreast."

Hunch did not reply. He also did not move away from the door.

Kim heaved an exaggerated sigh. "Well, I ain't goin' to stand here arguin' with you all night," she said. "And I ain't leavin' London half asleep, neither. If you ain't letting me out, I'll doss here."

She sat down on the chest with more confidence than she felt, remembering her previous experience. No explosions or purple sparks followed, so she swung her feet up and stretched out on top of it. It wasn't as comfortable as it might have been, but it wasn't cold and there weren't any rats looking to share it with her. It'd do.

She grinned at Hunch's fulminating expression and closed her eyes. He'd think she was shamming it, and he'd watch her closely to see that she had no chance to slip away. So she wouldn't sham. There was no point in wasting however much time Mairelon planned to take, and no reason not to take full advantage of a warm, dry, safe place to rest. She grinned again at the thought of Hunch's probable reaction, and let herself drop into sleep.

The wagon door opened, and Kim came awake all at once. She gave an instant's consideration to the possibility of pretending she was still asleep, in hopes of hearing something of interest, then rejected the idea. She'd do better to let them know she was awake, as a sort of expression of good faith. It wouldn't calm Hunch's suspicions, but at least it wouldn't raise any more of them. She opened her eyes and sat up.

Mairelon had just entered the wagon. He carried a large parcel under one arm and there was a worried crease across his forehead; aside from that, he looked like one of the grand swells Kim had occasionally seen going into the Drury Lane theater. He glanced from Hunch's dour face to hers. Kim grinned and stretched.

The worried crease vanished and the corners of Mairelon's eyes crinkled in amusement. "Wise of you to have gotten some sleep, Kim."

"I thought so," Kim said smugly.

Hunch snorted and rose stiffly to his feet. He had been sitting beside the door, Kim saw, presumably to block any attempt she might make to leave. "You're late," he said to Mairelon.

"Not as late as I might have been." The remaining traces of amusement disappeared from Mairelon's expression. "Are you ready to leave?"

"Now?" Kim said, startled. She glanced involuntarily at the tiny window in the top of the wagon's door. There was no sign of an approaching dawn.

"Now."

Hunch looked at Mairelon suspiciously. "There's three hours yet afore morning," he pointed out.

"Yes. And we should be at least two hours gone by then," Mairelon replied.

Hunch and Kim were both staring at him. "What 'ave you gone and done now?" Hunch demanded at last.

Mairelon's lips set in a grim line. Carefully, he puts his parcel down on top of the cupboards. After a moment, he looked up. "I haven't 'gone and done' anything," he said. "Unfortunately, Andrew isn't likely to believe that."

"You never went off Grosvenor Square!" Hunch gasped.

"Give me credit for some sense," Mairelon replied. "No, I met my esteemed brother outside Renée D'Auber's."

Kim's eyes widened. Everyone in London, from the Prince of Wales to the poorest mud-lark, knew of Mademoiselle Renée D'Auber. She was the only child of a

French wizard who had fled his country during the Terror
and an English Countess who had been generally considered to have married beneath her. Mademoiselle D'Auber
had kept a foot in both worlds. She was welcomed by all
but the most stiff-necked members of the *baut ton*. She kept
a select salon attended by magicians, bluestockings, and
intelligentsia, and she was rumored to be a dab hand at
spell casting herself. There were also whispers that she was
personally familiar with some of the less savory elements
of London society. The upper classes considered her wild
and not altogether respectable; the lower shook their heads
in fascinated wonder at the strange ways of foreigners and
gentry, and pronounced her too clever by half.

"You 'adn't ought to 'ave gone there," Hunch told Mairelon almost fiercely.

"Where else was I supposed to get willow root, black
alder, vervain, and rue at this hour?" Mairelon retorted irritably.

"You ain't a-going to 'ave a chance to use them 'erbs
much if word gets out you're in London."

"Renée wouldn't give me away. And how was I supposed to know Andrew would be there? He never used to
like Renée. He shouldn't even be in town yet; the Season
doesn't start for at least a month!" Mairelon ran a hand
through his hair in a distracted manner.

Hunch opened his mouth, then closed it again. Kim
thought he looked more worried and upset than angry, and
she filed that away in her mind for later consideration. At
last Hunch said, "I'll be getting the 'orses, then."

Kim glanced at Mairelon's face, then looked away. "I'll
help," she said quickly as Hunch rose.

To her surprise, Hunch did not object. He simply looked at her and nodded. Kim blinked and followed him out of the wagon. They started toward the end of the market where horses could be stabled for a fee. As soon as they were well out of earshot of the wagon, Kim looked up and demanded, "What was that about?"

"It ain't your affair," Hunch growled repressively.

Kim was ready to argue, but Hunch's forbidding expression made it clear that she would get no further information from him. She resolved to question Mairelon himself as soon as she could find a good opportunity. She looked up. Hunch was chewing on his mustache again. Kim snorted quietly and turned her attention to considering what little she had learned.

Mairelon the Magician knew more than stage magic, that was plain enough. And she'd bet every farthing she was carrying that he was the "Merrill" that the skinny toff at the Dog and Bull was so anxious to find. Odds-on, Mairelon was gentry, too, or at least very well breeched. Ordinary market performers didn't have brothers who owned houses in Grosvenor Square.

Then there was the matter of the men who had tried to follow Hunch. He and Mairelon seemed to consider it more of a nuisance than a threat, which implied that they were used to dealing with such things. And Mairelon knew Renée D'Auber well enough to expect a welcome at her home.

The whole thing had a havey-cavey look about it. Frowning, Kim considered piking off with her five pounds and leaving Hunch to explain her absence to Mairelon. The trouble was, she didn't want to go. She liked Mairelon. Furthermore, she trusted him. Whatever it was that he was involved in, she was certain he hadn't lied when he'd told her it wasn't illegal.

It might be dangerous, though. Kim's frown deepened. She didn't know anything about magic, but she'd been involved in smoky dealings before. Mairelon might be able to use her help. She blinked, surprised by the strength of her desire to go along with the magician, then pressed her lips together, determined to be objective. She shouldn't be staying with a couple of culls on a queer lay without a good reason. She'd had more than her share of close calls already. Her luck wouldn't last forever.

For a moment, she wavered, then she remembered Dan Laverham. With a feeling of relief, Kim stopped trying to convince herself that she ought to abandon Mairelon. She had to get away from Dan Laverham, and that meant getting out of London. That was a good enough reason for anything! Besides, if she sherried off now, she'd never find out what was really going on. Kim grinned to herself and hurried to catch up with Hunch.

SIX

They were on their way out of London within the hour. Hunch drove from a tiny ledge on the front of the wagon, while Kim rode inside with Mairelon. She would rather have been outside with Hunch, despite his suspicions, for she disliked the closed-in feeling of the darkened wagon. Mairelon's assurance that it was only until they were out of London, and her own thoughts of Dan Laverham, were all that stifled her objections. Kim was not anxious to be seen by anyone who might take word back to that slimy character, small though the chance might be.

The jolting of the wagon made her queasy at first, but the feeling passed quickly. Mairelon watched her closely. "All right now?" he said after a time.

"Right enough." Kim peered at him. "You couldn't do somethin' to make a bit of light in here, could you?"

Mairelon laughed. "I'm afraid you'll have to get used to the dark. No wagoneer would keep a lamp lit while the

wagon's moving, not even on the best road in England."
The wagon jounced across a rut and Mairelon grimaced.
"Which this manifestly is not."

Kim hadn't been thinking of a lamp, but she let it pass.
Mairelon's point was clear enough: a lighted wagon would
attract attention. She stared at the window with some dis-
quiet. She had no idea where they were going; she realized,
or even which direction. Well, they hadn't crossed the river,
so they weren't headed south, but that still left a lot of
possibilities. Suddenly she grinned. If she didn't know
where she was going, Laverham certainly wouldn't!

"Not going to sleep, I take it?" Mairelon said.

The wagon hit a bump that nearly threw Kim off the
chest. "Ain't nobody could sleep through that," she said
scornfully when she was secure once more.

"Sorry," Mairelon said. "This wagon wasn't built to be
ridden in."

"I never would of guessed," Kim said sarcastically.

Mairelon laughed again. "I suppose that it *is* a bit obvious. If you aren't going to sleep, why don't we start on
your lessons?"

"Lessons? You mean, reading and magic?"

"Eventually, yes. But you can't read if you can't see, and
the same thing applies to the kind of magic I'll be teaching
you. We'll start on those later, after it gets light."

Kim frowned. "How much you plannin' on teachin'
me?"

"If you're going to be of any real help with the show,
there are a number of things you'll need to know besides
stage magic," Mairelon said dryly.

"What things?"

"The way you talk, for one." Mairelon looked at her and hurried on before she could reply. "You see, people expect a performer to sound like a Duchess. You don't, of course, but I think that with a little training you could."

"Hunch don't talk like a gentry cove," Kim pointed out, nettled.

"He doesn't assist me on stage, either."

"Huh." Kim considered. She hadn't known any truly successful actresses, but she'd seen enough of the shows in Covent Gardens to know that what Mairelon said was true. On stage, at least, the better actresses aped the accents of nobility. The prospect of learning to do the same was not unappealing. "All right, then. What's first?"

Mairelon let out his breath as though he had been afraid she would think the suggestion insulting. "First, you stop using quite so much thieves' cant," he said briskly. "You'll have to practice all the time, until it seems natural."

"Practice *talkin'*? Just to sound flash? I—" Kim stopped. "Oh. That's what you meant, ain't it?"

"It's exactly what I meant," Mairelon said, and waited.

"Mmmm." This was going to be harder than she'd thought. "What else?"

She could hear the smile in Mairelon's voice as he went on with his instruction. There seemed to be an endless number of different things for Kim to remember to say, or not to say, or to say instead of something else. Mairelon was both patient and creative. He explained each of his directions carefully. He made up sample conversations and recited them in different styles, so that Kim could hear the difference between the speech of a London costermonger and that of a Sussex yeoman, a middle-class tradesman, or a north country Viscount. Then he had Kim imitate each of his voices, correcting her gently whenever she slipped.

It was an amusing way of passing the time; Kim didn't even notice when the interior of the wagon began to grow lighter. She was almost disappointed when, shortly after dawn, Hunch pulled into the yard of a coaching inn; temporarily ending the lesson.

While Hunch watered the horses, Mairelon produced the package he had brought back to the wagon the previous night. To Kim's surprise, it contained a boy's jacket, shirt, and breeches. They were nearly new, and much finer than the best clothing Kim had ever worn. "That's for me?" she said in disbelief.

"Of course," Mairelon replied. "It wouldn't fit me, or Hunch, either. I'd intended to get you a dress as well, but there wasn't time. We'll have to attend to that later."

Kim was reduced to near speechlessness. Mairelon waved away her attempts at thanking him and shooed her out into the inn's yard. There he insisted that Kim wash as much of herself as could be decently managed under the inn's pump. Hunch fussed with the horses and muttered into his mustache throughout the entire proceeding. Only then would Mairelon allow Kim to try on her new clothes.

Back inside the wagon, Kim shinned out of her own tattered clothing immediately and pulled on the garments Mairelon had brought her. The breeches were a little tight and the jacket was a little loose, but the clothes remained the best she had ever worn. She shrugged her shoulders, testing the movement of the jacket, then grinned and threw open the wagon door.

Mairelon was nowhere in sight, but Hunch was standing

beside the steps. " 'Ere," he said, and handed her a chunk
of fresh bread and a slice of cheese. "We ain't stopping
long," he added in response to her look of surprise. "Eat
while you can."

This was entirely in accord with Kim's philosophy, and
she bit into the bread with great satisfaction. "Where's Mairelon?" she asked as she munched. She was disappointed
that he had not stayed to see how she looked.

"There." Hunch jerked his head toward the stable, but
did not elaborate.

Kim nodded, her mouth full, and sat down on the steps
to finish her meal. Mairelon returned just as she swallowed
the last of the bread and cheese. She scrambled to her feet
so that he could get the full effect of her new finery, and
he nodded thoughtfully.

"You make a very pretty boy," he said. "But I don't think
you'll want to hike the roads in those. Try this."

Kim caught the bundle he tossed her and looked at him
in bewilderment. "Hike?"

"I told you the wagon wasn't meant for riding in, remember? Unless we're in a hurry, we walk. It's less work
for the horses."

Kim nodded and went back inside. The bundle was yet
another set of clothes, plain and much-mended, but clean.
They looked like farmers' wear, Mairelon must have gotten
them from one of the stable hands. She frowned suddenly.
She was glad she wouldn't have to wear the rags she'd had
on earlier, but she was rapidly becoming uncomfortable
with the number of things Mairelon was giving her. She
didn't like owing him so much, it gave him a claim on her,
and she still didn't know what he expected in return. Well,

she hadn't asked him for any of it. It was his own lookout if she sherried off with everything. She shrugged and reached for the clothes.

When she emerged, she found that Mairelon had changed his full-dress London evening garb for something very like a laborer's smock. Kim had to suppress a laugh; in the patched, brown homespun he bore a strong resemblance to a not-very-reputable tinker's helper. As soon as he was ready, they left the yard. Hunch led the horses instead of driving from the van, and Mairelon and Kim walked along behind the wagon.

Mairelon showed Kim some of his simpler magic tricks as they walked. He claimed that doing them on the move was more difficult than working them on stage, and therefore it was good practice. Kim was particularly fascinated by the various ways of tying knots that slid apart like oiled snakes if the right loop were pulled. She made Mairelon show her how they were tied, going slowly through the process several times. Then she practiced until she could manage a creditable performance.

She was disappointed to find that Mairelon's tricks owed more to his deft fingers than to real magic. But she hadn't expected him to teach her any *real* magic, she told herself sternly. And the things he showed her were certainly fascinating. She swallowed her regrets and concentrated on making a half-crown appear to vanish from one hand and reappear in the other.

Her language lessons continued as well. Mairelon had a way of looking at her and raising his eyebrows whenever she used a cant phrase or misplaced a word. It was far more effective than the scoldings and blows Mother Tibb had dispensed whenever her students were slow, Kim found herself learning more quickly than she would have dreamed.

They were well out into the country now, and Kim found the open fields and hedges very strange after the close confines of the London streets. Near noon they stopped to let the horses rest and graze on the verge. Kim helped Hunch unharness them, then Mairelon called her over to begin her first lesson in reading. She spent most of the two-hour stop scowling ferociously at the little brown book of letters Mairelon had produced. She emerged with a profound respect for anyone who had mastered this difficult art, and an even more profound determination to join their number.

The afternoon was occupied by more lessons, but this time Mairelon was the pupil. He asked Kim to teach him how to pick locks. Relieved to find that there was something he didn't know how to do, Kim readily agreed. She scornfully rejected, however, the notion of beginning with the lock on the chest inside the wagon. "You ain't—you aren't goin' to get nowhere—anywhere?—if you start in on a fancy job like that one," she told him.

Mairelon accepted the rebuke and brought out a smaller padlock from somewhere in the depths of the wagon. "Do we need anything else?" he asked.

"You mean, special keys and such?"

Mairelon nodded apologetically. "I've heard that they're useful."

"Maybe, but I just use a bit of wire. If you lose a key, you got to get a new one, and that takes time. A bit of wire's always easy to come by."

Mairelon nodded. Kim spent much of the afternoon demonstrating the twists and pulls that Mother Tibb had shown her so long ago. She was not as patient a teacher as Mairelon had been, but her student had the benefit of years of experience with sleight of hand, and he learned very quickly. By the end of the afternoon, she was ready to let him try his hand at the rusty-looking lock that held the rear doors of the wagon.

"Tomorrow, perhaps," Mairelon said. "I think I've had enough for one day."

Kim rather agreed with him. She was tired and very dusty from the long trek in the wagon's wake, and her brain whirled in an attempt to assimilate all the new things she had learned. When they reached the edge of a little village and pulled off the road to make camp at last, her main emotion was relief.

Hunch tended the horses while Mairelon and Kim gathered wood. When the fire was well started, Mairelon hung a pot above it on a wobbly tripod affair that he had cobbled together out of green branches and twine. Hunch went muttering through the grass and weeds along the road. He returned with several lanky plants, which he threw into the pot along with a little meat and some vegetables from the wagon. Kim was not sure whether it was Hunch's seasoning or the long walk, but the stew was the best she had ever tasted. There was plenty of it, too; Kim ate until she was stuffed, and there was still some left in the pot.

When the meal was over, Mairelon and Hunch began a low-voiced conversation on the other side of the fire. Kim quickly grew frustrated with her inability to hear what they were saying, and Hunch's occasional fierce glares made it quite clear that she had better not move any closer. Kim glared back at him, which accomplished nothing beyond providing her with some emotional satisfaction, then rose and wandered back to the wagon. She glanced at the rusty lock holding the rear doors, shook her head, and went on around to the steps.

Inside the wagon, she gave the chest a speculative look. She decided against it; Mairelon knew she could open it, and had undoubtedly taken precautions. *More* precautions, she amended, remembering the purple explosion that had thrown her across the wagon. Instead, she went to the rear of the van. She hadn't been able to investigate that area before, because Mairelon had been performing just outside, and she was curious about how the folding stage worked.

The curtain was heavier than its faded, threadbare appearance had led her to expect. She examined it more closely and found a series of lead weights sewn into the hem. Her surprise lasted only a moment. Mairelon wouldn't want a stray breeze to reveal the luxurious interior of his wagon while he was performing. Kim frowned, wondering why he hadn't put a folding panel behind the curtain for added security. She'd have to remember to ask him later; she was certain he had some good reason. She lifted one end of the curtain and peered behind it.

There was a foot-wide space between the curtain and the back wall. Kim slipped into it and let the curtain fall shut behind her. A little light filtered in around the edges, providing a gloomy reddish illumination. As she waited for her eyes to adjust, Kim ran her fingertips lightly across the rear wall. There was no break in the surface, this must be the floor of the stage, then. She crouched to study the base of the wall. Yes, there were hinges, carefully sunk into notches in the wood. They hardly showed at all, and when the stage was lowered, they would lie flush with the floor, providing no inconvenient lumps for a performer to trip over.

She completed her inspection and straightened, just as the sound of hoofbeats came clearly from just outside. Old habits took over; Kim froze, half crouched behind the curtain. She heard a shout and the muffled sounds of conversation, but she paid little attention. She was too busy reminding herself that she was doing nothing the nabbing culls could nick her for. She hadn't nicked anything for nearly two years, not since she'd been on her own. She had just managed to convince herself that it would be perfectly safe to go outside and see what was happening when steps sounded on the stairs and she heard the wagon's door open.

"—and you can take a look at it," Mairelon's voice said.

"Well, that's good news," an unfamiliar voice replied. "What's this Hunch says about you picking up another stray?"

Curiosity kept Kim motionless. "I would hardly call Kim a stray," Mairelon said. "And Heaven only knows what would have happened to her if I'd left her in the streets of London."

"Um. Still trying to make up for Jamie? No, no, I shouldn't have mentioned it. But you're certain she has nothing to do with the robbery?"

"Quite sure. Now, Edward, do you want to look at the bowl or not?"

"Yes, of course; let's have it."

Sundry clicks and thumps followed, the sounds of Mairelon unlocking the chest and throwing back the lid. Then light flashed brightly around the edges of the curtain, and the strange voice exclaimed, "My word!"

"Impressive, isn't it?" Mairelon replied. "Will you take it with you?"

"Not unless you want me to. The consensus is that it may help you find the rest of the pieces, but it may also make things more dangerous for you."

"How?" Mairelon asked sharply.

"Magic cuts in both directions. If you can use the bowl to find the platter and the spheres, they can be used to find the bowl. And you."

"Of course. But I thought you had more in mind than that."

"Marchmont thinks someone at the Ministry has been talking too freely," Mairelon's companion said reluctantly. "It may be deliberate."

"I see. And there's still the little matter of finding out which one of our colleagues at the Royal College planned the theft in the first place, isn't there?"

"You've no proof that anyone—"

"Don't be a fool, Shoreham! Someone arranged things very cleverly to make it look as if I were the one behind that theft. Someone *very* well informed. It was sheerest luck that I ran into you that night, or you'd be as sure I'm guilty as the rest of them."

"All right, all right. But I still wish you'd let me clear your name."

"And give whoever it is a reason to try again? No, thank you. Besides, as long as no one knows who is really responsible, there will still be those who believe I was behind it."

"I should think the word of the Earl of Shoreham will be enough to put an end to such gossip," Shoreham said stiffly.

Kim swallowed an exclamation and pressed herself against the rear wall of the wagon, wishing fervently that she had come out from behind the curtain as soon as Mairelon opened the wagon door. Robbery and intrigue were things she emphatically did not want to get mixed up in, particularly if there were Earls involved, too. The gentry were even more trouble than toffs.

Mairelon's laugh had little humor to it. "Nothing stops gossip, Edward; you ought to know that."

"If you would just—"

"Let it lie, Edward. What else do you have to tell me? I assume you didn't come all this way just to look at the Saltash Bowl and warn me that someone in the Ministry is too free with information."

"You're still determined to go through with this?"

"Would I be here, like this, if I weren't?"

"Oh, very well, then. We've finally traced the platter."

"And?" Mairelon's tone was eager.

"It's in the hands of one of those new druid cults."

"Druid cults?"

"There's been a sort of half-baked revival going on for the past year or two. It's all very fashionable—mistletoe and white robes under the new moon, with little golden sickles for everyone." Lord Shoreham snorted. "Quackery, all of it; no science at all. It's the sort of thing that gives magicians a bad name."

"Then why did it take you this long to find the platter?"

"This group has one or two members who dabble a bit in real magic."

"I see."

"They call themselves Sons of the New Dawn, I believe," Lord Shoreham went on. "They're located in Essex, near Suffolk, at a place called Ranton Hill."

"I'm familiar with the area. Edward, if I'm going to Essex, why in Heaven's name have you dragged me a day's trip in the opposite direction?" Mairelon demanded.

"To try and keep unwelcome attention centered in this area. The platter's been there for at least two years; there's no reason to hurry."

"Mmmm. It'll take me at least two days to get there now—"

"Three," Lord Shoreham said blandly. "I'd rather you went around London instead of through it."

"If you insist."

"Under the circumstances, I most certainly do."

"Very well. Tell me about these druids, then."

Kim heard a sound like a sigh of resignation, then Lord Shoreham's voice said, "There are only about ten members, mostly young men in it for a lark. The three most likely to have the platter are Frederick Meredith, Robert Choiniet, and Jonathan Aberford. I've brought a list of the others."

There was a rustling noise as the paper changed hands. "That will do, I think," Mairelon said with some satisfaction. "I'll leave in the morning."

Lord Shoreham cleared his throat. "Ah, there is one other thing. How well do you know the Viscount Granleigh?"

"I don't believe we've met."

"And St. Clair?"

"The Baron and I . . . have met. Where is this leading, Edward?"

Shoreham sighed. "I wanted to know whether you were likely to meet anyone who would recognize you."

"Then why didn't you just ask?" Mairelon's tone was infuriating in its innocence.

"Richard! The Runners *are* still looking for you in connection with the original robbery, you know."

"It's half the reason I left England. I take it Granleigh and St. Clair are likely to be in Essex?"

"Possibly Charles Bramingham is married to St. Clair's sister, and his son is St. Clair's heir. His wife is a bosom bow of Amelia Granleigh, the Viscountess, and is addicted to house parties. It's not beyond the bounds of probability that you'll run into them."

"I know. I've stayed at Bramingham Place a time or two. Don't go ruffling your feathers about it, it was years ago, and they're not likely to remember me. What is their connection with the Ministry?"

There was a moment's silence, then Lord Shoreham said ruefully, "Richard, you are uncanny. How did you know?"

"There must be at least a hundred people in London who might have recognized me, including my dear brother Andrew. You didn't ask me about any of them."

"Andrew's in London? You didn't see him, did you?"

"As a matter of fact, I did. Briefly. It needn't concern you."

"Nothing in this affair—"

"You're avoiding the subject, Edward. What's so special about Bramingham and the Granleighs?"

Lord Shoreham sighed again. "Stephen Granleigh is involved with the Ministry in a number of ways. Of necessity, he's familiar with the history of the Saltash Bowl. Has decided opinions on the subject, too."

"I see. And St. Clair?"

"Was elected to the College in your place."

"He must have been delighted." Mairelon's voice was utterly devoid of expression. "I must remember to congratulate him if I see him."

"Richard! Don't take foolish risks."

"Foolish? Never."

"I ought to take the bowl, after all, and let someone else recover the platter."

"You can have it if you like, but it won't keep me out of Essex."

"I was afraid of that. Richard, if the Runners catch you with the Saltash Bowl—"

"The Runners have criminals enough to deal with in London. What would one of them be doing in Essex?"

"Quite possibly looking for you," Lord Shoreham replied dryly. "I told you someone's been talking too much."

"I'll take the chance."

"Very well. I hope your luck holds, Richard. And don't hesitate to call on me if something happens."

"You may be sure of it."

The wagon door opened, and Lord Shoreham's footsteps sounded on the steps. Kim heard Mairelon moving about the wagon, then a soft thump as the lid of the chest closed. She held her breath, waiting for him to leave and wondering how she was going to sneak out unseen. But Mairelon did not leave. Kim was just beginning to wonder whether she would have to stay where she was all night when Mairelon spoke.

"I think you had better come out now, Kim, and explain why you've been eavesdropping on my conversation."

SEVEN

Kim swallowed hard and pushed the curtain aside. Mairelon was standing in the center of the wagon, watching her. His face was expressionless. Kim swallowed again and said nothing.

"You *do* have some explanation, I trust?" Mairelon said.

"I was just—it was an accident," Kim said lamely.

"I see. You just happened to hide behind the curtain at exactly the time Lord Shoreham was planning to arrive," Mairelon said with a cool politeness that was worse than sarcasm and far worse than open anger.

"Yes!" Kim said hotly. "You and Hunch didn't have no use for me outside, so I came in here to look at that stage you got in back. Which you got to get back of the curtain to do."

"The timing was remarkably convenient."

"You never said when that Shoreham cove was comin'," Kim said angrily "So how would I of known when to hide? You ain't told me nothin', neither one of you."

"Why didn't you come out?"

"With the two of you talkin' about me? And after that . . ." Kim squirmed. "It wouldn't of looked right."

"Wouldn't *have*," Mairelon said, sounding as if his mind were on something else. "No, I suppose not."

"How did you know I was there?" Kim ventured. She had been half afraid Mairelon would throw her out at once, but it seemed she had been wrong. He wouldn't be correcting the way she spoke if he'd made up his mind to get rid of her.

"The end of the curtain was hanging oddly, I noticed it when I was showing Shoreham the bowl. Then I remembered seeing you come around this way and that you hadn't come back. Simple, really."

"So why didn't you say something right then?"

Mairelon looked uncomfortable. "I had my reasons."

"You didn't want the gentry cove to know I was there!" Kim said triumphantly.

"Shoreham has a nasty temper at times. Besides, I prefer to deal with you myself."

"So what are you goin' to do?"

"I don't know." Mairelon studied her. Kim stared back, trying to gauge his temper. He looked tired, and Kim was suddenly sorry she had added to his worries, however inadvertently. She pushed the thought aside, she had worries of her own.

"I suppose I shall have to bring you along," Mairelon said at last.

"To Ranton Hill?"

"That far at least. Afterward—well, we'll see how things go."

"What if I ain't wishful to go?"

Mairelon's eyes narrowed. "I beg your pardon?"

"I said, what if I ain't wishful to go with you?" Kim repeated. She chose her next words carefully, aware that she might be jeopardizing whatever fragile trust in her Mairelon still retained. "You told me you weren't doing nothin' the nabbing culls'd be . . . lookin' out for. But it didn't sound that way when you were talkin' to the gentry cove."

"No, I suppose it didn't," Mairelon said, and some of the tension went out of his shoulders. He looked at Kim and shook his head. "I wish I knew whether you—" He stopped short and snapped his fingers. "Of course!"

Kim stared in surprise as Mairelon turned and pulled open the wagon door. "Hunch! Do you have any rosemary in that cache of herbs you cart around all the time?"

Hunch's response was muffled, but a moment later Kim heard Mairelon say, "Thank you. Kim will be with me; don't disturb us for an hour or so. I'm going to need to concentrate."

"Master Richard!" Hunch's tone was horrified. "You ain't going to . . . You wouldn't never . . ."

"There are days, Hunch, when you remind me forcibly of my excessively estimable brother," Mairelon said in a tone of mild irritation. "Is it her virtue or mine that you're worrying about?"

"You ain't a-going to gammon me," Hunch said severely. "What are you up to?"

"I'm going to take that suggestion you made just before Shoreham arrived, if you must know. I trust you don't expect me to do so outside the wagon, in full view of the road?"

Hunch snorted but did not answer. A moment later, Mairelon pulled his head and shoulders back into the wagon and closed the door. His right hand held a small packet, presumably the herbs he had gotten from Hunch. Kim eyed him warily. "What're you goin' to do?"

"Reassure myself," Mairelon said absently. He set the packet down on the counter, then crossed to the chest and opened it. He muttered a word and made a quick gesture with his left hand, hidden from Kim by his body. Then he withdrew the velvet-swathed bundle that had been Kim's downfall. He set it carefully on the counter and gently folded back the velvet.

Kim's eyes went wide as she stared at the heavy silver bowl nested in the ripples of black velvet. It was shallow and circular, like the soup bowls the gentry used, but more than twice as large. The rim was at least two inches wide and carved into intricate leaves, flowers, and vines. It shone softly in the lamplight.

Kim looked at Mairelon. "Is that the silver bowl you and the gentry cove were on about?"

"The Saltash Bowl. Yes." The magician opened a cupboard and removed several small jars. He measured carefully as he added portions of their contents to the bowl, then mixed them with a long wooden rod. Kim noticed that he was careful not to touch any part of the silver with his hands as he worked.

She started to ask another question, but thought better of interrupting him. She waited until he finished the mixing and laid aside the wooden rod. As he reached for Hunch's packet, she said, "You ain't explained nothin' about what you're doin'."

Mairelon paused in mid-reach and looked at her. "No, I haven't, have I?" He hesitated, studying her, then sighed. "I suppose you have a right to know what to expect. Very well, then. One of the uses of the Saltash Bowl is to compel people to speak truthfully."

"And you're goin' to use it on me?" Kim asked cautiously. It was not a welcome thought. There were any number of things she would rather not be forced to discuss truthfully: the uses to which she had put her expertise in lock picking, for instance. On the other hand, this was an opportunity to observe real magic at close hand, and she wasn't about to pass it up without a reason. Assuming, of course, that she had a choice.

"Not exactly. The magic of the Saltash Bowl can be used only under very specific circumstances. More important, it can be used only when the entire set is together."

"That platter the gentry cove was talkin' about?"

"Among other things. I cannot, therefore, use the bowl to force you to be truthful. However, I believe I can cast a similar spell, using the bowl as a focus, which will let me know whether or not you are telling the truth."

"So if I don't say nothin', you can't tell what's true?" Kim said. Mairelon's lips tightened, and she added hastily, "I'm just tryin' to understand. You ain't got no business knowin' everything about me."

"A reasonable objection," Mairelon said after a moment. "Very well. The spell is just an indicator. If you don't say anything, it won't have anything to work with, so it won't tell me anything."

Kim nodded. She understood the unspoken implication well enough. Mairelon would be able to tell a good deal by which questions she chose not to answer. "All right, then," she said. "I'm ready. What do I have to do?"

"Just stand there, for the time being." Mairelon turned back to the silver bowl. He smoothed a wrinkle from the velvet on which it rested and laid a twist of straw beside it, not touching the silver. Then he opened Hunch's packet and sniffed at it. He nodded in satisfaction, but to Kim's surprise, he did not dump it into the bowl with the rest of the herbs. Instead, he set it down and reached for the lamp that hung beside the door. He adjusted the wick, then did something to the hook that held it. When he pulled on it, the lamp came away from the wall on a long flexible arm.

Mairelon positioned the lamp to hang a hand's breadth above the center of the silver bowl. Then he looked at Kim. "If you have any other questions, ask them now. From here on, any interruption could have . . . unpleasant consequences."

"I understand." Every street waif in London had heard whispers of the fate that came to anyone foolish enough to interrupt a true wizard in the practice of his magic. Burning alive would be nothing to it. Kim might have her doubts about some of the things she'd heard, but she wasn't about to test them now.

Mairelon gave her a searching look, then nodded. He turned back to face the bowl and took a deep breath. The lamp above the bowl threw the magician's shadow against the opposite wall, large and dark, and made a mask of his face. Kim shivered, then froze as Mairelon began to speak.

The language was unfamiliar to Kim, but every word seemed to hang in the air, clear and sharp as broken crystal. She could almost feel their edges, and she was afraid to move and jostle their invisible presence. She understood, now, where the saying had come from, "deadly as a wizard's words." She wondered how there could be room in the wagon for the solid sounds Mairelon was speaking.

The magician's hands moved suddenly, sliding with exquisite precision into a gap in the growing lattice of invisible, razor-edged words. One hand seized the packet of herbs Hunch had provided; the other lifted the twisted straw on the opposite side of the bowl. The straw touched the lamp's wick and burst into flame. Mairelon's voice rose to a shout, and herbs and burning straw dropped together into the silver bowl.

Smoke billowed out of the bowl, spreading a strong, sweet smell throughout the wagon. The lamp went out with the suddenness of a snuffed candle, and the silver bowl began to glow. Mairelon lowered his arms with a sigh and looked at Kim. "What is your name?" he said.

Kim hesitated. "Jenny Stower," she said deliberately.

The glow of the silver bowl dimmed to an angry red point. "Your name?" Mairelon repeated. "And the truth, this time."

"Kim."

The bowl flashed into silver light once more. Kim stared at it, awed and frightened. "Where did you first hear of me, and from whom?" Mairelon asked.

"At the Dog and Bull, the day afore I snuck into this wagon. A skinny toff offered to pay me if I'd find out what you had in here." The bowl remained silver, and Kim relaxed a little.

"What, exactly, did he tell you?"

Kim repeated the story she had told Mairelon at their

first meeting. The bowl glowed a steady silver throughout the tale. Mairelon nodded when she finished, and made her repeat her reasons for eavesdropping on his conversation with Shoreham. Kim did the best she could, but the bowl's light faded slightly.

Mairelon frowned. "And were those your only reasons?"

Kim shifted uncomfortably. "Mostly."

"You'll have to do better than that," Mairelon said, watching her closely.

"All right! I was curious."

The silver light brightened. Mairelon's lips twitched. "Curious?"

"Why not?" Kim said indignantly. "Anyone as meets you can see you're a regular swell, and it queers me what your lay is. Bilking the culls in the markets ain't work for a gentry cove, and you ain't told me nothin'. I got reason for wonderin'."

Mairelon laughed. "I should have guessed. Well, I'll explain as soon as we're finished here. You've enough of the pieces to get us all into difficulty by accident if you aren't told the rest."

He asked Kim a few more offhand questions, but his suspicions seemed to be laid to rest. "That's all, I think," he said at last. He turned to the bowl and raised a hand, then paused and looked at Kim. "Why *did* you decide to leave London with us? Curiosity again?"

Kim swallowed. "Yes," she said, and the bowl flickered.

Mairelon looked from her face to the bowl and lowered his hand. "There is more, I think?"

"It ain't nothin' to do with you!"

The light held steady, and Mairelon nodded. "Perhaps it

is not, now. However, we will be returning to London eventually, and I don't like the possibility of a nasty surprise waiting for me."

"He ain't waitin' for *you*," Kim muttered.

"Nevertheless, I should like to know who 'he' is, and why you considered it so important to remove yourself from his vicinity. Particularly if the reason is something that is likely to interest the constables."

"It ain't the nabbing culls I'm worried on," Kim said, scowling. "It's Laverham." She sighed. "I suppose now I got to tell you."

"Have to. I would appreciate it. Who is Laverham?"

Kim took a deep breath and began trying to explain her antipathy to Dan Laverham. Mairelon waved her to silence after a few sentences.

"I'll take your word for it that the man is unpleasant," the magician said. "But what set you off?"

"He was at Tom's shop, where I took those flash togs you asked me to get rid of. He asked a lot of questions, and one of his men tried to follow me when I left."

Mairelon frowned. "He had you followed? How far?"

"Half a block in the wrong direction, I tipped him the double right off."

"And you're sure it was you he was interested in?"

Kim shrugged. "What else? Laverham's been aching to get his fambles on me since before old Mother Tibb stuck her spoon in the wall."

"Who is Mother Tibb?" Mairelon asked.

"She raised me and some others," Kim said shortly. "She's dead." She didn't want to talk about Mother Tibb. Even after two years, talking brought back memories of the skinny old woman's terrified howls as the constables hauled her off to prison, and of the hangman's steady tread and the sickening thud as the trapdoors dropped away beneath the feet of his line of victims. Kim preferred to remember the dubious safety and fleeting camaraderie of the earlier years, when she thought of Mother Tibb at all.

"I'm sorry," Mairelon said gently. He paused. "About Laverham—" He made her describe her brief encounter in as much detail as she could remember. At last he paused and said, "All right, I'll agree that he seems to have been after you. But if anything else like that happens, or if you run into Laverham or any of his men again, tell me."

Kim nodded. Mairelon turned to the still-glowing silver bowl and moved both hands in a swift, complicated gesture above it. The light gathered around the rim of the bowl, as though something were sucking it upward. Then, with a faint popping noise, the lamp flared into life and the glow of the bowl vanished.

Mairelon smiled in satisfaction and began setting the wagon to rights. The extended lamp hook folded neatly and invisibly back into the wall beside the door, the ashes of the herbs were thrown outside, and the Saltash Bowl was wiped and wrapped in velvet once more. Kim watched for a few minutes in silence before reminding Mairelon that he had promised to explain to her what was really going on.

"So I did. The story really starts about fifteen years ago, when old Lord Saltash died. He left a rather large bequest to the Royal College of Wizards. You've heard of the Royal College, I trust?"

"As much as anybody."

"Mmmm. Well, Saltash fancied himself a magician, and

he'd collected a tremendous number of odds and ends of things that he thought ought to be properly investigated. He dumped the lot on the College. Most of them turned out to be quite worthless, but—"

"That's why you called it the Saltash Bowl!" Kim said. "It was part of the rum cull's collection!"

"Yes, though I wouldn't call Saltash a rum cull. The bowl is only part of the grouping, there's a silver platter that matches it, and four carved balls of different sizes. Together, they're the key to a very interesting spell."

"Making people tell the truth," Kim said, nodding.

"I don't think you realize what that means," Mairelon said testily. "It's easy enough to bind someone *not* to do things, but a spell to force a person to *speak*, and to speak only the truth, without interfering with the ability to answer intelligently—well, it's remarkable. Most control spells are obvious; they make the people they're used on act like sleepwalkers. But the Saltash group—"

"All right!" Kim said hastily. "It's bang-up. What next?"

"The Royal College spent a good deal of time, here and there, trying to duplicate the spell on the grouping. No one ever succeeded, and the Saltash group became a curiosity. And then, four years ago, it was stolen."

Mairelon paused. "It was stolen," he repeated, "in such a way that it appeared that I was the thief."

"You were in the Royal College?" Kim asked.

Mairelon blinked, as if he had expected some other response. Then he smiled slightly. "Yes, I was. Under another name, you understand."

"Richard Merrill?"

"You *are* a shrewd one. Yes, that is my name."

"But you ain't the sharper who nicked the bowl."

"No. If I hadn't been lucky enough to run into Edward, though, I'd have no way of proving it. The evidence was overwhelming. Even my brother Andrew believed it."

Kim snorted. "He's a noodle, then."

Mairelon's face lost its set look, and he laughed. "A surprisingly apt description, I'm afraid."

"So why didn't this Edward cove tell anybody that you ain't the one who lifted them things?"

"Those things, Kim, not them things. At the time, it was . . . convenient to have an excuse for leaving the country quickly."

"How do you mean?" Kim asked suspiciously.

"I was spying on the French," Mairelon said baldly.

"Oh."

"And there was my pride, too. Hubris, the failing of the gods. I wanted to recover the stolen items myself, you see. I thought I'd find out who was behind the theft. Someone at the College was involved, I'm certain. I asked Edward to let me try."

"And that's how you got hold of that bowl?"

"It took me a year to track it down after the war ended. It was in a little town in Germany, property of the local Baron. He'd picked it up as a souvenir of England, and he was incredibly stubborn about selling it."

Kim thought back to the conversation she'd inadvertently overheard. "So now you're going to Ranton Hill to find the platter part. What about the rest of it?"

"I can use each piece to help find the others, and it gets easier the more pieces I have. With the bowl and the platter together, it won't be hard to locate the four spheres."

"What about—" Kim's question was interrupted by a peremptory knock at the door. Mairelon lifted an eyebrow in amusement and went to open it.

Hunch stood outside, his expression clearly disapproving. "You've 'ad your hour, Master Richard," he said. "And I'd like to know where 'Is Lordship's sending us off to this time."

"Essex," Mairelon said, and grinned. "Ranton Hill, to be precise. Did you have any other questions, Kim? Then, if you'll excuse us, we had better go and figure out what route will get us there with a minimum of delay. We can talk more in the morning."

EIGHT

For the next five days, it rained. Torrential downpours alternated with misty drizzle or bone-chilling showers that made even the best roads treacherous going. The seldom-frequented lanes used by Mairelon's wagon became a sticky quagmire which plastered the horses and mired the wagon wheels. Despite Mairelon's best efforts, their progress slowed to a crawl.

None of them rode; the wagon alone was nearly too heavy for the horses to tow along the roads. Hunch and Mairelon took turns leading the horses, sliding and stumbling through cold, oozy mud that sucked at their feet and weighted down their boots in inch-thick layers. Even Kim sank ankle-deep unless she kept to the verge and slid on the slippery wet mats of last year's grass instead.

By the time they stopped to camp each night, they were all exhausted, but Mairelon insisted that Kim continue her lessons no matter how tired she was. It was easier to agree than argue, so Kim applied herself as best she could to arts such as reading and legerdemain which could not be conveniently practiced while marching through the rain. During the day, Mairelon continued her instruction in what Kim privately called "flash talk." When her voice grew hoarse, he let her stop and listen while he recited poetry or plays, or rendered the same speech over and over in a variety of styles and accents.

They slept in the wagon, though Hunch muttered balefully and chewed his mustache over the arrangement. Kim was not really sure whether he was fretting over Mairelon's morals or the spoons, by the end of the second day, she no longer cared. Sleeping in a place that was even approximately dry was far more important than Hunch's disapproval. Mairelon appeared as unaware of Hunch's glares as he seemed unconscious of any impropriety, though Kim did not for a minute believe that he was as oblivious as he looked.

On the sixth morning, Kim followed Hunch out of the wagon to find a steady, soaking rain falling from an endless sheet of clouds the color of lead. With a snort of disgust, she pulled the collar of her cloak tighter around her neck in a hopeless effort to keep the water out. The cloak was Mairelon's, and much worn, and she had had to tie it up with a length of rope at her waist to keep it from dragging in the mud. It made a bulky, awkward garment and she was positive that she would slip and end up covered in mud before the morning was over.

"Cheer up," Mairelon said as he passed her, heading for the horses. "It will stop before noon."

"Hah," Kim said. She took an injudicious look at the sky, which was still uniformly leaden, and water dripped down her neck. "Ow!" she said, and glared after Mairelon. "If you're so knowin', why ain't you put a stop to it afore now?"

"Haven't," Mairelon said absently. "Why *haven't* I put a stop to it before now."

"All right, why haven't you?" Kim said crossly.

"Because weather magic is tricky, time-consuming, costly, and extremely noticeable," Mairelon replied with commendable patience. "I can't afford the time or the energy, and I certainly can't afford to be noticed. Not until we've gotten our hands on the Saltash Platter, at least."

He continued on and Kim scowled after him. "What's the good of traveling with a wizard if you have to get wet in the rain like other people?" she muttered.

Low as her voice was, Hunch heard her. "You'd ought to be glad you wasn't left in London!"

"Why?" Kim demanded. "At least there I could keep dry. And I wouldn't have to worry about no nabbing culls, either."

"Any." Mairelon's voice came floating over the heads of the horses. "If the two of you have finished exchanging pleasantries, it's time we left. Rear doors, please; Hunch, take the right side, the wheel's sunk a little deeper there, I think."

Kim and Hunch took up positions on either side of the wagon. "Ready? Now," Mairelon called, and they pushed while he urged the horses forward. After a brief struggle, the wagon rolled forward and they were on the move again.

To Kim's disgust, the rain soon dwindled to a light drizzle. By noon it had stopped entirely, and Mairelon was wearing a smug expression. Kim was more than a little inclined to snarl at him, but in the past few days she had learned that snarling at Mairelon did little good. He simply smiled and corrected her grammar.

They stopped early that evening, for travel was still muddy and exhausting. Then, too, they were less than an hour's travel from Ranton Hill, even with the mud, and Mairelon had not yet decided whether he wanted the wagon to be much in evidence when they arrived. With that in mind, he had chosen a campsite where a small wood came down to meet one side of the road, so that the wagon could be drawn in among the trees.

Hunch built a large fire while Mairelon and Kim hauled pots and buckets of water from an irrigation ditch on the other side of the road. When they arrived back at the camp, they found that Hunch had already hung the dampest of the cloaks and bedding around the fire, blocking most of the heat. Hunch accepted the buckets with his most dour expression, and Kim and Mairelon retreated at once to the far side of the wagon.

"What's got into him?" Kim asked, settling herself onto the footboard at the front of the wagon.

"Hunch is merely expressing his desire to continue his own activities without distraction from the two of us," Mairelon explained, leaning against the wall next to Kim.

"Does that mean he's goin' to start dinner soon?" Kim asked hopefully.

"Not soon, I'm afraid. First he'll want to get as many things cleaned and thoroughly dried as he can. Resign yourself to scorched bedclothes tonight."

Kim made a scornful noise. "Hunch ain't got no sense. Dinner's more important than blankets."

"Don't try to convince him of that," Mairelon said, smiling. "You won't succeed, and there's nothing to be gained from trying. Though perhaps I shouldn't be the one to make that argument, it's my dignity Hunch is trying to defend, you know."

"Ho! Hunch, worryin' over your dignity? After he's been naggin' at you for two days for wearin' that cloak instead of the one with the patches?"

"Yes, well, Hunch gets these notions from time to time. Have you practiced that handkerchief trick you were having trouble with?"

"I äi—haven't had time," Kim said. "I can't do it at all on the move, and we only just got here."

"Then practice it now, before the light goes," Mairelon said, handing her a handkerchief.

Kim rolled her eyes and spread the handkerchief out on her lap. She flexed her cold fingers several times, trying to limber them up a little, then began carefully folding and rolling the linen square as Mairelon had taught her. She was only half finished when Mairelon's head turned and she heard him murmur, "Now, I wonder who that is?"

Kim looked up. Through the screen of trees she saw a coach-and-four making its slow, soggy way up the lane; the heads of two postillions were clearly visible above the coach's roof. Kim blinked in surprise. What was a bang-up turnout like that doing on a quiet farm lane? And where was it heading?

"Exactly what I would like to know," Mairelon said, and Kim realized that she had spoken aloud. Kim glanced at him and saw that he was frowning slightly. "And we're not going to find out sitting here."

Without waiting for Kim to respond, Mairelon pushed himself away from the wagon, pulled his shapeless, still-damp hat farther down on his head, and started briskly off into the trees in the same direction that the coach was traveling. Kim blinked, then dropped the handkerchief and scrambled after him.

The coach passed them a few minutes later. Screened by the small trees and untrimmed scrub along the edge of the woods, Mairelon and Kim studied it. Kim could hear loud female laughter from the carriage windows, but the curtains were drawn and she could not see who was inside. The driver and postillions were wrapped in driving cloaks against the damp, and their faces were impassive.

"Blast!" Mairelon said softly as the carriage lurched on by. "Can you keep up with it, Kim?"

"I don't know about that coach, but I can keep up with you right enough," Kim answered. "But shouldn't we go back and tell Hunch where we're goin'?"

"If we do that, we'll lose it," Mairelon said, ducking under a low-hanging branch. "You're right, though; Hunch should know. Why don't you—"

"I ain't goin' back now," Kim interrupted in as firm a tone as she could manage while trying to follow Mairelon's erratic path among the trees.

"All right," Mairelon said to her surprise. "But when Hunch finds out—look, they're turning off!"

The coach was indeed easing its way off of the lane and into the woods. From where Kim stood, it looked almost as if the coach were trying to force its way through the trees, but when she and Mairelon reached the spot a moment later, they found another lane leading into the woods.

"That driver is good," Mairelon commented, eyeing the trail. "This is hardly more than a deer path."

"You goin' to stand there jawing or get on after that coach?" Kim asked pointedly. "It's gettin' dark."

"So it is," Mairelon said. "Come along."

The trail wound through the trees almost as erratically as Mairelon had, and the curves hid the coach from sight. Fortunately the imprint of the wheels in the soft ground was easy to follow, and they made better time now that they did not have to worry about being seen. Even so, walking became more difficult as the light faded. Kim was about to suggest that they turn back before they lost their way completely when Mairelon stopped.

"Look there!" he said in a low voice, pointing.

Kim, who had been concentrating on following the coach tracks through the deepening gloom, looked up. Light danced among the trees. "Some cull's lit a fire on the hill, looks like."

"It does indeed," Mairelon said. "And I'll lay you odds that's where our coach is headed."

"Doesn't look like it to me," Kim said, though without a great deal of conviction. The trail they followed did not, at the moment, appear to head in the direction of the bonfire, but that did not mean it would not shift its bearing on the far side of the next bend.

"Let's find out, shall we?" Mairelon said with his most charming smile, and, turning, he headed for the bonfire.

After a moment's hesitation, Kim followed. Sticking with Mairelon was certainly safer than trying to continue after the coach alone and in the dark, and she was decidedly uninterested in going back to the camp and explaining all this to Hunch without Mairelon's support. Besides, she was at least as curious about the bonfire as she was about the coach and Mairelon's interest in it.

The fire was farther away than it looked; it took ten minutes of brisk walking to reach the foot of the short, steep hill with the fire on top. Kim was a little surprised at the way the hill poked up out of the flat ground, but she supposed that things were different in the country than in London. The hill was bare of trees except for a single large trunk at the top, clearly visible in the firelight, and the grassy slope had been recently scythed.

Several young men stood around the fire in the positions of people waiting for something and rather bored with doing so. One was staring down the far side of the hill; three others squatted over a game of dice, while two more watched and contributed unrequested advice; another drank surreptitiously from a pocket flask. Their voices carried clearly to the edge of the forest.

"Meredith's late again," the man with the flask commented.

"So's Robert," one of the others said. "Maybe they've got better things to do on a cold, damp night like this."

"What, in the country?" said the man next to him.

"No main," said one of the dicers. "Throw again."

"It's Robert's turn to bring the girls," a fifth man spoke up. "He'll probably come along with them."

"I told you he had something better to do!"

"Eight for a main," announced the second of the gamblers. "Shoot again."

"Robert's coach is just turning in at the lodge," said the man who was watching the far side of the hill. "He'll be here in a minute or two. I hope he has sense enough to leave the rest of his party there. We don't need any bits of muslin giggling over the ceremony."

"Good, that's everyone but Meredith," said the man with the flask. "We can start without him."

"Not tonight," the watcher said without turning.

"Burn it, Jon, are you going to make us stand here all night?" the man with the flask expostulated. "Meredith may not even come! He's missed meetings before."

"Two guineas on the fader's point," said one of the dicers coolly.

"If you don't like it, Austen, finish your flask and go," the watcher said. "But remember that you swore an oath—"

"I didn't know it was going to mean standing out in a cold wind in the middle of the night, scorching my boots at a great stupid fire while you prose on at me!" Austen said in tones of deep indignation.

"If your boots are scorching, you've only yourself to blame," said a cheerful voice, and a new figure climbed over the far edge of the hill and into the firelight. His arms were full of something that strongly resembled a very large bundle of laundry. "You don't see anyone else standing close enough to the fire for ashes to fall on his coat, do you?"

"Ashes!" Austen leaped backward, brushing at his cloak. He peered closely at his garments, then gave the newcomer a reproachful look. "Burn it, Robert, if that's your idea of a joke—"

"Don't get in a stew about it," Robert advised him. "Here, take your robe before I drop the lot of them in the mud."

This thinly veiled warning caught the attention of the rest of the group, and for the next few minutes they crowded around the newcomer, laughing and shoving and tugging at the bundle in his arms. Kim glanced at Mairelon, to see whether he had had his fill of watching this strange gathering. By now it was too dark to make out much of his expression, but he seemed to be concentrating closely on the hilltop group.

"Who are those coves?" Kim whispered.

Mairelon glanced down as if he had just remembered her presence. "A pack of imbeciles," he answered. "And if I'm not mistaken—ah, yes. See for yourself."

Kim looked back at the hilltop. About half of the men were pulling long, baggy, light-colored robes over their heads. "They look like Bedlamites to me," Kim muttered. "Who—"

"Ssh!" Mairelon said as the man called Jon said something to Robert that Kim did not catch.

"No, I didn't," Robert said, evidently answering Jon's question. "The girls and the robes were almost more than I could manage as it was. I left it with Meredith after the last meeting."

"And Meredith's still not here." Jon's voice sounded grim. "If he doesn't come, you're for it, Robert."

"How much longer are you planning to wait, Jon?" one of the white-robed men asked. "Have we got time for a few more throws?"

"Can't you think of anything but your dice?" Jon snarled.

The man gave a cheerful, unrepentant shrug. "Well, there's the doxies at the lodge, but I have the feeling you wouldn't like that much of a delay."

Some of the others laughed. Jon looked as if he were about to explode, but before he could deliver whatever rebuke he had in mind, Austen said, "There! Isn't that him?"

Heads turned, and someone said, "That's Freddy, all right. Nobody else sits a horse that badly, you can spot him even in the dark."

"Hurry it up, Meredith!" Austen shouted.

"Quiet, you fool!" Jon said, rounding on him. "Do you want to be heard from here to the village? Do you want people to come spying on our Sacred Rites?"

"Oh, really, Jon, don't get carried away," Robert said. "There's a dozen light-skirts in the lodge who can see us from the windows if they want to bother."

"They are here by our permission," Jon said loftily.

His dignified effect was spoiled by someone at the back of the group, who snickered and said audibly, "I should hope so!"

Jon glared around him, but could not locate the speaker. He turned away, and a moment later another figure came panting over the crest of the hill. Robert handed him the last of the robes, and he struggled into it hastily while the others pointed out the difficulties his tardiness had caused them.

"Didn't mean to be so late," said the newcomer in a muffled voice from halfway inside his robe. "I . . . had to make a stop on the way here."

"There will be time to hear your explanations later, Meredith," Jon said. "Now we must begin. To your places, gentlemen!"

The white-robed figures spread out in a circle around the fire and drew the hoods of their robes up over their heads.

It made them look suddenly eerie, almost terrifying, and Kim shivered slightly. One of the anonymous figures raised his arms above his head, and Jon's voice cried loudly, "By the Sacred Oak, and Ash, and Thorn! By the Three Wise Birds and the Three Generous Kings! By the ineffable Name Itself! The rites of the Sons of the New Dawn are now begun!"

NINE

The white-robed figures lowered their heads and began a strange, droning chant. Kim shuddered again as sonorous phrases drifted down the hill, and she jumped when Mairelon touched her arm.

"I'm going to see if I can get a little closer," Mairelon said, looking at her quizzically. "You can wait here, if you're feeling jumpy."

"Wait here, with them frog-makers up there mumblin' spells?" Kim whispered indignantly. "What do you take me for?"

Mairelon snorted. "Spells? Don't be ridiculous. That's the most preposterous rigmarole I've ever had the misfortune to have to listen to. Don't let it worry you."

"Why not?"

"Because they're mixing magic at random, from the sound of it. Half of it's Welsh, half of it's Scottish, and half of it's cribbed from someone's classical education, with a few things that are entirely out of someone's imagination thrown in for good measure. They'll never get anywhere if that's the tack they're taking."

"That's too many halves," Kim said, frowning. "And whatever it is, it sounds pretty impressive to me." The words didn't have the crystalline quality of Mairelon's magic, but they had a portentous power of their own that was just as striking.

"That's because you've never read Homer in the original Greek," Mairelon said. His attention had returned to the hilltop, where the white robes were now marching solemnly around the fire. Kim reached for his arm, anticipating his next move, but she was an instant too late. Mairelon slipped out of the trees and started up the hill, crouching low to avoid the firelight. With a sigh and a string of mental curses, Kim followed.

To her relief, Mairelon did not try to sneak all the way up to the edge of the hilltop. He stopped about halfway up the slope, near enough to hear every word clearly but still well below the level where a casual glance might see a careless silhouette. Kim stopped beside him and flattened herself against the ground. Mairelon looked at her, then, with visible reluctance, did the same.

The cold and damp seemed to penetrate Kim's clothes almost instantly. She ignored the discomfort as best she could, knowing from years of Mother Tibb's somewhat irregular training that an unnecessary movement was likely to attract unwanted attention. Beside her, Mairelon lay just as motionless, and Kim tried to distract herself by wondering where he had learned the trick. Had someone told him about it when he went off to spy on the French, or had he figured it out for himself the hard way?

The chanting stopped at last, and Kim heard Jon's voice announce, "So is the beginning ended, and the Central Mysteries begun."

A murmur of agreement rose from the assembled figures. As the muttering died, Jon went on in a much brisker tone, "Tonight we are to dedicate the Sacred Dish, the first of the Four Holy Things. Austen, you're the Bearer; George, you and Quembly-Stark can do the Escorts, and Robert can act as—"

"Uh, Jonathan, I'm afraid there's a bit of a problem," someone put in tentatively.

"You forgot to bring the dish, didn't you?" Jon snapped. "Well, I'm not putting off the ceremony again just because you have a bad memory, Meredith. This time you can just ride home and bring it back."

"That'll take hours!" someone else objected. "Especially if he came on that broken-down nag of his; the creature can't move above a trot even with a good rider in the saddle."

"As long as we can wait down at the lodge instead of up here in the wind, who cares?" another of the men retorted.

"No reason to wait at all," Meredith said. Cautiously Kim raised her head. As she had expected, all eyes were on the bland and rather foolish-looking Meredith. "I can't get the thing, you see," Meredith explained. "So there's no point in my going back, and no reason to wait."

"Can't get it?" Jon's voice rose. He put back his hood and glared at Meredith. "What do you mean, you can't get it?"

"I just can't," Meredith answered with dogged stubbornness. "That's all, and there it is. No use going on at me about it, might as well finish up and go on down to the lodge."

"Explain this . . . this recalcitrance!" Jon commanded.

"Yes, Freddy, just why is it that you can't bring the dish out tonight?" Robert asked.

"If you must know, I haven't got it any more," Meredith, said. "Now can we go down to the lodge and eat?"

Jon goggled at him, all but speechless with rage. "You haven't *got* it?"

"Got a problem with your ears, Jon?" Meredith asked with interest. "M'grandfather's been having a bit of trouble that way, but you expect it in a man his age."

"What have you done with the Sacred Dish?" Jon grated.

"Lost it in a card game," Meredith said. "Debt of honor, pay or play, you know. So it's gone."

"How *dared* you!" Jon shouted, waving his arms for emphasis. "That dish was ours, the property of the entire Order! How dared you even *think* to appropriate it for your own uses!"

"Actually it wasn't," Meredith said almost apologetically.

"Wasn't what, Freddy?" Robert asked.

"Wasn't the property of the Order. Bought it myself, never been paid. Logically the thing was mine. All quite in order." Freddy Meredith nodded, as if to emphasize the logic and propriety of his actions.

Jon turned a fascinating shade of purple and opened his mouth. "Freddy's got a point, Jon," Robert said hastily. "If he didn't use the Order's funds to buy it with—"

"What funds?" Austen put in. "This Order hasn't got any

funds; nobody's paid their subscription fee in over six months. Including you, Jon."

"There, you see?" Freddy beamed.

"You idiot!" Jon said. "Do you know how long it took me to locate that platter? We must get it back!"

"It's quite all right, Jonathan," Robert said. "We'll just buy it back from whoever won it from Freddy. Who did win it, by the way? Not Lord North, I hope."

"No, no, I don't play at his table," Freddy assured him. "Been around long enough to know a flat from a leg, you know. No, I was playing whist with Henry."

"What does Henry Bramingham want with the silver dish of the Sons of the New Dawn?" someone asked.

The grass beside Kim quivered as Mairelon tensed, but she could not tell what had provoked the reaction from him. Surely it couldn't have taken him this long to guess that the "sacred dish" these culls were so nattered about was the Saltash Platter he was looking for?

"Only stake I had left by the end of the night was the platter," Meredith explained. "Henry cleaned me out. Last hand, that went, too."

"Who cares?" someone else said. "It's obvious that we're not going to dedicate the Sacred Dish tonight, so let's finish up here and get inside where it's warm."

This suggestion produced a round of enthusiastic cheers, and the entire group threw off their robes and started down the hill despite Jonathan's grumbles and the glowering looks he continued to throw at the oblivious Freddy Meredith. None of them bothered to check the far slope of the hill, so Mairelon and Kim escaped detection. Even so, Kim did not really relax until the last sounds of merriment were muffled by the solid closing of a door.

Kim sat up at last, feeling cold and stiff, and realized that Mairelon was still lying prone against the side of the hill. She crouched again hastily and hissed, "Somethin' wrong?"

"What?" said Mairelon in a normal tone. "No, nothing's wrong; I'm thinking, that's all."

"Think about gettin' us back to camp," Kim advised. "Or Hunch'll be comin' after us with a rope, like as not."

"Oh, Hunch won't start worrying until well after dark," Mairelon said, still without moving.

Kim looked at him with profound exasperation. "It is well after dark," she pointed out.

"Then we'd better get back to camp quickly, hadn't we?" Mairelon said. He pushed himself away from the hill with his hands, twisted sideways, and slid down the slope feet-first. Kim scrambled after him, muttering curses. She was beginning to understand how Hunch had acquired the habit.

Getting back to camp took nearly as long as Kim had expected. Mairelon got lost twice, forcing them to retrace their steps in the dark. Kim did not enjoy these detours. The noises of insects and the occasional rustling movement of small animals made her jump, where the calls of lamplighters and the rumble of the heavy drays would have been soothing. Stumbling over an uneven clump of grass and falling into a bush was somehow different, and more unpleasant, than tripping on a broken cobblestone and landing in a pile of litter. Even the darkness had a different quality, a clarity and depth that bore no resemblance to the foggy blackness of the back streets of London.

Hunch met them on the road. He was carrying a lantern and frowning heavily, and both ends of his mustache looked distinctly damp and ragged. "Master Richard!" he said in evident relief when Mairelon came close enough to be identifiable. "You ain't 'urt!"

"What? Of course not," Mairelon answered. "Why should I be?"

" 'Cause you 'adn't got no reason for a-goin' off and not tellin' me, if you ain't been 'urt," Hunch said, recovering rapidly. "Leastwise, I don't see as you did."

"That's because you don't know where we've been," Mairelon said in his most reasonable tone. "You really ought to have a little more faith in me, Hunch."

Hunch snorted expressively. "All right, where 'ave you been?"

"Finding things out," Mairelon said. "Among them, the reason why our friend Shoreham has such a low opinion of the Sons of the New Dawn. As well as a hint to the current owner of the Saltash Platter."

"And 'oo might that be?"

"According to the ersatz druids whose undeniably imaginative ceremony we observed this evening, Henry Bramingham. Not the best of news."

" 'Enry," Hunch said, frowning. "I ain't sure—"

"Later, Hunch, if you please. Later, and preferably warmer, drier, and much less hungry. I hope no one has stolen our dinner while you've been swanning about out here."

"You 'ad ought to be sent to bed without any," Hunch grumbled, "and that dratted girl, too."

"Really, Hunch!" Mairelon said in a shocked tone before Kim could do more than gasp in outrage. "And all this time I'd thought you were worried about the proprieties."

Hunch's tangled efforts to refute this deliberate misinterpretation lasted until they reached the wagon. Kim was sure that this was exactly what Mairelon had intended, and while she would normally have been annoyed at his highhanded method of taking over her battle, this time Kim was grateful. She was cold and tired, and her hands and face bore scratches that stung when she thought about them. She was in no condition for an argument with Hunch.

Dinner was waiting, and if the stew was thick enough to cut with a knife and the potatoes in it were so well cooked that they came apart at the touch of a spoon, Kim did not mind at all. Mairelon was either pickier or preoccupied; he settled himself on the bottom step of the wagon with a full dish and a spoon, but ate so slowly that Kim was halfway through her second bowl before he finished a quarter of his own.

When Kim paused long enough to notice this curious behavior, she glanced at Hunch. He was frowning and nibbling delicately on the left half of his mustache whenever he looked in Mairelon's direction. That was enough for Kim. She moved to a conveniently situated rock, rattled her spoon against the side of her dish, and when Mairelon glanced up, said, "What's got you so nattered, then?"

"Henry Bramingham," Mairelon said. He took a spoonful of stew and looked down at his bowl with a frown of annoyance. "It's gone cold."

"If you'd of eaten it right off, you wouldn't of noticed," Kim said without sympathy. "Who's this Bramingham cove?"

"Henry Bramingham is the son of Charles Bramingham and Harriet St. Clair Bramingham," Mairelon answered. Hunch made a strangled noise, and Mairelon looked up. "Yes, exactly."

"Exactly what?" Kim said, thoroughly exasperated.

"Exactly the problem," Mairelon said. "Harriet, you see, is the sister of Gregory St. Clair. And the Baron has, shall we say, very little liking for your obedient."

"E's the one as called in the Runners," Hunch said darkly. "*And* gave 'em Master Richard's name."

"So we think," Mairelon said. "He's also something of a wizard, and well known for his interest in unusual magical objects. If young Henry turns the platter over to his uncle, and I can think of no reason why he shouldn't, our chances of recovering it are small."

"So?" Kim said. The two men looked at her, and she shrugged. "I don't see what's the good in your havin' this platter you're so set on. If the Robin Redbreasts catch you with it, they'll be sure you cracked the crib and took it. I thought that was what you didn't want happenin'."

"You're right, but unfortunately there's no other way of finding out who really took the Saltash Set in the first place," Mairelon said. "If we can get all the pieces together, Shoreham and I can use one of the Ribensian Arcana to locate the person who stole them, but it won't work unless we have everything."

Kim shrugged again. "It's your neck. Which direction are you goin' to stick it out in next?"

Mairelon grinned. "The inn at Ranton Hill, I think I can pick up some gossip and get some idea of how things stand at the Braminghams', how recently Lord St. Clair has visited, that sort of thing."

"Not tonight," Hunch said firmly. "And this time you ain't a-going off alone, not if I 'ave to 'ide every pair of breeches you 'ave."

Mairelon looked startled, then thoughtful. "Yes, I think it will do very well," he said after a moment. "You can poke about in the stables and kitchens, Kim can sit in the public room, and I'll see what the news is in the private parlors. Someone's bound to know something, and this way we don't stand a ghost of a chance of missing it."

"Why're you so sure?" Kim asked.

"The country inn is the heart of every village, or at least its ears and tongue," Mairelon explained. "Think of it as a London public house, only more so."

"If you say so," Kim said dubiously. "Just what am I goin' to have to do?"

They spent the next hour or so discussing the exact methods each would use in their descent upon Ranton Hill's inn, what stories they would tell, and what clothes to wear to be convincing. Mairelon declared that he would pose as a fashionable Town buck, victim of a carriage accident while driving down to a friend's country house. Kim would be his Tiger, despite her protests that she knew nothing about horses and would be unable to convince anyone that she was what she pretended to be. Hunch was a groom who had been traveling with the baggage coach; he would lead the horses from the wagon, claiming that they belonged to the ostensibly demolished phaeton. Mairelon's confidence overrode his companions' misgivings, and by the time the fire began to die everything was settled.

TEN

anton Hill consisted of three shopfronts, two houses, an inn, and a stable. The buildings looked to Kim as if they had huddled together for protection from the empty farmland all around them. Not that the land was, technically, empty, but some low stone walls, a few trees, and a couple of sheep did not go nearly far enough, in Kim's opinion, toward filling up the space.

In addition, the village was so quiet that as they approached along the rutted dirt road Kim began to wonder if it was peopled by ghosts. The sound of the wind, the squeak of the harness leather, and the crunching of their feet and the horses' hooves against the road were the only noises. She was a little reassured when a dog began to bark as they reached the first house, summoning a stable hand in a well-worn smock from the rear of the inn.

Mairelon gave the man an offhand nod and disappeared into the inn. Kim looked after him, shifting her weight from foot to foot while the stable hand and Hunch eyed each other measuringly.

"What happened?" the man said at last, making a gesture that included the horse, Kim, Hunch, and the vanished Mairelon.

" 'E tipped 'is phaeton over trying to feather a corner," Hunch said with fine contempt. "Leastwise, that's 'ow I make it. 'E says a coach-and-four ran 'im off the road."

The stable hand spat. "Another one o' them wild uns. He stayin' the night?"

" 'Ow do I know?" Hunch said. "Even if 'e'd told me, 'e's just as likely to change 'is mind as not."

"That's the Quality for you," the stable hand said, and spat again. "Well, bring your horses around back, no reason they should suffer for their master's stupidity."

The man started walking as he spoke. Hunch tightened the makeshift leads attached to the horses' halters. The animals bobbed their heads, slightly out of sequence, and began to move. Kim shifted her weight again, wondering whether she should follow or wait and wishing Mairelon had told her a little more about the duties of a Tiger. She was just about to start after Hunch and the horses when Mairelon stuck his head out of the door of the inn.

"Kim! There you are. No need to stand about; the luggage won't be along for a couple of hours at least. Come inside and wait where it's warm."

Kim nodded, glad to have some direction at last. As she started into the inn, she noted that the village was showing a few signs of life at last: a large, round woman had emerged to sweep the step in front of the mercer's shop

(and get a look at the new arrivals), an open carriage was
descending a distant hill toward the town, and a second dog
had joined the barking of the first, prompting a volley of
curses from an unseen person on the second floor of the
inn. The last thing Kim saw before the door of the inn
closed behind her was a large jug hurtling out of the window in the general direction of the dogs. The crash was
audible even after the door closed.

Mairelon was standing just inside the door, in a short
hallway at the foot of a steep flight of stairs. Beside him,
the innkeeper darted uncertain looks at the mud-splattered
boots and breeches of his newest guest, clearly trying to
decide whether this was truly one of the Quality or only
some jumped-up Cit trying to pass himself off as gentry.
Kim could almost sympathize. Mairelon's cape was well
cut but, to her experienced eye, a little shabby and out of
fashion, and the mud made it difficult to determine whether
his boots were similarly well used. Had she been looking
him over on the London streets, she would have given him
a casual glance and gone on hunting for a better pigeon to
pluck.

"Get yourself something to drink while you wait," Mairelon said, seemingly oblivious to the innkeeper's worried
frown. He tossed Kim a coin that glittered silver in the air,
and the innkeeper's expression lightened. Kim suppressed
a smile and bobbed her head respectfully as Mairelon
turned to the innkeeper. "Now, since we're agreed, I'll just
go up and clean off a little of this dirt."

"Very good, Mr. de Mare," the innkeeper answered.
"Your lad can go on in there, my wife will be glad to see
to him. Now, if you'll just come this way . . ."

Mairelon followed him up the stairs without a backward glance, leaving a trail of damp and dirty footprints. Kim snorted softly. At least she would be able to find his room if she needed to. She looked down at the coin Mairelon had tossed her. It was a new shilling, more than enough for a pint of ale and perhaps a roll. She flipped it into the air, caught it, and went into the public room to listen to whatever local gossip there might be.

The room was nearly empty. Two weather-beaten men in farmers' smocks glanced up from their mugs as she entered, and a small, brown-haired man in the corner jumped nervously and then relaxed. Kim took a seat beside the door, where she could get a good look at everyone who might come in and still watch the rest of the big, square room. Once she was seated, she discovered that her view of the yard outside was limited to a slantwise glimpse of a corner, but she dismissed that limitation with a mental shrug. Nothing was perfect, and her job was to watch and listen to the coves inside, not the goings-on outdoors.

A large, grey-haired woman who was presumably the innkeeper's wife appeared a few moments later, carrying a tray of mugs. She replaced the farmers' drinks without comment, then looked over at the nervous man in the corner. He shook his head, then nodded and beckoned. "Make up your mind, Mr. Fenton," the woman said as she set a mug in front of him. "I haven't the time to be mucking about back and forth to the kitchen twelve times an hour, not for the likes of you."

"My money's as good as anyone's," the small man said. "And if you 'forget' to let me know when my . . . associate arrives, I'll see you regret it."

"Keep your hair on," the woman advised. "Nobody's come asking for you, not even Mr. Frederick. And what *he's* thinking of, letting you off your work like this—"

The small man flushed. "I have my half-day free, the same as anyone."

"Only more often," the woman shot back, and the two farmers chuckled audibly. "I'm surprised he doesn't turn you off, but there, he's always been the sort to put up with more than he ought."

"Mr. Meredith is kind enough to give me an extra holiday occasionally," the small man said, and Kim thought he sounded even more nervous than before.

"Yes, because you ask him straight out! You're abusing Mr. Frederick's trust, you are, and you ought to be ashamed."

"That's 'Mr. Meredith,' to you," the small man said with an attempt at a haughty sneer.

"Ho! 'Mr. Meredith,' to me that's known him since he was a lad? Next thing you'll be telling me what to call my husband! Drink up and hold your peace, *Mister* Fenton, or we'll see, that's all."

With this obscure threat, the woman picked up her tray and sailed back toward the door. She stopped long enough to give Kim a mug of warm, dark ale and collect the shilling, but Fenton did not take the opportunity to renew hostilities. He seemed content to glower over the top of his mug, alternating between dark looks at the grey-haired woman and equally dark but more apprehensive glances in the direction of the window overlooking the yard.

The innkeeper's wife left, and the farmers continued to sit in companionable silence. For lack of anything better to do, Kim studied Fenton while she sipped her ale and waited for someone else to come in and start another conversation for her to listen to. He was brown-haired and thin-faced, and he had an indefinable air about him that marked him as London-bred. From the conversation she had overheard, Kim guessed that he was in service with Mr. Meredith. A footman, perhaps; he was too well dressed to be a groom or stable hand, and not well enough turned out for a butler or valet.

Kim had just reached this conclusion when the serving room door flew open to reveal a dark-haired young man in fashionable riding clothes. He surveyed the room with an air of brooding intensity, then strode to the corner table and flung his gloves down in front of Fenton. "You sent me a message," the young man said.

Kim choked and slopped ale over the side of her mug. She recognized the young man's voice instantly; it was Jon, the most zealous of the druids she and Mairelon had observed the previous evening.

"I don't know that I would put it that way, Mr. Aberford," Fenton said, giving a significant glance in the direction of the farmers. "Merely, there are some things I think you ought to know."

"If your intention is to sell me the information that your master doesn't have the object he was commissioned to bring me, your luck is out," Jon said with gloomy relish. "I already know."

Fenton's shoulders hunched together as if he were bracing himself for a blow. "How did you find out—"

"He told me himself, last night. Blithering idiot! What

possessed him to play whist with Henry Bramingham, of all people?"

"Ah, I believe there was a wager involved," Fenton said. His shoulders relaxed, but he did not look at all happy.

"Well, he certainly didn't *give* Henry the Dish!" Jon snapped.

"Of course not, Mr. Aberford. I, ah, thought you ought to know, that's all. So if—" Fenton broke off in mid-sentence, looking out the window. He jumped to his feet, his face a pasty white color, and bolted for the door. Jon sat staring after him in simple astonishment, taken too much by surprise to remember any of his brooding airs.

Fenton reached the door just as it opened to admit an enormous man in ill-fitting new clothes. " 'Ere, now! Watch what you're about!" the man said in a deep, slow voice as Fenton skidded to a stop in front of him.

"Sorry!" Fenton gasped, then dodged under the big man's arm and vanished.

" 'E's in a bit of a rush, ain't 'e?" the big man commented to the room at large.

Kim rose quietly as the newcomer lumbered into the room and slipped out the still-open door of the serving room. There was no sign of Fenton in the hall, so she took a quick look out the front door to see if she could tell what had driven him to make such a dramatic exit.

The yard was full of activity. A landau had pulled up in front of the inn, its top open despite the cool weather. A handsome and vaguely familiar young man sat with his back to the coachman; facing him were an extremely elegant woman in her early forties and a stunningly beautiful blonde girl of perhaps seventeen. A second young man, whom Kim recognized at once as the bland and somewhat foolish Freddy Meredith from the druids' meeting, had pulled a large, placid bay horse to a halt at the edge of the innyard. He was sitting in the saddle as if stunned, gazing in admiration at the blonde. Standing next to him (or rather, next to his horse) was a shabby, sour-looking man, and Kim found herself first blinking, then squinting in surprise, and then sternly suppressing a strong impulse to take to her heels as rapidly and unceremoniously as Fenton had done.

Jack Stower! What was Jack Stower doing in Ranton Hill? Fortunately, his attention was fixed on the rider, and Kim had time to pull her head back into the inn. She shut the door far enough to hide her face and forced her frozen wits into motion. Dan Laverham *couldn't* have sent Jack after her, she hadn't known herself where she was going when she left London. Jack was on some other errand, then, and all she had to do was keep out of his way so that word of her presence in Ranton Hill wouldn't get back to Laverham. To do that, though, she needed to know what Jack was up to, so that she could avoid him. Hoping that no one would come into the hall to find her in so odd-looking a position, Kim opened the door a crack and peered out, listening with all her might.

"He's your man," Stower was insisting to Freddy Meredith.

Freddy did not appear to hear. "Bramingham!" he called with every appearance of delight. "Didn't expect to find you here."

The young man in the carriage twisted to look over his shoulder. "Freddy? Good Lord! I mean, what are you doing out at this hour?"

"Things," the rider said with a vague wave. He clucked to his horse, which ignored him. A faint frown creased his forehead, and he made a tentative movement with his heels. The bay bent its neck to eye its rider, then ambled over to the carriage, leaving Jack Stower standing with his fists clenched and a black expression on his face.

"Henry!" the elegant woman said in a peremptory voice as Freddy was performing this maneuver. "If you *must* stop to speak with your friend, at least send someone in to inquire about Jasper. At this rate, we shall never get to Swafflton."

"Yes, of course, Lady Granleigh." Henry nodded to the footman, who jumped from his perch at the rear of the landau and came over. "See if Mr. Marston is in, and have a note sent up to tell him we are here."

"Be better to go inside," Freddy advised from his perch on the horse. "Private parlor for the ladies. Much nicer than sitting out in the weather."

Kim missed Henry's reply, for she had to nip sideways and flatten herself against the wall to avoid the footman's entrance. He clumped past her without noticing, glanced around, then rang loudly for the innkeeper. Kim slipped back to the door and saw that Jack Stower had vanished. She heard the innkeeper's footsteps at the rear of the hall and made a quick decision. Better to have room to move than to be nabbed by Stower or the footman in the hallway. She slid out the door like a greased eel.

"Very well," the elegant woman was saying in a disapproving tone. "But I will have the proprieties observed. Present your friend to us, Henry."

"My pleasure, Lady Granleigh," Henry said in a harassed

tone. "Lady Granleigh, Miss Thornley, this is Mr. Frederick Meredith. Freddy, Lady Granleigh, and her ward, Miss Marianne Thornley. They're down for one of Mother's house parties."

"A pleasure," Freddy said, bowing.

"Meredith," Lady Granleigh said pensively. "Are you by chance related to Lord Cecil Meredith?"

"M'uncle," Freddy answered. "Stood godfather to me, or so they tell me. I don't remember it, myself."

"Indeed." Lady Granleigh's manner thawed noticeably. "Lord Cecil is a dear friend of my husband's."

"What brings you ladies out in all this muck?" Freddy asked offhandedly, though his eyes had returned to the lovely blonde girl.

"Since it is not raining, Lady Granleigh and I thought we would drive to Swafflton to look at ribbons," the blonde girl replied in a low, musical voice. "Mr. Bramingham was kind enough to accompany us."

"This ain't one of the stops on the road to Swafflton," Freddy said in a knowledgeable tone. "Sure Bramingham gave the coachman the right direction?"

"Freddy!" Henry said. "Don't be ridiculous."

"We are here to meet my brother," Lady Granleigh said in an icy voice.

"Oh, that's all right, then," Freddy said. "Didn't know you had one."

Miss Thornley giggled. Her guardian gave her a quelling look. "Really, Mr. Meredith—"

The door of the inn flew open. "Meredith I knew it was you," Jon Aberford said in threatening tones.

"Hullo, Jon," Freddy said mildly. "Bit of a surprise,

meeting you here. I must say, I didn't expect it."

"I should think not! How do you dare show your face in public?"

"Because I ain't a Turk," Freddy replied in reasonable tones. "Why should I care who sees it? Perfectly good face, besides, it's the only one I've got."

"Don't play the fool!" Jon said. "Henry, do you know what this . . . this blithering idiot has done?"

"No, and I don't much care to," Henry answered frankly. "It's nothing to do with me."

"Henry, you will do me the favor of *not* presenting me to your unpleasant and most unmannerly acquaintance," Lady Granleigh put in. "I must have the lowest opinion of anyone who would enact a scene in so public an arena."

"Ah, but it does!" Jon said, ignoring Lady Granleigh's interjection. He gestured at Freddy. "This *traitor* lost the Sacred Dish to you at play. Will you return it?"

"Here, now!" Freddy said. "Got no reason to go calling names! Everything was quite in order; told you so last night."

"Sacred dish?" Henry said, bewildered. "What are you on about now, Jonathan? You don't mean that big silver platter, do you?"

"Platter?" Lady Granleigh said with unexpected interest.

"What have you done with it?" Jonathan demanded.

"If you *are* talking about the platter, I haven't done anything with it yet," Henry snapped in evident exasperation. "It's sitting in a display case in the library, and it will *stay* in the display case until Lord St. Clair arrives tomorrow. At which point I am going to present it to him for his collection."

"What, your uncle's coming?" Freddy said to Henry. "You didn't tell me."

"Why should I?" Henry retorted. "It's nothing to you."

"No reason to keep it a secret, is there?" Freddy answered. "And it's bound to be of interest. Why, m'mother will want to call if Lord St. Clair is staying with you."

"Be quiet, Freddy!" Jonathan said. "Henry, be reasonable. You can't just give away the Sacred Dish!"

"Don't see why not," Freddy said, giving the matter due consideration. "*He* isn't one of the Sons; the thing don't mean anything to him. Unless St. Clair don't arrive. Hard to give something to someone who ain't there."

"Come by Bramingham Place tomorrow at three and watch me," Henry invited Jonathan cordially.

"You don't know what you are doing," Jon said, suddenly calm.

"I know enough."

"Quite," said Freddy. He had one eye fixed on Miss Thornley, who was beginning to look distressed. "Here, Jon, be a good fellow and come away; you're upsetting the ladies."

"You haven't heard the last of this," Jon said. With a parting glower he turned and reentered the inn.

"If that isn't just like Jon!" Freddy said.

"I trust we have seen the last of him," Lady Granleigh said. "Henry, are you quite certain that man of yours isn't carousing inside instead of delivering your message? Jasper ought to have come out by now."

Henry pressed his lips together. "I'll go and see, if you like, Lady Granleigh."

"If you do that, we'll lose you, too," Lady Granleigh

said. "Send that boy over there; he may as well be useful."

"Hi! You there!" Henry beckoned to Kim. "Pop inside and see what's holding up Mr. Marston, there's half a guinea in it for you."

"A shilling," Lady Granleigh said sharply. "No more than a shilling, and not until you come back. Really, Henry, you ought to know better."

Kim muttered something that would pass for "Yes, mum," and touched her hand to her cap, The respectful gesture might please the bracket-faced old cat, and it would screen Kim's face from unwanted notice. Reluctantly she turned and started for the inn.

Before she reached it, the door swung open and the footman emerged, followed by a tall man in a driving cape. Kim stepped aside without thinking, and froze as she got a good look at his face. It was the skinny toff from the Dog and Bull who had hired her to crack Mairelon's crib. Had all of London followed her to Ranton Hill?

"Amelia!" the toff said. "What d'you mean by arriving at dawn like this? I'd barely got my breakfast finished!"

"When we are in the country, we keep country hours, Jasper," Lady Granleigh replied. "I explained that to you yesterday; had I known you were going to be obstinate, I would have postponed our expedition until tomorrow. I am sure that Lord St. Clair would have been delighted to accompany us."

"Of course he would," Freddy said gallantly. "I mean to say, lovely ladies, pleasant company—anyone would be delighted."

Jasper Marston had by this time taken his place in the coach, and Lady Granleigh had had more than enough of

Freddy, nephew of Lord Cecil Meredith or not. "It is high time we were going," she announced. "Good day, Mr. Meredith. Driver!"

The coachman nodded and slapped the reins lightly against the horses' backs. The team snorted and began to move; in another moment, the landau had pulled out of the inn's yard and was on its way east to Swafflton.

ELEVEN

Kim drew a shaky breath as she watched the coach pull away, all too conscious that only good luck had kept Jasper Marston from noticing her. She wanted to run away, to hide, and she wished suddenly and passionately that she were back in London, where she might have had some chance of doing so. With both Jack Stower and the skinny toff in Ranton Hill, it was beginning to look very much as if staying in London would have been safer than leaving.

Freddy Meredith, who had also been watching the coach, chose this moment to turn and see Kim. "Hi, boy! Get someone out here to take this horse, will you?"

Glad of the excuse, Kim nodded and went inside. The innkeeper was coming out of the kitchen into the hallway, carrying a tray. "And where the devil have you been, boy?" he asked when he saw Kim.

"Man outside wants someone to take his horse," Kim informed him, ignoring his question.

The innkeeper rolled his eyes. "Quality! Well, I'll see to it. Your master wants you, third door on the right at the top of the stairs. Take this along with you."

The stairs were narrow and steep, and Kim had some difficulty in climbing them without dumping everything off the tray the innkeeper had handed her. She made it to the top at last, and stood balancing the tray against the railing while she caught her breath. Then she counted doors and kicked at the third one.

"Enter," Mairelon's voice called from inside the room.

"I can't," Kim called back crossly. "You'll have to open the door yourself."

She heard a scraping sound on the other side of the door, and then Mairelon opened it. "Kim! What are you doing with that?"

"The buffer downstairs said you ordered it," Kim replied, setting the tray on the table.

"And was too lazy to bring it up himself, hmm? Good Lord, you're white as a winding-sheet! Sit down, sit down, before you fall over." Mairelon took the tray from Kim's suddenly shaking hands and set it on the small table beside the window. Kim sank into the nearest chair. She was cold and her legs felt like jelly, she was too stunned even to think, though a corner of her mind marveled distantly at the strength of her reaction.

"Here," Mairelon said, pressing a glass into her hand. "Drink this. Will you be all right alone for a moment? I'm going to get Hunch."

Kim nodded, and Mairelon left. She took a deep breath, and the feeling of being far away from everything began to lessen. She sipped at the glass Mairelon had handed her, and coughed as a fiery liquid ran unexpectedly down her throat.

The door opened and Mairelon reentered the room. "Now, what's given you the wind up? Did your friend from the Dog and Bull see you?"

"I don't think so," Kim said. "But how did you know—"

"He's staying in the next room," Mairelon said. "I could hardly help noticing his presence, and I thought there was something familiar about his voice. So I contrived to get a look at him as he left. If it wasn't our skinny friend, what's upset you?"

"I ain't sure," Kim said. She was feeling more like herself, and her momentary weakness bothered her. "I ain't never done nothin' like that before, not even on my first crack lay."

"Really. And how long has it been since you did any housebreaking?" Mairelon asked.

"Couple years. Since old Mother Tibb died, anyways. After what happened to her, I lost the taste for it, sort of."

"What happened to her?" Mairelon said very softly.

"The nabbing culls got her. Most of the others, too. I was lucky I got away." She took a tiny sip from the glass and closed her eyes. "They got transported, mostly, but Mother Tibb swung because she ran things for the lot of us."

"I see."

"I shouldn't of gone to watch. It was stupid. And after that . . ."

"After that, you didn't feel as if you could go back to housebreaking."

Kim shrugged. "I never took to it much, not like some

of the rest. Besides, it ain't a good lay for a loner, and I couldn't join up with one of the other gangs because—" She stopped short and shook her head. Why was she telling Mairelon all this?

"Because they'd have discovered that you were a girl," Mairelon finished quietly. He was looking at her with an odd expression that she didn't have the energy to figure out. "Was it so important to you, staying a boy?"

Kim nodded wearily. "You ain't never seen the stews in St. Giles, or you wouldn't need to ask. Mother Tibb kept me on a good three years longer than most, because I had a knack for locks, but that wouldn't of lasted much longer. Anybody else would of packed me off as soon as they found out I wasn't a boy."

Mairelon went still. "Drink your brandy," he said, and his voice was harsh.

The brandy wasn't so bad, now that Kim knew what to expect. It was a great deal better than the cheap gin she had sometimes bought in London. She sipped it slowly, and in a few minutes more her grim mood began to lift.

"I found out some things you ought to know," Kim said to end the long silence.

"Wait until Hunch gets here," Mairelon said. "No sense in going over everything twice."

Fortunately, Hunch was not long in appearing. He snorted through his mustache when he saw Kim, which did more to make her feel herself again than even the brandy.

"Sit down and stop grumphing, Hunch," Mairelon said. "I've taken separate rooms for tonight, but we can hardly talk through the wall, and Kim says she's found out something of interest."

"That's as may be," Hunch said darkly. "But she 'adn't ought to be
'ere, and neither should you. Someone's been asking questions down at the stable."

"But it's such an interesting place," Mairelon said, waving in a general way at the walls of the inn. "Really, Hunch, you have no idea how fascinating this inn is."

"Maybe not," Hunch said "but I know when you're at one o' your queer starts, Master Richard. And you 'adn't ought to, not this time. Someone's looking for us."

"Oh, really, Hunch, how can you be sure of that?"

" 'Ow many people 'ave a yellow wagon with red wheels and a painting of a man in a top 'at on the back?" Hunch countered.

Mairelon frowned. "Someone's asking questions about the *wagon?*"

Hunch nodded. "It's us she's looking for, right enough."
"She?"

Kim though that Hunch was enjoying the effect his news was having, though his expression remained dour. "Aye. One of them grand ladies, they said. Offered a meg to anyone as 'ad news of it, and a shilling extra if she could be sure no one else 'ad the news afore 'er."

"What a good thing we left the wagon in the woods," Mairelon commented. He moved to the window and stared down at the stable.

"That ain't all, neither," Hunch said. "There was a cove nosing around, too, 'anging about in back of the inn and be'aving oddly. The 'ostler said 'is name was James Fenton."

"Fenton?" Kim said. "There was a Mr. Fenton in the

taproom for a while; he looked like a footman or somethin'. I think he works for that Meredith cove, the one who had that platter and lost it playin' cards."

"Does he," Mairelon said thoughtfully. "I wonder. What was he doing here, do you know?"

"He came to meet a Mr. Aberford," Kim said. "He wanted to sell him the news about Meredith's losing the platter, only Aberford knew already." Quickly she recounted the scene in the taproom. "When he took off, I followed him, and then—" She hesitated.

"And then?" Mairelon prompted.

"I think maybe I ought to go back to London," Kim blurted, staring down at her hands to avoid seeing Mairelon's or Hunch's expressions. "I'm goin' to be trouble for you if I stay."

"I see," Mairelon said after a moment of silence that to Kim seemed to go on forever. "Or rather, I don't see. Why don't you begin by telling us exactly what happened, and then perhaps I will."

"It was Jack Stower," Kim said. "He's one of Laverham's boys. I told you about Laverham."

"I remember."

"I swear I don't know how he followed me from London, I swear I don't. He didn't see me, but if he's pokin' about, he'll find out I'm here for sure, and—"

"Slow down and back up," Mairelon said. "Where and when did you see Stower? In the hall? On the stairs?"

"Outside, talkin' to that Meredith cove," Kim answered. Reminded of the task she had originally been set, she outlined the scene she had witnessed in the innyard. "Bramingham said his uncle was comin' down tomorrow, and he was goin' to give the platter to him as soon as he got there," she finished. "The Meredith cull got Aberford inside, and then the toff from the Dog and Bull turned up. He's the Friday faced mort's brother, name of Jasper Marston. They all drove off, and I came in."

Mairelon was staring into space with a heavy frown, looking as though he had not heard a word Kim had said for several minutes at least. "Stower, Laverham, Fenton," he murmured. "And a lady asking questions. A grand lady—Lady Granleigh, perhaps?"

"She acted grand enough," Kim said doubtfully.

"And her brother is the unpleasant but not altogether bright gentleman who arranged for my wagon to be broken into, thus beginning our acquaintance. And *he* obviously knows considerably more than he has any right to. Someone is playing a very deep game, I wonder whether it's him or her?"

"I don't see as it matters," Hunch said. "Ooever it is, we 'adn't ought to stay 'ere tonight."

"For once, Hunch, I believe you are right," Mairelon said. Hunch's jaw dropped. Mairelon did not notice; he was digging through the drawers in search of something. Not finding it, he went to the door of the room and opened it. "None of us will stay the night at the inn. Hi, landlord! Bring me up a pen and some paper."

"I thought you said we weren't stayin'," Kim said, bewildered.

"We are not staying the *night*. There is no reason not to stay the afternoon; it's a long drive to Swafflton, and the ladies will more than likely be shopping for hours. Besides—ah, thank you, landlord."

The innkeeper had arrived, carrying a scruffy-looking quill, an inkpot, and a sheet of paper. Mairelon took them with a charming smile and shut the door in his face. "Besides, I don't expect this to take long," he finished, setting the implements on the table.

"What are you goin' to do about Stower?" Kim asked as Mairelon made a face at the quill, dipped it in the inkpot, and began covering the paper with flowing, spidery letters.

"I am going to do nothing whatever, for the time being at least," Mairelon answered. He wrote another three lines and set the quill aside. "No sand? Our landlord seems singularly unprepared for Quality clientele; can it be that he seldom has any?" He picked the page up by one corner and waved it through the air to dry the ink.

"I'd better go back to London, then," Kim said.

"You will do no such thing. Hunch is the one who is going to London. He'll be quite all right; this Laverham fellow isn't looking for him." He folded the note and handed it to Hunch, who scowled and chewed absently on one end of his mustache. "Hire a horse and change whenever you have to. I don't want any more time wasted. Give this to Shoreham and tell him what we've found out so far. I've asked him to learn what he can about Laverham, Marston, Stower, and Fenton; stay til he has an answer to send. He'll be quicker about it if he knows you're waiting."

Hunch's scowl lessened slightly during this speech, but his expression remained gloomy. "All right, Master Richard. But you ain't staying 'ere, are you?"

"After what I have heard, I have not the slightest intention of doing so," Mairelon said with evident sincerity.

Hunch chewed more vigorously, and his frown returned.

"You ain't going to do nothing dreadful while I'm gone, are you?"

"That depends to some extent on how long you take, doesn't it?" Mairelon said, rising. "Come along, let's break it gently to the landlord that his newest guests are leaving already. I doubt that he'll be pleased."

The innkeeper was not nearly as unhappy about their abrupt departure as Mairelon had predicted, primarily because Mairelon informed him casually that he would, of course, pay for the rooms he had bespoken even though he would not remain to use them. He then hired a gig with which to drive to the next town and agreed to pay for the stabling of the horses until they could be sent for. A large purse changed hands, Kim had not known there was so much money in the wagon, and she wondered what else she had missed.

Three people were a tight fit in a gig, but they managed. Kim was almost grateful to be squashed between Hunch and Mairelon, they hid her very effectively from view on either side, and with her cap pulled low and her head tucked down she felt that Jack Stower was unlikely to recognize her, even if he should suddenly appear from around a corner.

Fortunately for Kim's peace of mind, Jack was nowhere to be seen, and once they were out of the village she relaxed a little. Mairelon was silent during the drive, staring out over the fields and hedges with an absent expression that made her think he was not really seeing any of them. Hunch chewed rhythmically on his mustache and scowled at the horse, casting intermittent glances in Mairelon's direction but saying nothing.

There was no one in sight when they reached the woods where they had left the wagon, for which Kim was grateful. She was tired of juggling roles; she did not want to have to think about whether she was supposed to be pretending to be a Tiger or a horseboy or a magician's assistant. She was tired of silent, empty spaces and the strange sounds and smells of the woods. She wanted London, and she realized that that, more than fear of what Jack Stower's presence might mean, was her real reason for suggesting she should go back.

She was still pondering this revelation as she stood beside Mairelon and watched Hunch drive briskly off. "Good," Mairelon murmured. "If he keeps up that pace, he'll be in London by tomorrow morning." He looked down at Kim. "Don't just stand there, come along. We have a great deal to do, and we had better get to it."

"I thought we were goin' to wait for Hunch to get back before we did anything," Kim said, all her homesickness swept away by a sudden wave of foreboding.

"Whatever gave you that idea?" Mairelon said in a tone of mild astonishment. "If we don't do anything, St. Clair will have the platter by tomorrow evening, and I can't have that. No, we're going to have a good meal and get a few things ready and then have a good nap, so that we'll be wide awake to burgle Bramingham Place at two this morning."

He turned and marched cheerfully toward the wagon, leaving Kim to stand staring after him openmouthed. She muttered a curse and plunged after him, already more than half resigned to the prospect. If Mairelon wanted to burgle Bramingham Place, burgle it he would, with or without her help. On the whole, she thought she would rather it be with, but she was not going to give up without an argument. Spluttering objections that she expected would be useless, she followed Mairelon into the wagon.

TWELVE

Bramingham Place was an enormous, rambling house that seemed to spread out in all directions. Mairelon, lurking with Kim behind an overgrown topiary duck while they waited for the last lights inside to be put out, explained in a whisper that building new wings had been a tradition in the Bramingham family for two centuries, hence the erratic sprawl. Kim wondered what they did with all the space. From the look of it, the house was larger than the entire village of Ranton Hill, and that was without considering the stables and gatehouse.

The last of the windows went dark, and Mairelon started forward with an exclamation of relief. Kim grabbed at his sleeve. "Give 'em time to fall asleep!" she hissed.

"It's all right; the library's at this end. They're far enough away that they won't hear a thing," Mairelon whispered back. "You did say Bramingham was keeping the Saltash Platter in the library?"

"That's what he told the druid cove, but what if he was gammoning him?"

"We won't know til we go find out, will we?" She could hear the smile in his voice, though it was too dark to see it clearly. "Shall we?"

Kim sighed. "How can you be so sure the library's at this end of the house?"

Even in the darkness she could see him stiffen. "I stayed with the Braminghams once, some years back," Mairelon said in a voice devoid of expression. "Just before the Saltash Set was stolen. I remember the visit . . . very well indeed."

"Oh." Kim searched for something to say, without success. She shrugged. "All right, then, let's bite the ken. But this is my lay, remember, don't go off on your own, or you'll muck up the whole thing."

"After you," Mairelon murmured, bowing. Kim shook her head, only half understanding, and slid through the night toward the house.

It was not, after all, much different from the jobs she had done so long ago in London. The house was bigger by far, but that was all. Mairelon pointed the way to a pair of long French doors near the room they wanted. Kim reached for the bit of wire hidden in her sleeve and opened the lock with a few deft twists of her wrist. They slipped inside, and Mairelon closed the doors softly behind them.

They were in a spacious sitting room. Kim could see the dim shapes of chairs and tiny tea tables scattered all around, deeper shades of darkness in the dark. Mairelon pointed toward a door in the opposite wall. Kim nodded and made a gesture which she hoped he would correctly interpret as a warning to be careful. Then she began picking her way across the room.

Three nerve-racking minutes later they reached the door. It was locked, but the mechanism was no more of a challenge than the one on the French doors had been. Kim had it open in a few seconds. On the other side was a hallway, thickly carpeted. Motioning Mairelon to keep to the center, Kim stepped cautiously into the hall.

The library was the second door on the left. It was unlocked, and Kim suppressed a snort of derision. That was gentry for you: they'd lock up half the doors and leave the rest wide open. They always picked the wrong half to lock, too. She pushed the door slowly inward, listening for creaking hinges. The door made no sound, and a moment later they were in the library with the door closed behind them.

"Well done!" Mairelon breathed in her ear, and she jumped. "You were particularly quick with that last door."

"Don't *do* that," she whispered back. "I was quick because it wasn't locked."

"Not locked?" Mairelon paused, and she could almost hear him thinking.

"Not locked," Kim repeated firmly. "And this ain't no time to chat. Find that thing you're lookin' for and let's get out of here."

"We'll never find it in the dark," Mairelon said. "A moment, please." He muttered a word.

A ball of cold, silver light the size of Kim's fist sprang into being just over Mairelon's head, casting threatening, sharp-edged shadows all around. Kim blinked, biting back a protest, and looked quickly about her. The library was a long room with bookcase-lined walls, its center was full of large chairs covered with needlework in bright colors that the silver light bleached to bearable pastels. A small table stood beside each chair on thin, fragile legs. Heavy curtains of a dark crimson shut out the light from the windows; unlike those in the sitting room, these came only to the bottom of the window. Below them, short bookcases alternated with glass boxes set on legs. Kim stared, then realized that these must be the "display cases" to which Henry Bramingham had referred.

Mairelon crossed to the windows and walked rapidly along them. He stopped a third of the way from the end and beckoned. "Here it is!" he whispered, and the strange silver light made an exultant mask of his face.

The Saltash Platter was a tray nearly two feet long, heavily ornamented around the edge with the same pattern of fruits and flowers and vines Kim had seen on the bowl in Mairelon's wagon. At either end a rope of vines twisted away from the edge and then back again, forming a handle. The silver shone brilliantly in the cold light, even through the glass of the display case. Kim looked at the case more closely. The top was hinged in back, and there was an unobtrusive gold lock at the front edge.

Kim pulled out her wire and paused, remembering what had happened when she tried to poke through Mairelon's chest. Of course, it wasn't the lock that had been enchanted, but still . . . She frowned and tugged at the lid, testing the strength of the lock.

It opened easily, cutting short Mairelon's impatient query. They looked at each other across the case, and Kim saw her own misgivings reflected in Mairelon's uneasy expression. "Magic?" she whispered.

"Possibly," Mairelon said softly. The sharp shadows magnified his frown. "If it is, touching the platter will set it off. Be quiet for a moment while I check."

He reached down, hands hovering just above the open case. The air grew heavy, and Kim held her breath, waiting for an explosion.

A soft crash sounded from the next room, and Mairelon jerked his hands away from the display case. He and Kim froze, and in the silence heard a well-muffled thud from the hall.

"We better get out of here!" Kim said, and started down the long room toward the door.

"Not that way; there's no time," Mairelon said, grabbing her arm. He gestured, and the light that hovered over his head shrank to a pinpoint; then he went swiftly to the bookshelf along the nearest wall. "Boccaccio, Boccaccio," he murmured. "Where—ah!"

Kim stared in astonishment as Mairelon reached out and tilted two books outward. She heard a small click, and then the sound of someone fumbling at the library door made her glance fearfully over her shoulder. The curtains were too short to hide behind. Perhaps if she curled up in a chair, she would be overlooked, but what about Mairelon? She turned back and almost forgot her fear in complete amazement.

"Inside, quickly!" Mairelon said. An entire section of the bookcase had swung outward, revealing a narrow, cupboard-like opening behind it. Kim pulled herself together and darted inside; Mairelon squeezed in after her, pulling the bookshelf to behind him. The silver light winked out.

Cracking a ken with a real magician certainly had advantages, Kim thought to herself as she wriggled into a more comfortable position. That book-achoo spell was one she'd have to be sure to learn. She felt Mairelon fumble at the wall and thought he was trying to latch the bookshelf in place. Then he breathed a nearly soundless sigh, and with a soft scraping a small panel slid aside, giving them a thin slot above a row of books through which to view the room they had just quitted with such haste.

Someone was moving slowly among the chairs, carrying a small dark-lantern that was three-quarters shuttered. The lantern beam swung toward them, and Kim wondered whether the bearer had heard Mairelon lower the panel. She heard a snort, and the contemptuous whisper "Mice!" and then the dark blob went on toward the display cases. The figure raised the dark-lantern and bent forward to peer through the glass, and for a moment his face was visible. Kim stiffened and stifled a gasp; it was Jack Stower again.

Mairelon put a warning hand on her shoulder. Angrily she shook it off. She wasn't such a flat as to make a noise that might reveal their presence, no matter how startled she was. Frowning, she watched Stower work his way slowly up the row of display cases toward the one that held the Saltash Platter.

Without warning, the library door swung wide. A pool of flickering amber light spilled through it, and an irritated masculine voice said, "Stuggs? Is that you? Confound it, where is the man?"

Jack Stower whirled, clutching his lantern, just as Jasper Marston, wearing a black and crimson brocade dressing gown and carrying a branch of candlesticks, strolled through the door. "Stuggs?" Marston said again, and then he saw Jack.

The two men stood staring at each other for a long moment; then a slow, deep voice from the hallway broke the stunned silence. "Right 'ere, gov'nor." An enormous figure loomed into view behind Marston. Stower cursed. He whirled and jerked the curtains from the nearest window aside, then yanked at the latch. The window did not budge.

Marston, shaking himself free of his paralysis at last, started forward (none too rapidly, Kim noted with scorn), brandishing the candlesticks like a weapon. "He's trying to steal the platter!" he cried. "Stop him, Stuggs!"

The figure in the hallway ran forward. He was unusually fast on his feet for a big man, but he had too much distance to cover and there were too many obstacles in the way. Stower, after one terrified look backward, hurled his dark-lantern through the stubborn window, snatched up the fallen curtains to keep from being slashed by the fragments of glass and broken window slats, and scrambled out, tipping over the nearest display case in his hurry.

Stuggs lunged after the fleeing Stower and grabbed his feet as the rest of him disappeared out the window. Kim heard a muffled howl of rage and fear, and Stower kicked backward. Stuggs lost his balance and crashed into another display case, his fingers still locked around one of Jack's boots, while the last of Jack Stower vanished.

Jasper picked his way across the broken glass to the window and squinted out it. Kim could hear distant noises; it sounded as if the commotion had roused the household, and somewhere a dog had begun to bark. Jasper did not seem aware of it. He turned and frowned at Stuggs. "He's gone! Why couldn't you hold him?"

" 'Is bootlace broke," Stuggs said mildly. "I got to 'and it to you, gov'nor, you 'ad it right about that there bowl being valuable. But you ought to 'ave told me there was other coves after it besides us."

"This is the platter, not the bowl, you idiot," Jasper Marston said. "But I suppose I should thank you for reminding me what we came for." He left the window and went straight to the display case containing the platter. He set the candlesticks down on the nearest table and beckoned to Stuggs. "Come here and open the lock, hurry, before someone else gets here."

As Kim had done, Stuggs tested the lid and made the same discovery. "It ain't locked."

"Not locked? That fellow we chased off must have opened it! We arrived just in time. Give it to me."

"No!" a familiar voice said in dramatic tones from the smashed window. Kim's eyes widened. What was the head of the druid group doing at Bramingham Place?

"What—" Marston turned his head and froze in mid-sentence.

Framed in the shattered glass and dangling splinters of the window were a man's head and shoulders. The man's eyes gleamed from the openings of a black mask, and a dark high-crowned hat covered his hair. His form was hidden beneath a driving cloak with several short capes, but the tone and timbre of his voice were unmistakable. "You are too late to further defile the Sacred Dish! Bring it to me, at once!"

Kim bit her lip to keep from laughing aloud. She should

have guessed that Jonathan Aberford would be after the platter, the same as everyone else. This was becoming altogether too much like a Drury Lane comedy. Mairelon seemed to think so, too; she could feel him shaking in silent amusement. She hoped they would both be able to control themselves. It wouldn't be funny at all if they were caught.

"Now, look here—" Marston began.

Jonathan raised a hand, and Kim saw the glint of candlelight on metal. Her amusement died instantly. "Bring it to me!" Jonathan commanded.

"Put that down, you young chub," Stuggs said. "Pistols ain't a thing to go waving around like that."

"Bring me the dish!" Jonathan cried. "I won't have any more delay!" He waved his pistol again. "Bring—"

Abruptly the masked face vanished from the window. There was a crash and the almost simultaneous sound of a pistol shot. Stuggs cursed and ran to the window. A moment later he pulled his head back inside and shook it in wonder. "Silly chub was standing on a bucket, an' it tipped over," he said. "The pistol must 'ave gone off when 'e fell."

"Never mind!" Jasper said. "Help me hide this before someone else comes in."

"What's going on?" a voice boomed from the doorway. "Hi, Marston! Looks like you've had a bit of a turnup."

"I don't care what he's been having, Mr. Bramingham, I won't have him making such *dreadful* noises in my house," said a shrill female voice from farther along the hallway. "He's wakened all the guests *and* the servants, and I won't have it. Even if he *is* your brother, Amelia, dear."

"Too late," Stuggs said in a resigned tone as the occupants of Bramingham Place, in various states of déshabillé, began pouring into the library.

THIRTEEN

The first person through the door was an older, heavier version of Henry Bramingham; Kim assumed he was the owner of the estate. Behind him came several other men in dressing gowns and a partially dressed footman carrying more candles. They were followed in turn by the ladies of the house, caps askew and clutching their dressing gowns about them, determined to miss nothing of whatever scandalous goings-on had been discovered.

Jasper dropped the platter onto the seat of a nearby sofa where it would be temporarily hidden by the back. "Housebreakers, that's what happened, Bramingham," he said, waving at the broken window and the chaos of shattered glass and broken furniture below. "I, ah, came down for a book and interrupted them—"

"Housebreakers!" A plump, grey-haired woman wrapped in layers of ruffles stiffened indignantly. "At my house party! I won't have it, Mr. Bramingham!"

"Of course not, my dear," the heavy man said, patting

her arm. "Good job, Marston; I see you've caught one."
He eyed Stuggs's bulk with evident misgiving. "He looks
a desperate rogue. Just hold him off a minute more, til
Henry gets here with the shotgun."

"What? No, no, Bramingham, that's not a burglar," Jasper said, clearly taken aback. "That's my man, Stuggs."

"Jasper!" Lady Granleigh pushed her way to the front of
the crowd and came toward him across the room, hands
outstretched. "Dear boy, were you injured?" Her expression
was at variance with her concerned tone, and as she came
nearer, Kim saw her soundlessly mouth the words "Did you
get it?"

"Yes," said Jasper. "I mean no, not at all. Ah, Amelia . . ." He gestured toward the sofa.

Amelia glanced down. She looked at Jasper and rolled
her eyes heavenward. "The very thought of your ordeal
makes me feel faint," she declared, and sat down on top of
the tray, spreading out her robe so that it was completely
hidden.

"Clever woman," Mairelon murmured. "Pity she's not on
our side."

"Shh!" Kim hissed. "You want to get us caught?"

"Amelia, dear!" Mrs. Bramingham said, hurrying over.

"Faint? Lady Granleigh never faints!" a bluff voice said,
and a distinguished-looking man pushed his way through
the crowd of servants and visitors. He was fully dressed,
which perhaps accounted for his tardiness, and there was
mud on his boots. "I'm afraid they got away, Bramingham," he said. "That boy of yours is still chasing
them, but I don't see that he has much chance of catching
up with them in the dark."

Mrs. Bramingham gave a faint, lady-like shriek. "Henry! My son is out there with those villains? I won't have it! Bring him back at once, Mr. Bramingham."

"Of course, my dear," Mr. Bramingham said, making not the slightest move to do so. "Did you see them yourself, Lord Granleigh?"

"*Somebody* was running off through the woods," Lord Granleigh replied. "I doubt that anyone got a good look at him, though. Now, what's this about Lady Granleigh fainting? You're not ill, are you, my dear?"

"I shall be quite all right in a moment," Lady Granleigh said, leaning back against the cushions. She looked nervous, and Kim wondered whether her husband knew that she and her brother were trying to steal Henry's tray.

"I can carry you up to your room," Lord Granleigh offered, plainly concerned.

"No, no, I shall do much better here," Lady Granleigh assured him. "Perhaps if you sent Marianne to me . . ."

"Mademoiselle Marianne is in the saloon, having the hysterics."

Heads turned toward a lovely young woman standing in the doorway. A lace cap lay like a snowflake on her auburn hair, and the pale green wrap that covered her nightdress set off her slender figure better than a ball gown. Kim felt Mairelon stiffen. "Renée?" he breathed in tones of horrified disbelief.

"Me, I do not see that having the hysterics is of any use whatever, and I have a great wish to know whether we are to be murdered in our beds, so I have left her with her maid," the auburn vision went on. "I think that her maid is very nearly as silly as she is, so they will go on well together. What has happened?"

A confused babble of voices greeted this question. Lady Granleigh objected that her dear Marianne was not in the least silly; Mrs. Bramingham offered some complaint about her son; Jasper launched into a highly colored and very jumbled account of the way in which he had run the ruffians off; Mr. Bramingham made a series of vague and contradictory statements that seemed intended to be reassuring. The auburn-haired woman listened with an appearance of polite interest, though it was impossible to understand more than one word in six. Finally Mr. Bramingham put a stop to it.

"Enough!" he roared. "Miss D'Auber, I must apologize; it has been a very trying night."

So the auburn-haired woman was the infamous Renée D'Auber, whom Mairelon had gone to visit the night before they left London! Kim could not keep from glancing in the magician's direction, but it was too dark in the cupboard to make out his expression. Frowning a little, she returned to her contemplation of the scene in the library.

"It seems to me that of a certainty someone has been trying something tonight," Mademoiselle D'Auber said into the silence that followed Mr. Bramingham's bellow. "But I do not yet know what."

Mr. Bramingham attempted a gallant bow, the effect of which was somewhat spoiled by the belt of his dressing gown, which chose that moment to come undone and flap around his knees. "Nothing that need cause you concern, Miss D'Auber."

"Father!" Henry Bramingham burst into the room with a

nod and a quick "Beg pardon" as he passed Renée D'Auber. His eyes were bright with excitement, and in one hand he held a dirt-covered pistol. Bits of earth and grass dropped from the pistol to the carpet as he waved it triumphantly before the eyes of the assembly. "We didn't catch him, but we found this on the South Walk."

"Henry!" shrieked his mother. "What do you mean by bringing that filthy object into the library?"

"I told you he had a gun!" Jasper said.

"Cool!" whispered one of the housemaids, who was standing wide-eyed in a corner, drinking in the uproar.

"Henry, you're upsetting the ladies," Mr. Bramingham said.

"I'm sorry; I didn't think." Henry looked down at the pistol as if he would have liked to hide it under his coat.

Mademoiselle D'Auber's eyebrows rose. "I see that Mademoiselle Marianne is perhaps not so foolish as I thought, unless your South Walk grows pistols, which is a thing unlikely. But do you say that this person has escaped?"

"Nothing to worry about, Miss D'Auber," Mr. Bramingham said. "If you'll just let us handle this—"

"But I do not see that you *are* handling it," Renée D'Auber pointed out. "And perhaps this villain has a second pistol and will come back to kill us all in our beds! I do not at all like this idea, me, and I will not spend another night in this house."

"Oh, *no*, Mademoiselle D'Auber, you mustn't leave!" Mrs. Bramingham turned in distress from her unwelcomed ministrations to Lady Granleigh. "Why, you've only just arrived!"

"I shall leave in the morning," Renée announced, and swept out of the room.

"There! See what you've done!" Mrs. Bramingham said crossly to Henry after a moment's silence.

"What I've done!" The look Henry gave his mother was full of righteous indignation. "I didn't break into the library and smash up the display cases. I didn't go dropping pistols in the South Walk. I suppose you'd rather I hadn't chased off the fellow who did!"

"I believe I am going to faint," Lady Granleigh announced loudly. The company turned to look at her and she sank back against the sofa, fanning herself with one hand. "If I could have a little *peace*," she said in failing tones, "I might be able to recover."

"Of course, Amelia, dear!" Mrs. Bramingham said. "Mr. Bramingham, take these people into the green saloon. I'll just get my hartshorn—"

"Alone," Lady Granleigh said with amazing firmness for a purported invalid.

"But, Lady Granleigh—" Mr. Bramingham began, frowning.

"Very well," Lady Granleigh sighed, cutting him off. "If you insist, I will allow Jasper to remain in case those villains reappear. But I must have *quiet*."

"But Mr. Marston was going to explain—"

Lady Granleigh raised a hand to her head. "Can it not wait?"

Mr. Bramingham blinked, then shook his head. "Yes, of course, Lady Granleigh, as you say. Come along, my dear. Henry, take that thing to the morning room; I'll come by in a minute or two. Come along, everyone, we must let Lady Granleigh recover."

Lord Granleigh gave his wife a penetrating look, but allowed himself to be shepherded out of the room along with the rest. Only Jasper and his "man" Stuggs remained behind. As the door closed behind the crowd, Lady Granleigh stood up briskly.

"Ah, Amelia, hadn't you better—I mean, what if someone comes back in and sees you?" Jasper stuttered. "You're supposed to be in a faint."

"I am not going to sit on that object for another instant," Lady Granleigh replied. "And if it had not been for your ineptitude, I would not have had to. What possessed you to rouse the household like this?"

"I didn't rouse the household, and if you'd listen for half a minute, you'd know it," Jasper said bitterly. "It was that Bedlamite in the domino with his pistol and his—"

"I am not interested in excuses," Lady Granleigh interrupted. "There will be time for that later. Right now we must decide what to do with this platter. We can't just carry it up to your room, you know. The halls are full of servants; it will be hours before things settle down."

"My room? Why my room? You're the one who was invited for the house party. You've got that hulking great wardrobe and at least two dressing tables to hide the thing in. I'm just an overnight guest; all I have is a shaving stand."

"You have neither a husband nor an abigail to pry into your things. I, on the other hand—"

"I should hope not!" Jasper said. Then he looked at his sister and snorted. "And if Stephen Granleigh has ever 'pried' in your things, I'll . . . I'll eat my cravat."

"If you dare to so much as hint any such thing about Stephen, I shall feed it to you myself," Lady Granleigh retorted. "Stephen is the soul of honor."

"Too honorable for his own good," Jasper muttered. His sister gave him a warning look, and he scowled. "Well, he is, and you know it, or why did you drag me into this mess in the first place? Granleigh stands to benefit as much as you do if he recovers the platter, but he wouldn't stand this havey-cavey nonsense for a minute." His expressive wave included the platter, the shattered window, the open display case, and his sister.

Lady Granleigh flushed. "That is not the point, and you are wasting time. What are we going to do with this platter?"

"Throw it out the window," Jasper said in a sulky tone.

"Don't be ridiculous, Jasper. There are still people combing the grounds in search of those housebreakers of yours; someone would be sure to find it before we could recover it."

"Why don't you 'ide it be'ind some of them books?" Stuggs suggested.

Lady Granleigh gave him a scornful look, but as no better idea was forthcoming, she and Jasper set to work removing books from one of the shelves. Unfortunately they did not think to check the platter against the size of the shelf before they did so, and when they tried to balance it on its edge against the wall, it proved too tall. They were forced to remove it and replace the books, reproaching each other viciously the entire time.

In the end, they hid the platter under the sofa cushions.

Lady Granleigh was not altogether pleased with this solution, and warned Jasper several times that he must make certain to remove it before the maids came to straighten up.

"And on no account are you to allow Mr. Bramingham and the others to search this room," she added.

"How am I supposed to stop them?"

"I leave that to you. Now, I think it is time I recovered enough to return to my room. You may escort me. After that, I suggest you rejoin Mr. Bramingham and tell them your story. You,"—she gave Stuggs a withering look—"had best stand guard outside the library door. It will look well, and that way we can be sure no one will come in and accidentally discover the platter before we have a chance to move it. Your arm, Jasper."

The three conspirators went slowly out of the library, Lady Granleigh clinging to her brother's arm as if she were about to collapse. The door closed behind them, and the room was empty at last.

Kim stirred, then poked Mairelon gently, somewhat surprised that he had not unlatched the bookcase door of their refuge. She felt him start at her touch. He let out a long breath and closed the little panel through which they had been looking. Kim felt him make a series of small movements, and then the bookcase swung wide.

Moonlight dribbled through the broken window, making Mairelon's magical light unnecessary. Kim darted out and began pulling cushions off the sofa. Mairelon pushed the bookcase back into place and followed, but more slowly. "Hurry up!" Kim whispered. "We ain't got much time."

"Yes," Mairelon said. "I know." He picked up the last

of the cushions and threw it viciously to the floor. Kim winced, glad that it had landed on the carpet and not knocked anything over. Even a small noise was likely to attract attention, now that the house was alerted.

Mairelon reached down and curled his hands around the handles of the platter. A moment later, he let go and stood staring down at it, a grim expression on his face.

"Someone got here before us," he said in a low, tight voice. "This is a forgery."

"A forgery? You mean it ain't the right *one?*"

"Exactly." Mairelon turned away. "We had better be going."

Kim looked back at the platter and hesitated. "Are you sure? That's real silver, I'll go bail. And it looks a lot like that bowl of yours."

"The silver's real enough, and you're right about the pattern, but it's not the Saltash Platter," Mairelon replied. "It wouldn't fool any magician for an instant, once he got close enough to lay hands on the thing."

"All right, as long as you're sure." Kim went to the broken window and peered out. "Don't see nobody. Let's pike off."

"We can't do it fast enough to suit me," Mairelon murmured, and waved her on.

FOURTEEN

Kim and Mairelon had no difficulty in evading the searchers who were still scattered here and there on the grounds of Bramingham Place. The servants were spread out and the lanterns they carried were visible for a long way, which made them easy enough to avoid, and there was plenty of cover among the hedges and trees of the sprawling gardens. Kim almost enjoyed dodging through the shrubbery and hiding in the formal borders.

The walk back to the wagon was long, cold, and silent. They kept to the roads, where the moonlight let them see to walk more easily. Mairelon seemed sunk in contemplation, and Kim was too tired to ask what he was thinking. When they reached the wagon at last it was nearly dawn. Kim fell into her makeshift bed at once, and was asleep before she had time to notice whether Mairelon was doing likewise.

She woke to full daylight and the sound of dishes rattling. "Hunch?" she said hazily, lifting her head to see over the mound of blankets she was huddled under.

"I'm afraid not," Mairelon's voice said from near the door of the wagon. "Hunch can't possibly be back before tonight, and I don't really expect him til tomorrow at the earliest. You'll have to put up with my cooking until then. Unless you have hidden skills?" he added hopefully.

"Gnngh," Kim said. She wormed one hand out from under the blankets and rubbed at her eyes. "No."

"Pity. You'd better come have breakfast before it gets cold."

Kim realized that she was hungry. Well, no wonder; she'd done a day's worth of walking since dinner last night, or at least it felt as if she had. She unwound herself reluctantly from the blankets and went out to correct the matter.

Mairelon was crouched over a smoky fire with a long stick in one hand. He was fishing for the handle of an iron pot that balanced precariously on top of two of the burning branches. "Just in time. Bring the plates over."

"I thought you said it would get cold," Kim said, picking up the plates. "Smells to me more like it's getting burned."

"Cold, burned, what's the difference? Ah!" Mairelon snagged the handle at last and lifted the pot out of the fire. He lowered it to the ground and picked up a spoon. "How much do you want?"

"How much is there?" Kim asked, eyeing the black pot dubiously.

"More than enough for two," Mairelon assured her. "I, ah, got a little carried away when I was adding things, I think. Here, take some. I'm afraid there isn't any bread. We'll just have to do without until tomorrow."

Kim frowned at the lumpy greyish blob on her plate, then

shrugged. She had eaten worse-looking meals in her life, and the worst any of them had done was to give her a stomachache. Hunch's savory stews were spoiling her. She took a spoonful. It tasted burned.

Fortunately, Mairelon did not seem to expect her to give her opinion of his cooking. Kim ate slowly, sneaking glances at the magician when she thought he would not notice. He was unusually quiet, but perhaps that was just because Hunch was not there to glower and complain.

Mairelon caught her eye on her fourth or fifth glance. "Have I sprouted horns or a third eye, or is it just that I have charcoal smeared on my forehead?" he asked mildly.

"No," Kim said. Rather than try to explain, she asked, "How did you know that platter last night was sham?"

"Any magician would have. I thought I told you that."

"You said you knew. You didn't say how."

"Ah. Well, I knew because there wasn't any magic in it." Mairelon stared into the fire and swallowed another spoonful of his breakfast blob. "When a wizard puts magic into an object, it's generally because he wants the object to *do* something. That means the magic has to be . . . accessible, and if it's accessible it can be felt by other wizards. If the magic is destroyed or removed it leaves traces, which can also be felt. The platter at Bramingham Place hadn't a farthing's worth of magic in it, and it never had."

Kim frowned. "But if any wizard who touched it would know it was a cheat, why would anyone bother makin' a sham platter?"

"A good question. Possibly the forger wasn't a magician, and didn't realize there would be any difficulty passing it off as the real thing. Or perhaps she only wanted to keep people from realizing it was missing right away. After all, she couldn't have known there'd be such a parade of burglars to blame it on."

"She?" Kim straightened, staring at Mairelon. "You know who put it there?"

"I think so." Mairelon poked at his breakfast. "Renée wasn't part of the parade, you see, and she has more than enough information to have had the platter copied. I can't think of any reason why she'd have come to one of Harriet Bramingham's house parties, either, except to steal the Saltash Platter. She hates house parties."

"Renée? You mean that French lady? I thought she was a friend of yours," Kim said cautiously.

Mairelon's laugh was without humor. "So did I. But she must have been planning this for a long time, certainly since before we left London. So why didn't she tell me?"

"Maybe that Earl cove told her not to," Kim ventured.

"Shoreham?" Mairelon frowned, considering. "I hardly think it's likely. He wouldn't have sent me here if he knew Renée was going to have a go at it."

"He might of—"

"Might *have*."

Kim smothered a relieved sigh. If Mairelon was correcting her speech again, he must not be feeling quite so downhearted. "He might have sent you anyway, if he wanted to get you out of London."

Mairelon looked up with an arrested expression. "Quite true. In fact, it would be just like Edward. I wonder . . ."

His voice trailed off and he stared at the air above the fire. After a moment, he shook himself. "Well, there's only one way to find out. Finish your breakfast, Kim. You'll want it."

"Why?" Kim said warily.

Mairelon gave her a winning smile. "You're going back to Bramingham Place, to take a message to Renée before she leaves."

"I'm *what*?"

"Well, I can't go. Gregory St. Clair is arriving today, and I don't dare chance his seeing me. Don't worry, you'll do fine."

Kim rolled her eyes and went back to eating. Burned and blobby or not, it was safer than talking to Mairelon.

Two days of relatively dry weather had done wonders for the roads, at least as far as travel on foot was concerned. Water still stood at the bottoms of the deepest ruts, and wagons and carriages continued to have a rough, sloppy time of traveling, but the edges of the lanes gave only a little under Kim's feet and no mud dragged at her boots to make walking a weary chore. If she had not been so worried about the task Mairelon had set her, she might even have enjoyed the walk.

"Message for Miss D'Auber, sir," she muttered under her breath. "The master said I was to give it only to her."

She frowned, wondering whether she sounded flash enough. Remembering the words wasn't hard, but the rhythms and the slightly different pronunciation Mairelon had insisted on were difficult indeed. And what if someone started asking her questions? She had some chance of getting the accent right for the sentences she'd practiced, but could she keep it up if she had to say anything else?

Firmly, Kim dismissed her doubts. She had agreed to run this rig, and fretting wouldn't make success any more likely than it already was. Practice, on the other hand . . . "Message for Miss D'Auber," Kim repeated in a low voice. "The master said I was to give it only to her. Message for Miss D'Auber."

So intent was she on her muttered repetitions that she did not hear the sounds of the approaching carriages until they were almost on her. A shout and the crack of a whip startled her into attention at last, and she glanced over her shoulder. Two high-perch phaetons were heading full tilt along the road, side by side. Their drivers crouched intently over their reins, shifting their weight automatically to compensate for the dangerous sway of their vehicles, oblivious to everything save their horses and each other. The one on the left pulled ahead, but his advantage was a matter of inches. The other driver's arm rose and fell, cracking his whip, and his horses leaped forward, bringing him even with the left-hand phaeton once more.

Kim dove for the ditch, praying that these Bedlamites wouldn't overturn or run off the road until they had gone safely past her. The thudding of the horses' hooves and the rumble of the carriage wheels grew louder, then passed by above her in a spray of water, mud, and flying gravel. As the sound began to fade, Kim looked up and saw the phaetons vanish around a curve in the road ahead, both of them still moving with furious speed.

She spat a curse after them as she picked herself up. Her left foot had landed in the muddy water at the bottom of the ditch, and some of it had gotten into her boot. The knees of her good breeches were wet and smeared with dirt and grass, and her hands were scratched and gritty. She cursed again and brushed herself off as best she could, then resumed walking, hoping darkly that something would teach those madmen a lesson. Maybe one of them would overturn his carriage and break a leg. Maybe both of them would.

As she drew near the curve, she heard shouts ahead. Prudently, she stepped off the road in case the phaetons were returning. The noises did not sound as if they were moving in her direction, but Kim took no chances. She trudged along the side of the ditch, sliding on the grass from time to time, until she rounded the curve and got a clear view of the road ahead. She stopped short.

Her wish had been granted: one of the phaetons had indeed overturned. It lay in a tangle of harness and broken wheels across the side of the road, while its owner, scowling ferociously and muddy to the eyebrows, tried to calm his frightened horses. On the opposite side of the road, a coach-and-four lay half in, half out of the ditch. A liveried postillion was tugging at the door of the coach, unconscious of the blood trickling down his face from a cut above his eye. His efforts only made the coach rock precariously. A second postillion was doing his best to control the four coach horses, which were plunging and rearing in a manner that threatened to reduce harness pole, coach, and all to splinters. The coachman lay motionless on the far side of the ditch, evidently thrown from his seat when the coach tipped over.

A little farther on, in the exact center of the road, the second phaeton had drawn to a halt. The driver was concentrating on his horses, and despite her poor opinion of his good sense, Kim had to acknowledge that he knew how to handle a team. Anyone who could come through such a tangle as this had been, at the speed he had been traveling, in a vehicle as notoriously unstable as a high-perch phaeton, without overturning his carriage or losing control of his horses . . . Kim could think of one, or perhaps two, hackney drivers in London who might manage such a feat if they were lucky. This gentleman did not appear to have turned a hair.

"Burn it, Robert!" The driver of the overturned phaeton backed up two hasty steps as one of the chestnut horses he was trying to calm half reared in the traces. "If either of them is hurt—"

"The master appears uninjured," the postillion at the carriage said, temporarily abandoning his pulling at the door to peer through the carriage window. "And I believe John Coachman is not seriously hurt."

"Not them, you imbecile, my chestnuts!" the infuriated driver cried. "Robert—"

"I would be happy to help you, George, but I can hardly leave my horses, can I?" Robert said, half turning without taking his attention from his restive greys. His voice and the outline of his face came together in Kim's mind, and she recognized him as one of the druids she and Mairelon had spied on. George's voice was familiar, too; he was probably another of them. Kim started to roll her eyes, only to be brought up short.

"Who, exactly, is responsible for this outrage?" said a cold, hard voice authoritatively.

Every drop of Kim's blood seemed to congeal into ice. She knew that voice; she had fled from London to get away from its owner. First Jack Stower, now Dan Laverham, she thought in despair. She would never get away from them. She wanted to dive for the ditch and the hedge beyond, but she could not make her muscles obey her. It was all she could do to force her head to turn in the direction of the speaker. When she did, she suffered a second shock.

The tall man who was in the act of climbing out of the ruined coach was not Dan Laverham. He had the same narrow jaw and sharp eyes as Dan, and the same long nose, but his dark hair had less grey in it. Under the superfine coat he wore, his shoulders were broader and more muscular than Dan's. He could have passed as Laverham's brother, if Laverham had had one who dressed like a toff, but he was *not* Dan Laverham. Relief made Kim's knees feel weak.

"Accident, not outrage," Robert said politely. "I am Robert Choiniet, and my friend with the unspeakable chestnuts is George Dashville."

"I take it you were racing on a public thoroughfare," the man from the coach snapped. "You should be horsewhipped for such carelessness."

"Possibly," Robert said with unimpaired calm. "I doubt that anyone will do so, however. May I take a message to someone for you, sir? I must go by Stavely Farm first, but after that I am at your disposal."

"Robert, you traitor!" George had finally succeeded in getting his animals under control, but his angry cry startled them into another round of sidling and head-tossing. "You can't mean to go back to Austen and claim you *won*!"

"Why not? Just because your driving was so bad that you overturned instead of merely losing by an inch or two?"

"Enough." The man from the coach spoke with a quiet deadliness. "I have no interest in your disagreements, and you will oblige me by saving them for another time and place." He turned to Robert Choiniet. "You will go by Bramingham Place and inform them that Lord St. Clair has met with an accident on the road. I trust you are capable of giving them sufficient directions. Beyond that, all I require of you is that you do not return."

"I understand perfectly, sir," Robert said coldly. "Give you good day."

He raised his hands a quarter of an inch. His horses sprang forward, eager to be away, and the phaeton swept off down the road. George Dashville stared after it, spluttering incoherently, while the Baron straightened his cravat and brushed at his coat and breeches. Kim shook herself out of her daze and eased herself farther down the slope of the ditch. A low stone wall ran along the far side; if she could get over it, she had a good chance of getting around the entire muddle of men and carriages without being seen.

Her luck held. The chestnut horses took exception to the Baron's abrupt movements, and George's efforts to keep them from bolting occupied both his attention and St. Clair's while Kim slid over the wall unnoticed. She bent over and crept along it, keeping her head low despite her curiosity. She didn't want St. Clair to catch her, even if he wasn't Dan Laverham. From the way Mairelon acted, St. Clair was as bad as Dan. She didn't straighten up until the Baron's caustic observations regarding George's horsemanship began to fade with distance.

FIFTEEN

Kim's back was sore and stiff from her long, crouched-over walk to avoid Baron St. Clair, so she took things easier on the last mile to Bramingham Place. Once she reached the drive leading up to the house, she slowed even further. She enjoyed looking about at the bushes through which she and Mairelon had dodged the night before, though the manicured lawn and meticulous placement of the trees made her nervous. Besides, she was in no real hurry to complete her errand.

Slow as she went, the house drew inexorably nearer. Kim sighed and straightened her jacket. She had better get this over with before her nerve failed her. She went up to the door and knocked.

The door opened at once, and Kim thought she saw a faint, fleeting expression of surprise on the face of the butler who had opened the door. "Message for Miss D'Auber," Kim said, touching her cap respectfully.

"Very good." The butler held out his hand.

"The master said I was to give it only to her."

The butler's features stiffened into cold disapproval, but all he said was, "I will see that she is informed. Wait here."

The door closed, leaving Kim standing on the step outside. Kim frowned at it. She had a vague idea that there was something not quite right about the butler's action, but her knowledge of gentry kens was limited to the most likely location of the silver. She shrugged. Wait, the man had said, well, she would wait, then. She sat on the step and stared out across the drive.

Several minutes later, Kim heard the door behind her open. She could practically feel the butler's disapproving stare digging into her spine, and smiled to herself. She twisted her head and shoulders around without rising and looked up with an expression of hopeful inquiry.

"Miss D'Auber will see you," the butler said. His mouth was turned down at the corners and he was standing rigidly erect, as if to make up for Kim's informality.

"Good," Kim said cheerfully, and scrambled to her feet. "How soon will she get here?"

The butler winced. "She will see you in the green saloon. I would not presume to say how soon. This way."

Kim tried to suppress a grin as she followed the butler. She was only partially successful, but as the man's back was toward her it did not really matter. He led her down a short hall and showed her into a large room with pale green walls and spindly-legged chairs covered in green-and-gold-striped silk. There were two gilded pier tables between the windows, each with a large gold-rimmed mirror hanging on the wall above it, and at the far side of the room stood a small writing desk.

As the door clicked shut behind her, Kim eyed the chairs dubiously. They did not look as if they were meant to be sat on, but the two footstools did not look any sturdier and she couldn't sit on the pier tables. She finally settled herself on a footstool, reasoning that if it collapsed under her she would be closer to the floor. She had hardly sat down before the door latch clicked again, and Renée D'Auber walked into the room.

"I am Mademoiselle Renée D'Auber," she announced, frowning at Kim. "You have a message for me, yes?" Her auburn hair shone in the sunlight and her figured muslin morning dress was the height of elegance. Looking at her made Kim feel small and rumpled and unpleasantly aware of the dust and grass stains her clothes had acquired on her walk to Bramingham Place.

"Yes," Kim said shortly. She rose and reached into her jacket for the letter Mairelon had given her. As she did, she saw Renée's eyes widen.

"But what is this? You are a girl! Of what is it that Monsieur Merrill is thinking?"

"You ask him, if you want to know," Kim said. French or not, this woman was altogether too fly for comfort. Kim scowled and tapped Mairelon's letter with her forefinger. "And how'd you know this was from him?"

"It is of all things the most likely," Mademoiselle D'Auber replied. "Who else would know I was here? Also, I have been asking for him, and he would of course hear of it. It is unimportant. Give me the message."

Reluctantly Kim held the letter out to her. Mademoiselle D'Auber took it and tore it open at once without stopping to look at the seal. She turned away as she began reading, a moment later Kim heard a brief exclamation in what was presumably French. Kim had no idea what the words meant, but the tone in which they were spoken was one of surprise rather than anger or annoyance.

Renée D'Auber glanced over her shoulder at Kim, then returned to the letter, this time studying it with evident care. Kim wondered what Mairelon had said about her and what this Mademoiselle D'Auber thought of it. She shifted uncomfortably, wishing she could sit down again but not daring to do so for fear of offending Mademoiselle D'Auber.

Mademoiselle D'Auber finished reading and turned back to face Kim. "Of a certainty, this is not at all good," she said, waving the letter.

"That's what we thought," Kim said, emphasizing the "we" slightly.

"To find the real platter becomes a thing most necessary," the Frenchwoman went on as if she had not heard. "I do not at all see how we are to go about it."

"We?" Kim said.

"But of course! It is why I am here, to help."

Kim's frown returned. "Hold on! I thought you was the one that nicked the real platter. Mairelon said nobody else could of got to it before we did."

"Monsieur Merrill is not altogether right," Mademoiselle D'Auber replied. "I looked at Monsieur Bramingham's so-remarkable platter yesterday afternoon, yes, but at once I saw that it was only a copy. I thought, me, that Monsieur Merrill had been very clever, but now I find that it was not him at all, but someone else. It is most annoying. This business is not well arranged, I think."

"It ain't no fault of ours," Kim muttered.

Renée had crossed to the writing desk and did not hear. "I shall write something for you to carry back to Monsieur Merrill," she said, taking out a sheet of heavy, cream-colored paper. "And you must take his letter with you as well. I will allow Madame Bramingham to persuade me to stay here for another day or two." She made a face as she spoke, then shrugged and bent over the page.

"Why do you want me to take Mairelon's message away again?" Kim asked.

"But it would be most awkward if it were found!" Mademoiselle D'Auber said, writing busily. "Monsieur Bramingham would of a certainty call the Bow Street Runners. He has already spoken of it. It was very foolish of Monsieur Merrill to take the copy of the platter, I think."

So Mairelon's letter had not included all the details of the previous night's events! Kim considered the implications of that while Renée finished her letter, and she began to feel more cheerful. "Why did you come—"

"A moment." Mademoiselle D'Auber sanded her letter, then folded it neatly and sealed it with a blob of wax, muttering under her breath as she did. Her voice was too soft for Kim to hear what she was saying, but each word had a sharp, crystalline quality that distance and muttering could not disguise. Kim remembered the spell that Mairelon had cast to test her truthfulness, and backed up a pace.

Mademoiselle D'Auber finished and straightened up with a smothered sigh. She studied the paper for a moment, then turned and held it out to Kim along with Mairelon's unfolded letter. "Here, take this to Monsieur Merrill and tell him that I will be at the inn down in the village tomorrow morning at, oh, ten o'clock precisely."

Kim nodded and took the letters, doing her best to hide her reluctance. Renée D'Auber had put some sort of spell on that letter, Kim was sure of it. And she, Kim, was going to have to carry the thing all the way back to Ranton Hill at least, and maybe farther, if Mairelon had given up waiting at the inn and gone back to the wagon. Kim wasn't normally squeamish, not even about magic, but she didn't like not knowing what kind of spell she was carrying.

Mademoiselle D'Auber watched closely as Kim stowed the letters away beneath her jacket, which did nothing to improve the state of Kim's nerves. "There is one thing more," the Frenchwoman said. She fixed her eyes on Kim's face and said with great seriousness, "It is of all things the most important that Monsieur Merrill not leave before I see him. You understand? So if he thinks to go, you must try to stop him. I think he will listen."

"Be the first time, if he did," Kim said, shrugging. "I'll tell him, though."

"Good." Renée D'Auber gave Kim a long, measuring look, and Kim found herself wondering once again just what Mairelon had said about her in his letter. Then the Frenchwoman went to a long, embroidered bellpull and gave it a vigorous tug. A few moments later, the door opened and a footman stepped into the room. "Mademoiselle?"

"See this . . . boy out," Mademoiselle D'Auber said.

"Mademoiselle." The footman bowed. With a single, sidelong look at the enigmatic Frenchwoman, Kim followed him out of the room and down the hall to the door of Bramingham Place.

When Kim arrived back at the inn late that afternoon, she found Mairelon in the public room playing cards with Freddy Meredith. They were the room's only occupants, and judging from the litter of coins near Mairelon's left elbow, they had been at it for some time. An empty wine bottle lay on the floor beside the table, a second bottle, barely a third full, stood next to the pile of coins that had been wagered on the current hand.

Kim paused in the doorway, wondering what the magician could want with a cloth-head like Meredith. Her eyes flicked from one to the other, and she frowned. Both men were impeccably turned out, from the stiff folds of their cravats to their gleaming Hessian boots, they looked the perfect picture of a pair of gentry. That, Kim realized, was what was bothering her. She had seen Mairelon in his gentry togs before, but she had never realized how well they suited him. No, not quite that, either. She had never realized how well the whole role suited him.

Still frowning, Kim stepped into the room. As she did, Meredith looked up and saw her. He blinked blearily in her direction. He was, Kim saw, more that a little bit on the go. "Who's this, Merrill?"

Mairelon turned. "Kim! What news?"

"Message for you, sir," Kim said, remembering just in time that she was still playing the part of an errand boy.

"Can it wait?"

Kim hesitated. What on earth was she supposed to say to that? "I think you should look at it, sir," she answered at last.

"Ah, well. Let's have it, then." Mairelon held out a hand expectantly.

Kim froze. "Uh—" She couldn't tell him straight out that Renée D'Auber had set a spell on the letter, not with Freddy Meredith sitting there, but she couldn't let him open it without warning him, either. "Sir, I, um—"

"Bailey didn't write it down? I see." Mairelon shoved his chair away from the table and rose, tossing his cards faceup as he did. Kim was relieved to see that there was nothing wrong with his balance or his speech, she had been afraid that he would be as bosky as his companion. "Sorry, Meredith, but duty calls."

Meredith muttered something and began gathering up the coins from the center of the table. Mairelon scooped his own winnings into his hand and thrust them into one of his pockets, then turned and followed Kim out of the room.

"That's a relief!" he said as the door shut behind him. "I was wondering how to get out of there without winning too much from him. You caught on very quickly. Where's Renée's message?"

"Here." Kim took the sealed paper out of her jacket. "She put a spell on it."

"What? Nonsense! There's no reason for her to do that." Mairelon twitched the note out of Kim's hand and reached for the seal. He stopped, frowning, and set his forefinger gently against the dull red wax. "You're right, though," he said after a moment's concentration.

Kim let out her breath in a soundless sigh of relief. "Can you do anything about it?"

"Not here. We'll have to take it back to the wagon."

"You sure we should?"

Mairelon looked irritated. "There's no other way to find out what she's done. I'd also like to read whatever she's written, that is why you went to Bramingham Place, after all."

"I was just askin'."

Mairelon tucked the note into his breast pocket and started for the door. "There's no point in waiting. You can tell me what happened on the walk back. Come along."

Kim rolled her eyes, shook her head, and followed.

Between Kim's desire to include every detail of her journey to Bramingham Place and Mairelon's periodic interruptions, Kim's tale took up most of the walk to the wagon. Mairelon commended Kim for avoiding the Baron St. Clair and frowned over his strong resemblance to Dan Laverham, but Kim could see that he was not giving her his full attention. When she began to speak of Bramingham Place and Renée D'Auber, however, the magician's preoccupation vanished. Kim found this extremely annoying until she noticed Mairelon's right hand rise to touch his breast pocket from time to time. He was more worried about that spell than he wanted to let on.

As soon as they reached the wagon, Mairelon began rummaging in the large chest. Kim sat on the floor beside the door and hugged her knees, watching with great interest. She was cold, tired, and very hungry, but she did not mention it. She was, after all, used to being cold, tired, and hungry, and if she said anything, Mairelon might remember she was there and send her away while he read Renée's letter.

Mairelon laid a white silk scarf and a small crystal globe on the counter and closed the lid of the trunk. He turned and spread the scarf out, smoothing it carefully until not a wrinkle remained. He drew Renée D'Auber's letter from his pocket and set it in the exact center of the scarf, with the blob of sealing wax facing him. Then he lifted the crystal globe with the tips of his fingers and set it on top of the letter. It showed a strong tendency to roll off the lumpy surface of the wax, but he got it positioned at last.

Finally he was satisfied. He raised his hands slowly and extended them, cupping them around the precariously balanced globe without touching it. He bent his head and began to whisper. The words hissed and sizzled in the confined space of the wagon, rough and saw-edged. Kim held her breath.

Orange light flared from the crystal globe, and Renée D'Auber's voice filled the wagon. "My friend, there are things that you must know, and even this means of communication is not entirely safe. I will meet you two hours before the time I told your young companion, in the hollow below the oak hill southwest of Ranton Hill. Do not fail me in this."

Slowly the orange light faded. Mairelon stood motionless, staring down into the crystal, even after the last of the light was gone. Kim twisted to get a better look at his face and realized that he was not looking at the globe in front of him. His eyes were focused on empty air, and he was frowning.

Kim cleared her throat, then cleared it again. Mairelon did not respond. At last she said loudly, "Hey! Is that all?"

"What?" Mairelon said, then shook his head and turned to look reproachfully at Kim. "Don't ever interrupt a wizard in the middle of a spell, Kim. Magic requires a great deal of concentration, and breaking it can be very dangerous."

"I wasn't interrupting a spell," Kim said. "You were just thinkin', far as I could see."

Mairelon blinked and glanced at the crystal. Then he rolled it to one side and picked up Renée's letter. He stood staring at it for a moment, tapping it gently against his left hand, until Kim was afraid he was going to go back into a brown study. She tried to clear her throat again and started coughing in earnest as she inhaled something the wrong way.

This attracted Mairelon's full attention at last, though his first inclination was to proffer cups of water instead of explanations. As soon as Kim got her breath back, she pushed the cup away and demanded, "What was it that was takin' you such a lot of thinkin' on? You ain't goin' to meet that gentry mort like she says to, are you?"

"Meet Renée? Of course I'm going to," Mairelon said. He looked down at the note, which he had still not read, and his frown returned. "I was just wondering why she chose that particular place."

"What particular place?" Kim said, exasperated.

"The hollow by the oak hill where those ridiculous 'druids' had their ceremony the other night," Mairelon said. "Feeling more the thing? Good, because we're going to have a busy evening. I want to get a good look at that hollow while there's still light, and after that—well, we'll see. Come along." He was out the door of the wagon before Kim could respond.

"Hunch ain't goin' to like this," Kim muttered as she limbed to her feet.

"Isn't," Mairelon's voice corrected. A moment later his head reappeared in the open doorway. "And since Hunch isn't here, it doesn't matter. Bring the lamp and the little sack in the corner, I may want them." The head disappeared once more.

Kim rolled her eyes, picked up the lamp and the sack Mairelon had indicated, and started after him.

SIXTEEN

or the rest of the afternoon, Kim and Mairelon
tramped through the wood at the foot of the druids'
hill, peering under bushes and up into trees. Kim
had only the vaguest idea what they were looking for, but
after several attempts to pry an explanation out of Mairelon
she gave up and simply copied him. Half-remembered
warnings about mantraps and poachers made her move warily, but she found nothing. Mairelon seemed to do no better
than she had, but he was preoccupied on the walk back to
the wagon, and Kim was positive he had noticed something
she hadn't.

At Mairelon's insistence, Kim spent the evening working
on her lessons. Her fingers were growing more used to the
moves and twists that made coins seem to vanish from one
hand and appear in the other, and she had mastered the art
of tying knots that slid apart when the proper bit of rope
was pulled, but she was not doing nearly so well at reading.
She pored over the stubborn little black marks for hours,

muttering to herself, while Mairelon prowled restlessly up and down the wagon. Once she ventured a question about his meeting with Renée, but he was so completely uninformative at such length that she did not try again.

Mairelon was up at dawn the next morning, blundering around the limited space inside the wagon in a way that made sleep impossible for anyone else. Kim tried muffling her head under the blanket, but it was no good. Finally she gave up and rose, yawning, to see whether breakfast was one of the things Mairelon had been getting ready during his annoying rambles.

It wasn't. Kim had to make the porridge herself, which did not improve her mood. Her irritation increased further when she noticed that Mairelon had put on his flash togs, rather than his smock or stage clothes, to go to his meeting with Renée. He looked very well in them, which somehow annoyed Kim even more. To top things off, she didn't do much better with the porridge than Mairelon had the day before. "I'll be glad when Hunch gets back," she muttered as she spooned the lumpy grey mixture into her bowl.

"What? Not already!" Mairelon said. He glanced around hastily, then turned a reproachful expression on Kim. "Don't scare me like that."

Kim stared at him in complete bewilderment. "What're you talking about?"

"I thought you said that Hunch was back," Mairelon explained.

"No, I said I'd be glad when he was," Kim said. Then, in response to Mairelon's skeptical expression, she added, "So we can get some better grub."

"Oh." Mairelon looked thoughtful. "You have a point.

Perhaps we should dine at the inn tonight if Hunch hasn't arrived by then. I rather hope he hasn't."

"Why? Hunch cooks better than that fat cove," Kim said.

"If Hunch gets here today, it'll be because he's in a hurry," Mairelon answered. "And he'll only hurry if he thinks Shoreham's information is important. I'd prefer not to have any startling news about any of the people connected with the Saltash Platter. Or its copy."

Kim mulled that over while she finished her porridge. She scraped the last few lumps from the sides of her bowl and surreptitiously shook them off her spoon and onto the ground beside the steps where she was sitting. She scowled down at the bowl, dropped her spoon into it with a muffled clink, and said, "We ought to leave if you want to be the first one at that hill."

"Yes," Mairelon said. "Thank you for reminding me." He rose and brushed at his pants, as if to dispose of non-existent crumbs. "Practice that handkerchief trick while I'm gone; you still haven't got the last twist right."

"You ain't leavin' me here!" Kim said incredulously.

"I most certainly am," Mairelon replied. "When Renée says alone, she means alone. I shouldn't be long."

"You shouldn't be goin' at all," Kim told him. "And you particularly shouldn't be goin' alone. What if that druid cull shows up wavin' his pops, the way he did the other night?"

Mairelon looked amused. "Jonathan Aberford? I doubt that he's even out of bed at this hour, much less wandering about in the woods with a pistol."

"How do you know? He's dicked in the nob, if you ask me, and there ain't no knowing what notions a Bedlamite'll get."

"All the more reason for you to stay here," Mairelon said. To Kim's indignation, he still looked more diverted than concerned. "If he shows up, you can bar the wagon door. No more arguments, Kim, if you please. You're not coming, and that's that."

"It don't please me at all," Kim muttered, but she could see that Mairelon was determined, and she knew from experience that once he took a notion, he was stubborn as a costermonger defending his route through the market. She sat and glowered at him while he straightened his jacket and brushed his hat, but she did not make any further remarks until he had disappeared into the woods. Then she burst out, "Bubblebrained, pigheaded, sapskulled gull! Muttonheaded flat! Nodcock. Goosecap. It'd serve him well enough if I up and followed him. Bufflehead. Shab—"

She stopped suddenly, staring at the place where Mairelon had vanished. She *could* follow him, as easy as not. She scrambled to her feet, then hesitated, considering. Mairelon was a wizard, and in spite of the abuse she had just been showering on him, Kim had to admit that he was sharp as two needles. That ginger-pated D'Auber mort was a wizard, too, and she had a powerful reputation. She was foreign into the bargain, and therefore unpredictable. What would they do if they caught Kim spying on them?

The thought gave Kim a moment's pause. Then she shrugged. She'd just have to make sure they didn't catch her, that was all. Stay hid and sherry off if they looked like suspecting anything. It was no different from being on the sharping lay in London. And if there *was* trouble, Mairelon would excuse her obstinacy in following him. Besides, given Mairelon's idea of "explanation," there was no other way she could be sure of finding out what happened at the meeting.

That decided her. She threw some dirt on the fire, kicked her bowl under the steps of the wagon, and started off. She did not take the same route as Mairelon had, but cut sideways up to the road. After all, she knew where he was going. There was no point in risking discovery by sticking too close.

The road was dry enough for comfortable walking, and there was no sign of approaching vehicles, but Kim, remembering her experience the day before, stuck to the far edge anyway. "What am I doing?" she asked herself as she trudged along. "Goin' off to spy on a couple of frog-makers? I must be madder than *he* is!" But she continued walking in spite of her misgivings.

The sound of hooves and the rattle of a carriage brought Kim out of her reverie. Glancing up, she saw a landau coming briskly toward her from the direction of Ranton Hill. She sighed and angled down the verge, hoping that the driver would not pay any heed to a shabby boy heading into town. When she looked up again, the carriage had slowed and begun to turn down the lane that led to the druids' meeting place. It was close enough now to give Kim a clear view of the occupants, and she nearly choked trying to smother an exclamation. Lady Granleigh sat stiffly erect in the rear seat, while her brother Jasper made shift with his back to the horses. The driver was the heavyset Stuggs, and he was frowning in evident concentration as he tried to maneuver the landau around the corner.

"This is the outside of enough!" Lady Granleigh said in

a carrying voice as the landau lurched forward. "On our return, you will drive, Jasper."

"Really, Amelia, I don't see why you think I'll do any better than Stuggs," Jasper replied. "I'm no Corinthian. You should have let me bring the coachman."

"You are, at least, a *gentleman*," Lady Granleigh said firmly. "And the fewer who are aware of this excursion, the better. Since you have seen fit to confide in this . . . person, we have no choice but to utilize his admittedly second-rate skills. And I must say, Jasper, that I think you could have found someone with more ability if you had only applied yourself properly."

The landau lurched again and rolled reluctantly into the lane, and Lady Granleigh's complaints were lost among the trees. Kim shook off her paralysis and sprinted forward. That skinny toff and his sister were trouble, whatever their lay was, but Kim was willing to bet sixpence that they'd be a particularly whacking great lot of trouble if they found Mairelon and Renée D'Auber at the druid hill. Fortunately, the lane was rough and curving, and with Stuggs driving they wouldn't make good time. Kim might, just possibly, get to the hill first with a warning if she ran.

She didn't manage it. The uneven ground, the constant need to dodge inconveniently placed trees, and the thin branches of the young trees and brush that whipped her face, all combined to slow her more than she would have believed. As she neared the hill, she heard voices ahead of her and cursed under her breath. In London she would have gotten there in plenty of time.

Kim slowed and began to pick her way with more care. It would do Mairelon no good at all if she made too much noise and Jasper or Stuggs discovered her. She reached the fringe of bushes below the hill and started working her way toward the voices. As she came around to the far side, she heard Jasper's voice with sudden clarity, saying, "—question is, who are *you?*"

"Tell him to come down here, where we can talk without shouting, Jasper," Lady Granleigh put in imperiously.

As Jasper repeated his sister's command, Kim stopped and peered through the bushes. Lady Granleigh and her brother were standing at the foot of the hill. Stuggs was a little behind them; beyond, the landau and horses were a sketchy outline between trees. The dark bulk of the druids' lodge was barely visible, though Kim knew from yesterday's explorations that it was only a few steps from the hill.

Mairelon was sitting on the ground halfway up the hill, careless of the damage his fine clothes must be suffering. His face was in shadow and Kim could not make out his expression, but his pose conveyed polite but bored attention.

"Well?" Jasper said when Mairelon did not reply. "Who are you?"

"No, no," Mairelon said. "I asked you first. I also, if you recall, asked how you found this place and what you intend to do here, and you haven't told me that, either."

"We might ask you the same thing," Jasper retorted.

"You might, but I don't recommend it," Mairelon said. "You'll get a reputation as a poor conversationalist if all you can do is repeat what other people say to you."

"This is absurd," Lady Granleigh said. "Tell us who you are and what you're doing here, or be off about your business. I haven't time to waste on this nonsense."

Mairelon rose to his feet and bowed. "It is impossible to refuse such a charming request. My name is de Mare, and I'm here by way of guarding the Sacred Hill."

Jasper and Lady Granleigh looked at each other. Behind them, Stuggs stiffened, and Kim saw his right hand rise toward his chest, as if to touch something underneath his coat for reassurance. Kim frowned. Mairelon had done a perfect imitation of Jonathan Aberford's tone, and both Jasper and his sister seemed to recognize the phrasing. Stuggs's reaction was more difficult to interpret, and more ominous.

"Well, you can go along now," Jasper told Mairelon grandly. "Jonathan Aberford said—"

"If I may speak with you a moment, Jasper," Lady Granleigh interrupted.

Jasper turned his head and glared at her.

"*Now*, Jasper," Lady Granleigh said with unruffled calm. Without waiting for him to respond, she turned and walked straight toward the bushes where Kim was hiding. Kim froze. She was certain she hadn't been seen yet, but if she tried to move now, Lady Granleigh would spot her for sure.

Lady Granleigh stopped a few steps short of the bush and tapped her foot impatiently as she waited for her brother to join her.

"What are you playing at, Amelia?" Jasper said irritably. "And what are we going to do now? Burn it, Miss Thornley never said anything about a guard!"

"Marianne is far too innocent to think of such a thing, and Frederick Meredith was clearly too shatter-brained to mention it," Lady Granleigh replied. "You should have talked to him yourself, Jasper, instead of leaving it to Marianne."

"That was your idea! You were the one who said Meredith would tell more to a pretty face. I never liked the idea of letting my fiancée empty the butter pot over that nodcock, and so I told you."

"Miss Thornley isn't your fiancée yet, Jasper, and you'd do well to remember that before you take that tone with me," Lady Granleigh said. "If you want my help in winning her—and her fortune—you will have to earn it. I must point out that so far you have been precious little help."

"How do you expect me to help when you ruin everything I try to do?" Jasper waved his arms indignantly. "I was about to get rid of that fellow so we could go ahead with your precious scheme, only you stopped me."

"You were about to make yet another muddle, you mean." Lady Granleigh shook her head. "Really, Jasper, sometimes I despair of your intelligence. Don't you see that Mr. de Mare's presence changes everything?"

"No, I do not," Jasper said. "If we could just persuade him to go away—"

"He would remember us, and when the platter was found, he would connect us with its reappearance. That could be very awkward for us."

"Well, what do you think we should do?" Jasper asked in a sullen tone.

"We shall give Mr. de Mare the platter," Lady Granleigh answered serenely.

"What?!" Jasper all but shrieked the word, and both Mairelon and Stuggs turned interested eyes in his direction.

Jasper scowled back at them and lowered his voice. "Amelia, have you gone mad?"

"Do you want to have Jonathan Aberford lurking about Bramingham Place for the remainder of our stay?"

"No, but—"

"Can you suggest some other way we might be rid of him?"

"We've already been over this, and you know I haven't. But you just told me a minute ago why we can't give this de Mare fellow the platter!"

"I explained why we cannot simply leave the platter here for Mr. Aberford and his friends to find, as we had originally planned," Lady Granleigh corrected him. "If you had been listening, or thinking, you would have understood. Presenting the package to Mr. de Mare is another matter entirely."

"I don't see how. He's bound to remember us, and you already said that that would be awkward."

Lady Granleigh sighed. "The platter is well wrapped, tied up, and addressed to Mr. Jonathan Aberford. If we tell Mr. de Mare that a young man, whom we took to be one of Henry Bramingham's friends, gave us the parcel in town and asked us to deliver it here, it will not matter whether he remembers us. Once they discover that the platter is a forgery, Mr. Aberford and his friends will look for the mysterious young man, if they look for anyone at all. You and I will be mere innocent go-betweens."

"And how are you going to explain it if anyone asks why Miss Thornley was prying into Meredith's business?"

"I shall say that she finds him interesting," Lady Granleigh replied. She frowned slightly. "I shall have to see that she continues to spend time in his company for the next day or two. After that, it will not be thought wonderful if she tires of him."

"Interested in *Meredith?*" Jasper snorted. "That won't fadge, Amelia. *Nobody* could be interested in that simpleton."

Lady Granleigh gave him a cold look. "Are you hinting that I will not be believed? I assure you, no one will think twice about it. Mr. Meredith is no more foolish than most young men, and Marianne is no less so than most girls, so it is quite plausible."

"Yes, but look here, Amelia, how am I supposed to pay court to Miss Thornley if you're forever telling her to talk with Meredith?" Jasper said hastily. "I don't like it."

"I did not ask you to like it," Lady Granleigh said. "I simply wish you to refrain from interfering. Keep quiet, and let me talk to Mr. de Mare."

"Amelia—" Jasper was too late, Lady Granleigh had turned and started back toward the hill as she finished her sentence. "Friday-faced harpy!" Jasper muttered, so low that Kim almost missed the words. He raked his fingers through his hair, patted his cravat, and smoothed the front of his coat, then started after his sister.

Lady Granleigh reached the foot of the hill and raised her chin to study Mairelon. "Mr. de Mare," she said as Jasper, still glowering in disapproval, joined her, "you have an honest face, and your reasons for being here interest me. Are you by some chance acquainted with Mr. Jonathan Aberford?"

"He is the leader of the Company that meets here," Mairelon said cautiously.

"Very good," Lady Granleigh said. "My brother and I are on our way to Swafflton. A young man in the village requested that we deliver a package to this place, and we agreed. The package is addressed to Mr. Aberford; presumably he will know what to do with it. I trust you can see that he receives it?"

"I am quite capable of doing so, madam," Mairelon replied.

"Then we will entrust the package to you. We have spent far too much time on this errand already. Stuggs!"

"Ma'am." The large man lowered his eyes as Lady Granleigh turned to face him, transforming his expression from one of intent interest into one of bored resentment.

"Fetch the parcel from the carriage at once, and give it to Mr. de Mare, with my compliments," Lady Granleigh commanded.

Kim frowned as she watched Stuggs nod and walk off. Unless she'd forgotten the difference between a sharper and a flat, there was something about that cove that didn't fit. He smelled of the back streets and rookeries of London, and gentry didn't hire servants there if they wanted to keep their silver. If only she could pike off to the Hungerford Market for a few hours and ask Red Sal or Tom Correy what they knew about Stuggs! One of them was bound to have heard something . . . Kim put the thought firmly aside; there was nothing to be gained by wishing for the impossible.

Stuggs returned, carrying a large brown package. He paused at the foot of the hill, but one glance at Lady Granleigh set him climbing. Mairelon waited where he was and accepted the package with a solemn half-bow. Kim, still watching Stuggs closely, saw a crease form between his eyebrows as he turned and came down the hill, and realized that Mairelon's bow had prevented Stuggs from getting a good look at his face.

Kim brooded over the possible implications while Lady Granleigh and Mairelon exchanged polite farewells. Jasper's concession to good manners took the form of a curt nod, which drew a glare from his sister and another half-bow from Mairelon. Lady Granleigh hesitated, looking as if she would have given her brother a rare trimming then and there, except that she would then have been guilty of even worse conduct than his. In the end, she turned and swept away without saying anything, but her lips were pressed together in a manner that boded ill for Jasper's peace during the coming carriage ride. Jasper followed, still scowling, and a moment later Kim heard the sounds of the coach departing.

SEVENTEEN

Kim let out a long breath as the noise of the carriage died away among the trees. She could hardly believe she had gone unnoticed. "Well, well," Mairelon's voice said meditatively from the hillside. "How very interesting."

Kim jerked at the unexpected sound, and her arm grazed the bush in front of her. Mairelon's head snapped in the direction of the rustle. "Renée?" he called.

"No, it's me," Kim said, rising. She walked forward, brushing dead leaves from her coat.

"You were supposed to stay at the wagon," Mairelon said without heat.

"That's what you said," Kim agreed. "I never told you I would."

"True." Mairelon pursed his lips and gazed at Kim thoughtfully. "I can see I'll have to listen to you more carefully in the future. How long have you been here?"

"Since right after the bracket-faced gentry mort and her

brother came," Kim answered. "I saw them on the road, but I couldn't hop it fast enough to get here first."

"You didn't by any chance see Mademoiselle D'Auber as well, did you?"

"No," Kim said with some satisfaction. "I didn't."

Mairelon eyed her sharply, then frowned. "It's not like Renée to be late." He tucked Lady Granleigh's parcel under his arm and pulled a watch from his pocket. As he glanced at it, his frown deepened. "Certainly not this late."

"Maybe she saw them two on their way here," Kim suggested, jerking a thumb in the direction Lady Granleigh's carriage had gone. There was no reason for Mairelon to get in a taking over Renée D'Auber. She was a wizard, after all; she could take care of herself.

Mairelon looked up, still frowning. "Yes, that would explain it," he said. "And it's 'those two,' not 'them two.' "

"Those two, then," Kim said, obscurely comforted by this offhanded correction. "What are you goin' to do with the platter?"

"Platter?" Mairelon's expression went blank; then his eyes followed Kim's pointing finger. "Oh, is that what's in this package? How convenient."

"It's the cheat they nicked from the library at Bramingham Place," Kim added. "I heard them talkin'."

"Indeed." Mairelon took the parcel out from under his arm and studied it. "Why would Lady Granleigh want to give the fake platter to Jonathan Aberford? And why deliver it here? He lives in the vicinity, his direction can't be particularly difficult to discover."

Kim shrugged. "They didn't say."

"Mmmm." Mairelon continued his examination of the

parcel for a moment. Suddenly he flipped the package end for end, tucked it back under his arm, and started briskly down the hill. "Time to be going. It wouldn't do for someone to get into the wagon while we're away."

"Or catch us hangin' about here with that thing," Kim muttered, eyeing the package Mairelon was carrying. As he reached the base of the hill, she fell into step beside him and added in a louder voice, "There's somethin' smoky about that Stuggs cove, that drove the carriage."

"Do you think so? He's not the usual gentleman's gentleman, I'll admit, but then, Jasper Marston doesn't seem very good at being a usual sort of gentleman."

"I don't know what his lay is, but he's no flat, that's sure," Kim said positively "He pokered up when you said your name was de Mare, and he was watchin' everything too close. And he wasn't keen to give you that package, no matter what the bracket-faced mort said."

"Wasn't he, now," Mairelon said "How interesting. You know, Kim, this whole business is beginning to look extremely odd."

"*Beginnin'* to look odd?"

"Marston, who has no reason I can think of to even be aware of the existence of the Saltash Set, hires the unlikely Mr. Stuggs to run errands and you to find out whether I have the bowl. Not, mind you, to steal it, but only to discover whether the thing is hidden in one of my cupboards He and Lady Granleigh go to a great deal of trouble to steal a copy of the Saltash Platter from Bramingham Place, in spite of interruptions from several people who ought not to know anything about it, either. Then when they get it, they immediately set out to give it to Mr. Aberford, whom Marston, at least, must have recognized as one of the inept housebreakers"

"Maybe he didn't," Kim said. "And they've had the platter since night before last. That ain't givin' it back very immediately"

"Isn't," Mairelon corrected. "The real question is, why would Lady Granleigh want to turn the fake platter over to Aberford instead of giving it back to Henry Bramingham? Bramingham is, after all, the person from whom she stole it."

Kim shook her head. "There's no accountin' for gentry folk."

"Nonsense," Mairelon said firmly. "She must have had some reason. Your Mr. Stower is another puzzlement. I doubt that he is in league with Lady Granleigh, but given Marston's obvious penchant for unusual servants, I don't think we can rule out a connection there."

"He ain't my Mr. Stower," Kim said. "If he's anybody's, he's Dan Laverham's."

"So you've said. In which case, the question that leaps immediately to mind is, is Stower on his own in this or not? And either way, why is he, or Laverham, interested in the Saltash Set? And how did they find out about it?"

"The last part's easy," Kim said. "Laverham's got an eye for anything that'll bring in money, and London's full of coves as would put him in the way of nicking the platter just to get on his good side."

Mairelon gave her an indecipherable look. "Possibly Hunch will have more to say about it when he returns from London. Then there's Mr. Aberford, whose desire for the platter is the only one that appears simple and straightforward. I therefore distrust it on principle, particularly given Mr. Aberford's, ah, unorthodox attempts to retrieve the thing"

"You weren't above breakin' into that Bramingham cove's library yourself," Kim reminded him. "Unless that ain't—isn't—what you meant by 'unorthodox.' "

"*Everyone* broke into Bramingham's library," Mairelon said testily. "Including Renée. Everyone who was anywhere near Ranton Hill, that is. I suppose I should be glad St. Clair didn't arrive until a day later, or we might have seen him bumbling around with everyone else."

Kim suppressed a shiver "I don't think so. He didn't look like no bumbler to me, and for sure he's no flat."

"Quite true," Mairelon said with another sidelong glance at Kim. "I stand corrected, I've been acquainted with St. Clair long enough to know better. He would undoubtedly—"

Mairelon broke off as they came within sight of the wagon. A curl of smoke was rising past the far side of the roof, and Mairelon looked reproachfully at Kim.

"I put the fire out before I left!" Kim protested. "I'm not sapskulled."

"Then it appears we have company," Mairelon said. His stride lengthened, and Kim had to skip twice to catch up. "Perhaps Renée has found us, after all."

Kim, who had been thinking of Jasper Marston and his sister, or the unpleasant Lord St. Clair, was surprised and not altogether pleased by this suggestion. She was even more surprised, but considerably relieved, when they came around the corner of the wagon and found Hunch feeding medium-sized sticks into a new fire. A placid-looking roan, presumably Hunch's means of transportation, was tied to the back of the wagon, chewing quietly on an invisible wisp of hay.

"Hunch!" Mairelon said, stopping short. "Well, that was always a possibility. You haven't seen Renée around anywhere, have you?"

"*If* you mean that Miss Doo-bear friend o' yours, no, I ain't," Hunch answered. "Nor I ain't likely to. She's in London, laid up with a chill."

"No, she isn't," Mairelon said, frowning. "She's a houseguest at one of Mrs. Bramingham's interminable parties. I've seen her myself. I wonder why she thought she had to pretend she was staying in London?"

"You've seen 'er?" Hunch frowned. "Now, 'ow would you 'ave done that when you was supposed to be a-staying 'ere out of trouble while I was gone?"

"These things happen," Mairelon said, waving a hand in airy dismissal.

"Don't you gammon me, Master Richard," Hunch said severely. "What 'ave you been up to now?"

"This and that," Mairelon answered "What did Lord Shoreham have to say? Or did he send you off without any information? I hope not; I did tell you to wait."

" 'E 'ad a lot to say." Hunch's expression was grim, and he paused for a moment to chew on the right side of his mustache. "And I ain't repeating any of it til you tell me what you've been doing!"

"Oh, we've been keeping busy, haven't we, Kim?"

"Don't go draggin' me in!" Kim said quickly. "It ain't none of my lay."

Hunch scowled at Kim, then turned his attention back to

Mairelon. "You 'adn't ought to—what 'ave you got there?"

Mairelon shifted the parcel under his arm and smiled. "This? I'm not sure. Kim says it's the Saltash Platter, but I haven't looked yet to see whether she's right."

"I never—" Kim gasped, only to be cut short by a look from Mairelon.

"Let's find out, shall we?" Mairelon said, holding the parcel out to Hunch.

Hunch tried to glare at Mairelon, but his eyes kept returning to the package. At last he took it. With a final glare and considerable muttering, he sat down on the step of the wagon and began undoing the knots. Kim realized suddenly that Hunch was just as curious about things as she was, and as little able to resist the opportunity to find something out.

The strings fell apart and Hunch unfolded the wrappings. A silver platter lay across his knees, shining even in the leaden sunlight that crept through the clouds. It was very like the one Kim had glimpsed at Bramingham Place, but she wouldn't have wagered a farthing one way or the other on this being the same article.

"Where did you come by this?" Hunch demanded suspiciously.

"One thing at a time, Hunch," Mairelon responded. "Let me have a look at it first."

"No, you don't," said a new voice as Mairelon reached for the platter.

The surly tone was unmistakably Jack Stower's, and Kim's stomach sank as her head swiveled in the direction of the voice. There was no chance that he wouldn't see her now. Then she got a good look at him, and froze where she stood.

Jack Stower was standing at the rear corner of the wagon beside the roan. He had a large sack strapped over one shoulder. In each hand he held a pistol, and his face wore a forbidding scowl. "I'll have that there wicher cheat, and no gammon," he snarled.

"Just so," said Mairelon without moving. "Do I bring it to you, or do you come and get it"

"Put it on, the ground, there," Stower said, gesturing with one of the pistols. "Then you and the turnip-pated cove get over by the fire. Hop it!"

With exaggerated care, Mairelon lifted the platter and set it in front of Stower. Then he backed away, his eyes fixed on Stower's face. "Hunch," he said without turning, and the dour servingman rose and joined him.

Stower stuck one of his pistols through his belt and swung the sack down from his shoulder. The coarse fabric stretched and shifted around something large and flat and rectangular as he lowered it to the ground. Kim stared at the sack in sudden wild surmise.

"Now you, boy," Stower said, taking the second pistol from his belt and aiming it at Mairelon and Hunch once more. "You take that wicher cheat and—Kim!"

"Surprise," Kim said sourly. "Long way from London, ain't it, Stower?"

Stower's face darkened. "I'll London you! You think you're going to nick a few of the yellow boys Laverham's offering, don't you? Well, you ain't getting nothing. This is my lay, see? How'd you get here ahead of me, anyways?

You didn't follow the old cove from the inn. I'd a seen you."

"Just luck," Kim managed. She felt sick. After Stower's hints, Mairelon and Hunch would never trust her again.

"Sorry, Master Richard," Hunch said in tones of chagrin. "I thought as I 'ad shook 'em off the trail in London."

"But Mr. Stower wasn't in London," Mairelon said, and Kim nearly jumped when she felt the unmistakable crystalline quality of the words. Surely Mairelon couldn't mean to try a spell on a man holding two pistols at his head?

"He was in Ranton Hill," Mairelon went on, and the sharp edge of magic was clearer and more threatening than before. "He should still be in Ranton Hill. He should go back to Ranton Hill before something happens to him, *tzay min po, katzef*!"

Jack Stower's face contorted, as if in fear or pain. He gave a strangled cry and hurled one of his pistols at Mairelon. Instantly Hunch dove sideways, knocking Mairelon out of the way as Stower turned and plunged into the wood behind the wagon. Kim threw herself down as the pistol hit the ground and went off, sending a bullet whistling through the empty air where Mairelon's chest had been a moment before.

"The shotgun, Hunch," Mairelon said, panting slightly. "He's still got one pistol, and that spell was only a makeshift. It won't hold him long."

Hunch rolled to his feet and ran for the wagon without wasting time on words of acknowledgment. Kim picked herself up and followed, pausing just long enough to scoop up Jack's bag and the silver platter that lay beside it. Mairelon was the last one inside. He barred the door behind him, then reached up and pressed a knothole in the ceiling.

There was a barely audible click. Mairelon set his palms flat against the ceiling and pushed, and a two-foot section lifted up half an inch, then slid back out of the way. "The gun and a lift, Hunch, if you please," Mairelon said softly.

"You 'adn't ought to be doing this, Master Richard," Hunch grumbled, but he handed Mairelon the shotgun and knelt. Mairelon set a hand on the edge of the opening in the ceiling and a foot in Hunch's cupped hands, and a moment later slid noiselessly out onto the roof of the wagon.

Kim watched this performance with considerable admiration. The speed and smoothness with which it was done spoke of much practice, and she was impressed by the forethought that had designed the hidden panel in the ceiling. After a moment, it occurred to her to wonder just how often Mairelon and Hunch had had to make use of this particular device. It threw a whole new light on their possible doings in the past.

The minutes ticked slowly by. At last, Mairelon's head reappeared in the opening. "No sign of him," the magician said. "He's gone for now. Here." He handed the shotgun down to Hunch, then climbed down through the hole. "I'll have to see about setting up some wards; we can't have people popping in and waving pistols around whenever they feel like it. It's becoming altogether too popular a sport to ignore."

"Like that Aberford cove the other night," Kim said, nodding.

"And just what 'as that got to do with all this?" Hunch demanded. "What 'ave you been at while I've been gone, Master Richard?"

"Back to that again? Really, Hunch, I'm beginning to think you're prudish, and I see no reason for Kim and me to elaborate on our relationship merely to satisfy your vulgar curiosity. Particularly when we have more important things to do." Mairelon smiled beatifically at Hunch's outraged expression and waved toward the sack Kim was holding. "Just open that up, Kim, so we can see what our Mr. Stower has been hauling about the countryside."

Kim deposited the silver platter on the floor and began wrestling with the knots at the mouth of the sack. She got them loose at last and reached inside. A moment later she held up a large silver platter, to all appearances identical to the one on the floor.

"Well, well," said Mairelon. "What have we here?" He reached out and took the platter from Kim, and a frown creased his forehead.

"It looks like this other one," Kim said, nudging the first platter with her toe.

"That's exactly what it is," Mairelon said. "Exactly."

"What does that mean?" Hunch said in a resigned tone.

"It means that it's another fake," Mairelon replied.

EIGHTEEN

Munch stared at the platter in Mairelon's hands. "*Another* fake?" he said at last. "You mean that one—" he nodded at the platter on the floor, "—ain't the Saltash Platter, *either*?"

"That is correct," Mairelon said. He turned the second copy over in his hands, studying it with a thoughtful expression. "Kim," he said suddenly, "bring it over here and hold it up so I can look at them both."

Kim did as she was instructed. Mairelon peered intently at a section of the platter he held, then turned to Kim's. After a moment, he returned to the first platter and repeated the process. There was a smear of dust above his left eyebrow, and Kim wondered how he could keep from noticing it, even if his reflection was blurred by the intricate patterns incised on the surface of the platters.

Finally Mairelon set his platter on the counter. With a relieved sigh, Kim did the same; Saltash Platter or not, all that silver was *heavy*. Mairelon stared absently down at them both.

"Well?" Hunch demanded.

"Two copies," Mairelon said, more as if he were thinking aloud than as if he were answering Hunch. "Two *identical* copies. Identical right down to the scuffs and scratches. Whoever made these wasn't working from a description or from drawings."

"Then he had the real one to copy?" Kim said tentatively.

"I would be willing to bet on it," Mairelon replied. "So if we find the silversmith, we'll find the Saltash Platter."

Hunch snorted. "Sounds to me as if you're back where you started, Master Richard."

"Not quite," Mairelon said, and smiled. "There's only one person in this area who's had the platter long enough to make copies. Freddy Meredith."

"*Meredith?*" Kim said incredulously. "You're bammin' me! That sapskull?"

"I'll admit it doesn't sound likely," Mairelon conceded. "But who else is there? Bramingham only had the platter for a day or so; he couldn't have gotten *one* copy made in that time, much less two. None of the other, er, interested parties has even been in Ranton Hill long enough, much less had the platter in his possession."

"What about that Aberford cove?" Kim objected.

"Well, yes, I suppose he ought to be considered a possibility," Mairelon said. "But I don't think he would have tried to burgle Bramingham Place the other night unless he thought the platter there was the real one."

"Burgle Bramingham Place?" Hunch said. His lips tight-

ened, causing his mustache to wiggle alarmingly. "Master
Richard—"

"Yes, I hadn't forgotten about you," Mairelon interrupted. He seated himself on top of the chest and looked
at Hunch with an air of expectancy. "I assume Shoreham
told you something worth hearing, or you wouldn't have
come back so promptly. Let's have it."

Hunch rolled his eyes. Kim suppressed an impulse to
grin, as much at Mairelon's tactics as Hunch's reaction. She
wondered how long Mairelon would be able to keep from
explaining to Hunch just what he had been doing in his
henchman's absence. She sat down cross-legged on the
floor and waited for Hunch to begin.

" 'Oo do you want to 'ear about first?" Hunch asked.

"Jack Stower, since he has intruded on us so recently."

" 'E's a nasty piece o' work," Hunch said. " 'E lives in
St. Giles, far as anyone can tell, thieving and suchlike. Lord
Shoreham says 'e ain't no different from most of the scum
as follows 'is profession, and the most interesting thing
about 'im is 'is master."

"Who is Dan Laverham," Mairelon said. "We'll have
him next, but not before we're finished with Mr. Stower.
Did Shoreham find out when Stower left London?"

" 'E left the day after we did," Hunch replied. "Lord
Shoreham found someone 'oo was drinking Blue Ruin with
'im the night afore 'e left, and 'e says Stower was mum-
bling 'ints about some errand 'e was going to do for Mr.
Laverham."

Mairelon looked interested. "Hints? What sort of hints?"

"Mysterious 'ints," Hunch said. "Lord Shoreham didn't
say no more than that."

"How like him," Mairelon murmured. "Very well. What about Mr. Laverham?"

" 'E's a bit of a puzzle. 'E lives in the rookery, but 'e dresses and talks like one o' the *ton*. And 'e went to 'Arrow."

"Harrow!" Mairelon looked startled. "How did a boy from St. Giles get into a school like that? He *is* from St. Giles?"

"Far as Lord Shoreham knows," Hunch said, nodding. "As for 'Arrow, somebody paid 'is fees."

"He's probably the by-blow of someone with both a conscience and the money to indulge it, then," Mairelon said thoughtfully. "Unfortunately, the combination is not so unusual that it is instantly apparent who Laverham's presumed parent is."

"That's what Lord Shoreham thought," Hunch said. " 'E said 'e'd talk to some of 'is friends in the City and see if one of 'em could track the money, but it ain't much of a chance."

"I wonder how well Laverham did at Harrow? They're strong in Latin and Greek and wizardry, as I recall."

Kim chocked. "You mean Dan Laverham is a *wizard*?"

"If he was educated at Harrow, he ought to know the basics, at least," Mairelon replied. "Don't let it trouble you."

"Easy enough for you to say," Kim muttered. She didn't know what a first-class frog-maker could do to someone, but half-formed images of the horrible possibilities whirled through her mind. Their very vagueness made them worse than actual knowledge would have been.

"Anything else?" Mairelon asked, turning back to Hunch.

"Mr. Laverham 'as a name in some parts as the man to see if you want something done and you ain't fussy about 'ow. 'E ain't never been caught doing nothing wrong, though."

"That's Dan, all right," Kim said in an undertone.

"Yes, thanks to Kim, we probably have more information about Mr. Laverham's criminal activities than Shoreham does," Mairelon said. "Did he have anything to say about Marston or Fenton?"

"Mr. Jasper Marston is 'ead over ears in debt," Hunch told them. " 'E's supposed to be rusticating right now, to get away from 'is creditors."

"And Lady Granleigh has promised to assist him to a rich marriage if he helps her with whatever labyrinthine plans she has set in motion," Mairelon said.

Hunch looked startled. " 'Ow do you know that?"

"Kim overheard them talking," Mairelon said.

" 'E's Lady Granleigh's younger brother, and Lord Shoreham said 'e was a bit of a slow-top," Hunch resumed. "When 'e ain't wasting 'is money on cards and 'orses, 'e does what 'is sister tells 'im."

"That has become fairly evident. Shoreham didn't mention Marston's man, Stuggs, did he?"

"No."

"Ah, well. One can't have everything, and I didn't ask." Mairelon stared pensively at the window for a moment. Then he looked up and said, "I believe that leaves James Fenton."

Hunch grinned. The unaccustomed expression made him

look positively fiendish, and Kim was completely taken aback by the change. Mairelon took one look and came to attention like a skilled sharper sighting a promising dupe.

"Fenton's the black sheep of 'is family," Hunch said, still with that disturbing grin. "They're mostly respectable tradesmen. 'E seemed clever, so they 'ad 'im put into service. 'E started off as a footman."

"Indeed." Mairelon's eyes narrowed. "And what house was he in service to?"

"Lord St. Clair's," Hunch said with great satisfaction.

"St. Clair!"

"*And* 'e was dismissed the day after the *Colony Queen* left the docks," Hunch added.

"Huh?" said Kim.

"The *Colony Queen* was the ship Hunch and I took when we, er, fled the country after the Saltash Set was stolen," Mairelon said. "So Fenton was dismissed right after the theft was blamed solidly on me, was he? I wonder if he knows something about it."

"Lord Shoreham thought 'e might," Hunch said. " 'E also thought you'd be interested in knowing that on the night the Saltash Set was stolen Fenton 'ad some unscheduled free time."

"Unscheduled? You mean he took French leave?"

"No, 'e 'ad Lord St. Clair's permission," Hunch said. " 'E just wasn't supposed to 'ave that night off, Lord Shoreham says."

"Well, if Shoreham says Fenton was supposed to be working that night, he's probably right," Mairelon said. "I don't know how he comes up with these things, but he hasn't been mistaken once in five years. What has Fenton been doing since he, er, left St. Clair?"

"Mucking about 'ere and there. 'E did a few jobs for some of them 'ousebreakers, but 'e ain't 'ad no honest work until six weeks ago, when 'e upped and 'ired on at Meredith's 'ouse."

"Six weeks," Mairelon said, frowning. "Time enough for him to find out about the platter and notify St. Clair, if that was why he was here. But if St. Clair let him go—"

"Couldn't it have been a blind?" Kim said. "That Lord St. Clair, he sounds like a fly cove; maybe he didn't want any ties to a looby like Fenton. If the two of them nabbed that silver stuff you're always on about, then—"

Mairelon shook his head. "No, no, I can't believe St. Clair was involved in the original theft. He'd have to be completely lost to all sense of honor."

"And I suppose he wasn't a Captain Sharp if all he did was peach on you to the nabbing culls?" Kim said scornfully.

"It's not the same thing," Mairelon said.

"I don't see why not," Kim told him. "Anyway, lords aren't that different from other folks. If they want somethin' bad enough, they'll try to get it however they can, and never mind the right and wrong of it."

"What a remarkably cynical philosophy to find in one so young," Mairelon said, staring at Kim.

Kim shrugged, only half understanding. "I'm not that young; I'm rising seventeen, I think. And I don't see what my age has to do with how people are."

The muscles in Mairelon's jaw tensed, and for a moment he looked positively angry. Then he said gently, "It's not a matter of how people are, Kim; it has to do with how they ought to be. We'll discuss it some other time, perhaps. Though I still don't think St. Clair had anything to do with the theft, if only because he'd have kept the Saltash Set for himself instead of splitting it up and selling it. He'd had his eye on it for years; he wouldn't have given it up easily."

"Oh," Kim said, disappointed. "Then we still don't know who stole it?"

"Don't look so cast down," Mairelon said. "We'll find out eventually. Meanwhile, we have a few other things to take care of."

"What things?" Hunch asked, squinting suspiciously at his master.

"St. Clair is staying at Bramingham Place," Mairelon said. "So is Renée D'Auber. And it is evidently no secret that the Saltash Platter—or rather, an exceedingly good copy—was in Henry Bramingham's possession until the night before last. I doubt very much that all this is merely a coincidence."

"So?"

"So I want to know how Shoreham's secret information on the whereabouts of the Saltash Platter managed to reach so many people in so short a time," Mairelon said. "Also, I'm worried about Renée. She was supposed to meet me at the druids' hill over an hour and a half ago, but she never arrived. I'm going to Bramingham Place to see if I can find out why."

"I thought you didn't want that Lord St. Clair seein' you," Kim objected. "Ain't—isn't that why you sent me over there yesterday?"

"It is, which is why you're coming with me. Don't argue,

Hunch; you've had a long ride and you should rest. Keep the shotgun handy in case that Stower fellow turns up again. I'll set up the warding spells when we get back."

"Now, see 'ere, Master Richard!" Hunch said. "You ain't a-going to take that girl with you, not if I 'ave anything to say about it. Like as not, she's working for that Mr. Laverham."

Kim scowled fiercely at Hunch to hide a sudden, strong inclination to cry. Stower's accusations hadn't gone unnoticed, after all, and she had no way of proving that he was wrong. "I ain't!" she said, but she had little hope of being believed.

"Really, Hunch." Mairelon's tone was mild, but Hunch stiffened and sat back, eyeing his master warily. "You forget," Mairelon went on, "I questioned Kim myself, with the Saltash Bowl to compel her to be truthful. Or do you remember that, and doubt my skill?"

"I'd forgot," Hunch said, plainly chagrined. "But—"

"No," Mairelon said in the same mild tone. "No buts. Spell or no spell, Kim has earned the right to be trusted. You owe her an apology."

"No, he don't," Kim said hastily. Hunch looked at her in surprise, and she hurried on, "I'd forgotten about that spell myself. I thought sure you'd take Stower's gab for truth. I would have. So he don't owe me nothin'."

"Doesn't," Mairelon said.

"What?" Kim said, momentarily at sea.

"Hunch *doesn't* owe you *anything*. We'll leave it at that."

Hunch nodded, still wearing a faint expression of surprise. Mairelon looked at Kim and added in a severe tone,

"You have been doing well with your lessons, but you tend to fall back on cant phrases and poor grammar when you get excited about something. Try to be more careful."

Kim fought down a desire to laugh in relief. She felt positively light-headed and didn't trust herself to say anything, so she simply nodded.

"Good. We'll be going, then." Mairelon paused and looked at Hunch, who was chewing on his mustache but wisely refrained from commenting. Mairelon smiled. "I'll send Kim back if I need you for anything, but I doubt that I will. And perhaps you'd better pack while we're gone; we might want to move the wagon in case Stower takes it into his head to come back with a friend or two. Assuming, of course, that he *has* a friend or two. Don't forget the shotgun."

"I won't," said Hunch. "And don't you forget to watch for that there Stower, neither. 'E might follow you instead of coming back 'ere."

Mairelon nodded and beckoned to Kim. With some caution, he opened the wagon door, but there was no sign of Jack Stower. "Come along," Mairelon said to Kim, and started briskly for the road. Kim stared after him for a moment, realizing suddenly that she had let herself in for another two-hour walk out to Bramingham Place and back. Cursing mentally, she ran to catch up.

NINETEEN

The walk to Bramingham Place was every bit as long as Kim remembered. To make matters worse, Mairelon decided that Kim needed more practice with her speech lessons and drilled her mercilessly as they hiked along. He stopped only when an approaching rider or cart distracted his attention, but as they saw only three during the entire trip this did not give Kim much respite.

At the edge of the manor grounds, Mairelon turned down a narrow side lane along a tall hedge. Kim followed, relieved by the end of the lessons and equally glad that she would not have to face the long trudge up the formal drive. All those rows of trees and carefully positioned shrubs made her uncomfortable.

"There ought to be a gap along here somewhere," Mairelon muttered a few minutes later. "I didn't think it was this far."

"Maybe they've plugged it up since you were here," Kim said.

Mairelon looked at her, then at the hedge. "You know, I think you may be right. Well, we'll just have to push our way through, then."

"Couldn't we go around?" Kim asked without much hope. When Mairelon took a notion, he was stubborn as a hackney coachman wanting full fare in advance. "This ain't—isn't the way we came the other night."

"It isn't dark now, either," Mairelon pointed out. "Unless Bramingham has replanted the entire grounds since I was here last, there's a wood on this side that will screen us from the house. The other way, there's a vista from the South Lawn. We'd be seen at once."

"Right," said Kim gloomily. "What are you plannin' to do when we get up by the house?"

"I'll work that out when we get there," Mairelon said. "I think the bushes are thinner here, follow me, and mind your head."

With considerable difficulty and more than a few scratches, they forced their way through the thin spot in the hedge. When they emerged into the little wood on the other side, Mairelon's clothes were covered with leaves and twigs, there were several snags in the previously smooth surface of his coat, and one sleeve sported a long smear of mud that ended in a small tear. Kim had fared little better, but she hadn't been wearing gentry togs.

"Hunch isn't going to be happy when he sees what you've done to them clothes," Kim said.

"Do you think so?" Mairelon said. He brushed the leaves and twigs from his shoulders, ignoring the ones caught in his hair, and studied his mud-flecked sleeve. "It is a little extreme, I suppose. Well, there's no help for it now. I think the house is—"

The echo of a shot from somewhere nearby cut Mairelon off in mid-sentence. His head whipped around and his eyes widened. "That was a pistol," he said, and started running in the direction of the noise.

Kim choked back a shout of dismay and ran after him while her mind listed in a remarkably clear fashion all the reasons why this was intensely foolish. Shots were something you ran *away* from, not toward. Someone else might have heard and roused the house. They would be taken up for poachers. They should sherry off while they had the chance. *She* should sherry off while she had the chance.

The list came to a sudden end as she broke out of the woods into one of the tree-lined alleys she so disliked. Mairelon was several steps ahead of her, slowing to halt beside an anonymous figure in a dark blue coat that lay sprawled on the ground at the edge of the woods. As Kim skidded to a stop next to him, she caught a glimpse of someone running off through the trees. The distance was too great for her to get more than a vague impression of a dark shape, but Kim didn't care. What mattered was that he was going in the right direction: away.

Mairelon went down on one knee and reached under the collar of the blue coat with one hand. "He's dead," he said. He shifted and bent to grip the corpse's shoulders, then gently turned it over.

"Fenton!" said Kim. She felt very odd, looking down at the empty, staring eyes and slack face. She had seen dead men before, and even robbed a few, but a fresh corpse in a shadowy London alley, wreathed in yellow fog, was somehow very different from the same sight in the calm green countryside.

"Get back, Kim," Mairelon said sharply, as though he had just remembered her and was not at all pleased to find her standing next to him.

Nothing loath, Kim backed up a few paces and looked around. A large canvas bag lay on the ground a few feet away. She stared at it with a sinking feeling, then went over and picked it up. It was much heavier than she expected, and she frowned as she tugged at the strings. If it wasn't another platter, what *was* it? She got it open at last, looked inside, and made a strangled noise.

"What's that?" Mairelon asked, looking up. "Another platter?"

"No," Kim said. "It's two of them."

"*Two* of them?" Mairelon stood and came over to her. He took the sack and put his left hand inside for a moment, then shook his head. "And both fakes. Well, at least now we know who was responsible for making them."

"We do?" said Kim.

"Well, nearly. It has to have been either Fenton or the man who shot him," Mairelon said. "One of them brought that bag here, and who would have two false platters except the man who's been making them?"

"You do," Kim pointed out. "Or you did until just now. Now you've got four."

"Yes, well, that's different. We've been collecting them, not making them."

"Why couldn't Fenton do that, too?"

Mairelon sighed. "True. It doesn't seem likely, but it's possible." He stared into the trees for a moment, then shook his head again. "There's no help for it. I shall have to send you back to get Hunch."

"*What?* No! I ain't goin'!" Kim barely stopped herself from shrieking. Leave Mairelon alone for over an hour with a dead body and a killer lurking in the woods, more than likely? Leave without having any idea what Fenton had been doing—or what Mairelon was going to do next? Leave now, and have to pry the story out of Mairelon later?

"I'm afraid you must," Mairelon said. "In case you had forgotten, there is a man around with a pistol. Once he's had time to reload, he'll probably recover his courage, and when he does I would like to have Hunch—and the shotgun—near at hand."

"Then you better go to the wagon yourself," Kim advised. "It ain't goin' to take an hour for the cove to reload, and it'd take that long just for me to walk back."

"True," Mairelon conceded. He frowned down at the bag. "I don't like leaving bodies lying around, but I can't very well march up to the door of Bramingham Place and explain matters, can I?"

Kim stared at him, amazed that he would even consider such a foolish action. "With the Runners after you? Not hardly!"

"Yes, there's that, too," Mairelon said absently. He was still frowning. "Well, let's finish here first, and then decide." He handed the canvas sack back to Kim. "Hold this."

Feeling a bit bewildered, Kim took the sack and watched as Mairelon returned to Fenton's corpse. Her bewilderment deepened when Mairelon began going through Fenton's pockets with the brisk professionalism of a London cutpurse. He ignored Fenton's handkerchief, shook his head over a gold snuffbox and an expensive-looking pair of gloves hidden inside Fenton's waistcoat, and frowned at a note he found in Fenton's jacket. Then, to Kim's complete confusion, he began patting Fenton's sides and pulling at the hems of his clothes.

"What are you doin' that for?" Kim demanded at last.

"I'm checking for—ah!" Mairelon stopped and took a penknife from his pocket. Carefully, he made a slit along the left seam of Fenton's waistcoat, a moment later, he pulled a folded paper from inside the lining.

"Well, well," Mairelon said, shaking the paper open. "What have we here?"

"How should I know?" Kim said. "How did you know to look for it there, anyways?"

"It's a trick the Frenchies used now and then when they had something important to send," Mairelon said. "If it comes to that, it's a trick I've used myself a time or two . . . well, well."

"Well what?" Kim said crossly. "What's it say?"

"Unless someone else finds out about this and gets there before we do, which seems unlikely, I believe we have discovered the location of the Saltash Platter at last," Mairelon said with great satisfaction. He refolded the paper and tucked it into an inner pocket, then rose, dusting his hands.

"You mean he really *was* makin' those fakes?" Kim asked, feeling a little chagrined.

"Probably, but it doesn't matter much any more. The important thing is that Fenton knew where the real platter is, and now we do, too."

"Then we can leave?"

"Not just yet, my dear," said a new voice. "Particularly

not if your friend's most recent statement is true. I have a great deal of interest in the Saltash Platter, you see."

Kim whirled and felt the blood drain from her face. "Dan Laverham!" she said.

Dan was standing next to one of the tall, grey-barked trees that lined the avenue. He held a pearl-handled pistol in each hand, and beside him stood Jack Stower, similarly armed. Jack's eyes were fixed warily on Mairelon, and as Laverham stepped into the avenue he said, "Be careful, Mr. Laverham! That there's the frog-maker I told you about."

"Really." Dan smiled. "Richard Merrill, I assume?"

"The same," Mairelon said, inclining his head. "May I inquire how you guessed?"

"Oh, come, now. There aren't many first-class wizards who'd be out chasing after the Saltash Set. You're far too well behaved to be one of the Sons of the whatever, and I am . . . familiar with Lord St. Clair's appearance. Who else could you be?"

"You are uncommonly well informed," Mairelon observed.

"It is necessary, in my business," Dan replied. "Don't try any spells, by the by. After Jack told me his little tale, I prepared a few odds and ends especially to take care of that sort of impromptu effort. You wouldn't have a chance." He gave Mairelon a long, appraising look that made Kim feel cold inside, then said in quite another tone, "Move over by Kim."

Without comment, Mairelon did so. Dan Laverham took two steps forward and glanced down at the body. "James Fenton. Dear me, how dreadful. And just when I thought he was finally going to be of some use to me, after all.

Well, it can't be helped. By the way, why did you kill him?"

"I didn't," Mairelon said.

"How interesting," Dan said. "Jack, go get that bag from Kim, there's a good fellow, and see what's in it. Then I think we had all better be going. You can't depend on amateurs to do the sensible thing; whoever shot Fenton might decide to come back and take a shot or two at us, and that would never do. Assuming, of course, that Mr. Merrill is telling us the truth."

Jack stuck one of his pistols into his belt and swaggered over to Kim. Silently she handed him the sack. If she hadn't been so scared, she would have enjoyed the way his expression changed when he opened the bag and saw what was inside.

"It's *two* of them wicher cheats, Mr. Laverham!" Stower said. "That there frog-maker's gone and doubled the thing!"

"Bring it here," Dan commanded.

Stower did so, eyeing Mairelon nervously the whole time as if he thought the magician might make twins of himself if he were not watched carefully. Dan felt around inside for a moment, just as Mairelon had, then shook his head. "They're forgeries. Fenton was probably hoping to pass one of them off as the real thing. Leave them."

Stower gaped at Dan in disbelief. "*Leave* them? But they're *silver*."

"I said, leave them," Dan said sharply. "I don't need any more complications. This—" he gave Fenton's body a casual kick, "—is more than enough."

The canvas sack hit the ground with a thud and a clatter. "Very good," said Dan. "Now, drag our late friend back into the woods a little, where he won't be so likely to be noticed. I don't want him found until we're well on our way back to London.

"I see you were acquainted with the late Mr. Fenton," Mairelon said as Jack Stower, glowering, complied with Dan's commands.

"James was one of my least reliable men," Dan said. "I was positively looking forward to disposing of him myself. If I'd realized he was getting ideas above his station, I'd have done so long before this." He gave the canvas sack a disapproving look.

"Then Fenton *was* the one who made all the fakes!" Kim said before she could stop herself.

"All the fakes? You mean there are others besides these?" Dan gave the sack a look that should have made it crumble to dust on the spot. "My, but he was ambitious. Or perhaps greedy is the proper word; under the circumstances, it's difficult to be sure. It was James, all right. His eldest brother is a silversmith."

"The black sheep of 'is family; they're mostly respectable tradesmen,' " Mairelon murmured. "I should have asked Hunch for details."

"Speaking of platters, I think it's time you told me where the real one is," Dan said pleasantly. "It's what I came for, after all."

"I'm afraid your Mr. Fenton didn't say," Mairelon said with equal affability.

"I don't care whether he told you where he put it or simply gestured so eloquently that the knowledge sprang into your mind unbidden," Dan said dryly. "I want to know the location of the Saltash Platter. I'm sure you don't need a list of the various painful things I could do to your young companion to make you talk."

"Quite so," Mairelon said in the gentle tone he used only when he was particularly angry. Kim glanced apprehensively at Dan, but he seemed oblivious to Mairelon's reaction, and Kim realized with a sense of shock that Dan did not know Mairelon at all. She was so used to taking for granted that Dan Laverham knew everyone and everything better than she did that she barely heard Mairelon continue, "It's somewhere in the druid lodge. I'm afraid he wasn't any more specific than that, but a little searching should turn it up without too much difficulty. The place isn't that large."

"Very good," said Dan. "Jack! Leave that and come along." He gestured with one of his pistols. "That way, Mr. Merrill, and not too fast. Follow him a little to the side, Kim."

"What d'you want them for?" Jack demanded, emerging from the woods with a sour expression. "Pop them and leave them with the other cove."

"You have no imagination," Dan responded. "Get that sack out of sight and meet us at the carriage. And don't linger; I won't wait for you."

As they started up the avenue in the direction Dan had indicated, Kim glanced back and saw Jack glare after Dan. He bent and grabbed the open end of the sack, and, with a strong heave, sent it flying into the trees before he ran to catch up with Laverham.

TWENTY

Dan Laverham directed them down the tree-lined avenue and along a bridle path to a wooden gate in the hedge. Kim, remembering how difficult getting through the hedge had been, gave Mairelon a reproachful look as Stower opened the gate and waved them through. Mairelon did not seem to notice; he was studying Stower in a way that made Kim very nervous. After all, Dan was still behind them with a pair of guns.

To Kim's relief, Mairelon did nothing to annoy Dan, and they reached the lane with no more than a few dark looks from Jack Stower. A closed carriage waited near the roadside, the driver's perch occupied by a figure muffled in a shabby, ill-fitting coat that, to Kim's experienced eye, had the indefinable aura of the London back streets. The horses were placidly chewing wisps of grass, and Mairelon gave them the same long, considering look he had just given Jack.

"Ben!" Dan called as he came through the gate. "We

have another stop or two to make. Mr. Merrill will give you the direction."

Mairelon glanced back over his shoulder at Dan. Dan smiled very slightly and lifted one of his pistols a fraction of an inch. "And they will be clear and without any deliberately misleading bits. Won't they, Mr. Merrill?"

"Of course." Mairelon inclined his head, then turned and went forward to speak with the coachman. Dan kept his eyes—and his pistol—fixed on them as he waved Jack forward with his other hand.

"I think you had better ride with Ben," Dan told him. "Put the guns under your coat; we don't want to attract attention."

"You ain't riding in there with two of 'em!" Jack protested. "What if they jump you?"

"A point," said Dan, showing no signs of concern. "Have the goodness to hold your gun on Mr. Merrill while I see to it that they won't."

Jack nodded with unnecessary force. He stepped forward and pointed both of his pistols at Mairelon's stomach. Dan looked at him, nodded, and turned to Kim. "I trust you will not attempt to do anything foolish in the next few minutes," he said. "It would have most unpleasant consequences."

Kim didn't trust her voice, so she nodded. Dan smiled coldly and set his right-hand pistol on the step of the carriage. "This will only take a moment," he said, putting his hand in his pocket. He withdrew it almost immediately, and when he uncurled his fingers, Kim saw two balls resting in his palm. One was a silver sphere, covered with tiny vines and fruit, that would have fit comfortably in the circle of

Kim's thumb and forefinger. The other was a small, faceted crystal the size of her thumbnail.

Behind her, Kim heard a sharp intake of breath from Mairelon. Dan looked past her and said, "I see you recognize these, Mr. Merrill. I hope that means you will be sensible enough not to interfere. The pieces of the Saltash Set are temperamental to work with when they aren't together."

Without waiting for a response, Dan stretched his hand toward Kim and began murmuring sharp, crystalline words. They hung in the air, twisting over and under and around each other like the streets of London, making an intangible net between Kim and Dan. Kim shuddered and took an involuntary step backward. Dan Laverham raised his left hand and made a complicated gesture, his voice rising as he did so. The invisible web of words swirled and swept forward, settling around Kim. She froze, waiting for it to do whatever it was meant to.

Dan gestured again, commandingly, and shouted a final phrase. The two spheres began to glow with a clear, silver light. Kim felt the razor-edged words close in, but the air between her and the spell was full of a strong, sweet, smoky scent, and the net of magic could not touch her. She swayed, light-headed with relief, and the spell swayed with her, maintaining its fractional distance.

"There," Dan said. He sounded breathless, as if he had been running, but he spoke in a tone of great satisfaction. He returned the two still-glowing balls to his pocket and bent to pick up his pistol.

"An interesting demonstration," Mairelon said in a cool

voice from behind Kim's shoulder. "But what is it supposed to accomplish?"

"Dear me, I thought you would be able to puzzle that out for yourself," Dan replied, straightening. "Even under these admittedly adverse conditions."

"You have a high opinion of me," Mairelon answered. "I recognized parts of it, but I've never seen anything quite like the whole. You adapted the Saltash truth spells to do something else, didn't you?"

"Shut your gob," Jack Stower growled, gesturing with his pistols.

"Now, now, don't get carried away, my dear," Dan said to Jack. "After all, he's quite right." Dan turned to Mairelon. "It's a control spell, or rather, a minor reworking of the control portions of the Saltash spells. It therefore has the same limits as its original, an annoyance I hope to correct once I have the whole set to study."

"The same limits as the Saltash spells?" Mairelon looked from Kim to Dan and shook his head. "That can't be very convenient. Only one person at a time, only one use per person, time limit—what is the time limit on your control spell, by the way? I know how long it is for the Saltash spells."

"Two hours," Dan answered. "Long enough for me to retrieve the Saltash Platter and Bowl and be well on my way back to London. Providing, of course, that we don't waste any more time. Into the carriage."

Kim blinked, realizing that this last command was directed at her. She felt no particular compulsion to follow Dan's orders, though she could still sense his spell hovering around her. She stared at Dan for a moment, her mind whirling, and suddenly the pieces came together. Dan had adapted the Saltash spells into a control spell, but his spell still had the same flaws as the Saltash spells. It only worked once on any particular person. And over a week before, on their first night out of London, Mairelon had cast the Saltash truth spell on Kim to find out what her lay was. That was why Dan's control couldn't touch her!

There were, however, two pistols still pointed at Mairelon, and he and Kim were outnumbered three to two, counting the phlegmatic coachman. It would clearly be much better to follow Dan's directions for a while. As long as he thought his spell was working, he wouldn't pay too much attention to Kim, and she might get a chance to pike off and get Hunch. Kim took a deep breath and climbed into the carriage.

"You next, Mr. Merrill," Dan said. "Sit there, next to Kim. Good." Dan climbed in after Mairelon and settled onto the seat opposite him. He pointed his pistols at Mairelon, then called out the window, "Up on the box with Ben, Jack. Keep your pistols handy, but try not to let anyone see them. We don't want to attract attention, remember."

Jack said something Kim could not hear, and Dan frowned. "Nonsense. Don't dally, my dear; I haven't time to waste."

There was a muffled curse, followed by an assortment of thumps as Jack climbed up to sit with the coachman. A moment later, the coach jerked and started off. "Not much of a driver, your man Ben," Mairelon commented. "Did you bring him out of sentiment, or economy?"

"Neither," Dan said with unimpaired good humor. "He

has talents other than driving that I thought I might find useful."

There was an undercurrent in Dan's voice that made Kim shiver. She was all too conscious of the various unpleasant ways a man could find to survive in London's rookeries; Jack Stower was the Archbishop of Canterbury compared to some. She knew nothing of the driver, but she knew enough of Dan to be sure that she didn't want to learn. Anyone he spoke of in those tones was sure to be an ugly customer.

Dan either did not see Kim's quiver or attributed it to the motion of the carriage. Mairelon shot her a flickering glance, then returned his attention to Dan as if he had noticed nothing. A moment later, however, the carriage lurched as he was shifting his position, and he fell sideways against Kim's shoulder.

"Don't fret," he breathed into her ear, his lips barely moving. "Sorry, Kim," he added in a louder tone as he straightened and resumed his seat.

Kim forgot her worries long enough to glare at him. "Don't fret" was probably his idea of a reassuring message, but he couldn't have picked a more ridiculous thing to say if he'd thought about it since the day they met. Don't fret, with Dan Laverham pointing a pistol at them, Jack Stower on the box with a gun of his own, a dead man in the woods behind them, and not the faintest hope of a way out of the mess that she could see? Don't fret, when Dan was about to get his hands on the blasted platter that all the rogues and half the gentry for miles around were chasing after? Did he take her for a Bedlamite, or hadn't it occurred to him that any reasonable person would fret himself to flinders in a situation like this?

"I think you should stay firmly seated from now on," Dan said to Mairelon. "It would be unfortunate, don't you think, if you were to career into me that way and my pistol were to go off."

"Unfortunate is certainly one word for it," Mairelon agreed. "You know, as long as we have time for a chat, I was wondering whether you'd tell me a little more about that control spell of yours. It's terribly interesting. Don't you think it's terribly interesting, Kim?"

"A more tactless comment I have seldom heard," Dan said.

"What?" Mairelon blinked, then looked from Dan to Kim for a moment and back to Dan. "Oh, yes, I see what you mean. But even so—"

There was a loud report from outside the window, and the coach jerked to a sudden and unceremonious halt. For a moment, Kim was convinced that Jack Stower had fired at something or someone; then she heard an all-too-familiar voice cry in ringing tones, "Stand and deliver! In the name of the Four Holy Things!"

"Jonathan Aberford," Kim said, feeling stunned. "That bufflehead!"

"Oh, Lord, not again," Mairelon said, rolling his eyes.

Laverham's eyebrows rose. "A holdup, in broad daylight? On a country road going from nowhere to nowhere else? It seems unlikely, on the face of it."

Jack Stower seemed to share Dan's opinion. "You're dicked in the nob," they heard him shout. "Mr. Laverham's in this coach!"

"Stand and deliver!" Jonathan cried again. "Drop your weapons, or I fire!"

"We've stood, we've stood," Jack snarled. "Now what?"

"An excellent question," Mairelon murmured. "I wonder whether he's thought of it?"

"If this is some trick of yours—" Dan raised a pistol.

"It's not a trick," Mairelon said. "It's a druid. In a manner of speaking, that is. He's harmless, I think, unless he happens to have taken the notion that highwaymen always shoot someone just to prove they're serious."

Before Dan could respond, they heard a wordless yell, a horse's shrill, frightened neigh, and the sounds of a scuffle outside. Dan leaned over and glanced out the window. When he returned his gaze to Mairelon, his expression had not changed, but there was an air of satisfaction about him. A moment later, Jack's face appeared at the window. He was breathless, and there was a smear of mud across his left cheek.

"We got the rum padder, Mr. Laverham," Jack panted. "What d'you want us to do with him?"

"Kill him," Laverham said.

"Right." Jack smiled, showing crooked brown teeth. "Now?"

Dan nodded, then, as Jack turned to go, he frowned and said, "No, wait. Are you—" he gestured at Mairelon with his pistol, "—quite sure this person is a druid?"

"Well, you can see that he's not much of a highwayman," Mairelon said in a reasonable tone. "It probably didn't even occur to him to bring a spare pistol."

"It don't matter," Jack objected. "The cull tried to pop the lot of us!"

"With only one pistol?" Dan said. "I think not. In any case, if this inept highwayman is a druid, he'll know where to look for the platter once we get to the lodge. We'll bring him along."

"But, Mr. Laverham—"

"Don't argue, my dear, just do it." Dan studied Mairelon for a moment, then smiled unpleasantly. "You'll have to be tied, of course," he said to the magician. "I'm not fool enough to leave you free with the carriage as crowded as it's going to be. Kim!"

Kim jerked, startled by the unexpected command. "What?"

"There's a bit of rope under the seat." Dan pointed with his left hand. "Get it and tie your companion's hands. And see you do a good job of it. I won't—"

The carriage door swung open, and Jack Stower shoved the unfortunate Jonathan forward, so that he staggered against the step. "Where do you want him, Mr. Laverham?" Jack asked.

"In a moment, Jack," Dan replied. "Tie him, Kim."

Remembering suddenly that she was supposed to be under Dan's spell of control, Kim bent and rummaged under the seat for the rope. She straightened and turned sideways to face Mairelon. "Hold out your hands," she said in a flat voice.

Mairelon did so, his gaze fixed on Kim's face. Kim dropped her eyes, wondering whether Mairelon knew she was faking. Well, he'd figure it in another minute. She looped the rope around his wrists and pulled hard for Dan's benefit, then fed the ends through the complex pattern Mairelon had shown her on their first day out of London.

When she finished, she looked up. Mairelon was still staring fixedly at her face, his expression unreadable. "There," Kim said. "You won't get out of *that* in no hurry."

"No?" Mairelon said. He looked down at last, and went still as he recognized the trick knot. He raised his head to look at Kim again and said very deliberately, "I see."

"Kim learned to tie knots down on the docks," Dan said, misinterpreting Mairelon's reaction. "Now, Jack, let's have the druid highwayman."

Jack shoved Jonathan again, and it was more by luck than planning that this time Jonathan stumbled up the step and into the carriage. He was hatless, one of the capes on his coat was torn, and there was a reddened area on his left cheek that would make a splendid bruise in another day or so. His awkward progress was due to the sock he had used as a mask. At some point during his encounter with Dan's men, the sock had slipped to one side, and the holes Jonathan had cut in it were now centered over his nose and right temple. Kim almost laughed aloud.

"This is entirely unnecessary," Jonathan said in a calm voice, but his hands shook as he raised them to pull the sock off his head. "I'm Jonathan. It was just a bet, and—" He stopped short as the sock came off and he saw the occupants of the coach.

"I see you weren't expecting us," Dan said, pointing his pistols impartially at Jonathan and Mairelon. "Not that it matters. Tie him, too, Kim."

"What?" Jonathan stared as if he couldn't believe what he had just heard. "You don't mean it! Look, my name's Aberford; if you stop at the next house, they'll vouch for me. You don't have to bring a magistrate into it."

"I don't intend to," Dan said. He lifted his pistol again for emphasis and added, "Just hold still while Kim works."

"What's going on here?" Jonathan demanded, finally taking in Mairelon's bound hands and rumpled appearance. "This is an outrage!"

"No more so than a holdup in the middle of the morning," Dan said. "You're hardly in a position to criticize. Jack!"

While Jonathan spluttered and Kim repeated her performance with another piece of rope, Dan held a brief conversation with Jack through the open carriage door. According to Jack, Jonathan had come galloping out of the trees, blazing away with his pistol. The frightened carriage horses had reared, tangling their harness and causing the coach to bounce to a halt. When Jonathan, with typical single-mindedness, had turned his back on the coachmen in his eagerness to open the carriage door, Jack had jumped him.

"Not badly done," Dan said. "However, we've wasted enough time here. Go help Ben with the horses."

"I ain't no horse coddler," Jack grumbled, but did as he was told, and in a few minutes the coach began to move again.

TWENTY-ONE

"**N**ow, Mr. Aberford," Dan said, settling back against the rear wall of the coach, "tell me what you thought you were going to accomplish with your little masquerade. And please, don't try to put me off with that tarradiddle about a bet. What were you really after?"

"I had a bet," Jonathan repeated doggedly. "With—with Robert Choiniet. He said I couldn't pull it off without being recognized."

"He was right," Mairelon murmured.

"Quiet," Dan said. "I'm afraid I don't believe you, Mr. Aberford. I think you were after something else. The Saltash Platter, perhaps?"

"The what?" Jonathan's puzzlement was unfeigned. "I've never heard of it."

"You call it the Sacred Dish," Mairelon put in.

Jonathan jerked upright in his seat as if someone had stuck a pin in him, banging his head against the roof of the coach. "What do you know of the Sacred Dish?"

"Not nearly as much as I'd like," Mairelon said. "For instance, how did you and your druids get hold of it? And how does it happen that you don't have the smallest notion what it really is?"

"I told you to be quiet," Dan said.

"When Queen Dick rules," Kim muttered, her annoyance with Mairelon momentarily getting the better of her fear of Dan. She was as curious as Mairelon about the druid's behavior, but *she* knew enough to keep her mouth shut when someone had a pistol pointed at her.

Dan gave her a piercing look, but just then the coach slowed and lurched through a sharp turn, distracting him. He leaned sideways and peered out the window. "It doesn't matter now. We appear to be arriving."

"Not quite yet, but soon," Mairelon said. "The lodge is around the back side of the hill."

"You aren't—you can't—what are you going to do?" Jonathan said.

"Look for something I . . . mislaid a few years ago," Dan answered. "And you are going to help."

Jonathan's jaw tightened. "No. I won't. I won't let you desecrate our meeting place."

"Let? My dear boy, how do you propose to stop me?" Dan said, shifting his pistol just enough to call attention to its presence.

"Yes, and what do you expect us to do?" Mairelon asked Jonathan in tones of great interest. "Or to put it another way, just what would 'desecrate' a place where you and your friends drink, dice, and wench until almost dawn?"

Jonathan turned a dull red and did not answer. The coach

bumped to a stop and Dan reached through the window and unlatched the door. "Out," he said. Mairelon shrugged and climbed out, steadying himself awkwardly with his bound hands. Jonathan sat back, looking stubborn.

Dan sighed. "Don't be foolish, dear boy. If you stay here, you have no hope of keeping me from doing whatever outrageous things you think I am planning. And I assure you that if you decide to be obstinate, I shall make it a point to think of something particularly outrageous."

Jonathan hesitated, then gave in. Wearing a ferocious scowl, he crawled out of the coach. Kim started to follow, but Dan put out an arm and blocked her. "After me," he said. "And from now on, you are to do nothing and say nothing unless I tell you. Do you understand?"

"I understand," Kim said sullenly.

"Good. Now, after me."

When Kim came blinking out into the light, she saw Jack Stower holding his pistol on Jonathan Aberford while Dan kept Mairelon covered. She glanced longingly at the woods, but she did not try to run. There was no cover close by, and Dan wouldn't so much as pause to consider before shooting her. Even the unexpected failure of his control spell wouldn't slow him down. She'd stand a better chance of nicking the Queen's garters at high noon on the steps of Buckingham Palace than she would of getting away now. Reluctantly she joined the others.

"Ben, you wait for us here," Dan commanded. "The rest of you will come inside and help look for the platter. You first, Mr. Merrill."

Mairelon walked over to the door of the lodge. "It's locked."

"It shouldn't be. We never—" Jonathan stopped short and pressed his lips together, as if he were afraid he was giving vital secrets away to an enemy.

"No matter," Dan said. He waved his free hand in a sweeping invitation. "Kim! Open the door."

Even more reluctantly than before, Kim walked forward and pulled her bit of wire out of her pocket. As she knelt in front of the lodge door, Mairelon gave her an encouraging wink. She did not dare respond, for Dan was watching her, but her hands did not shake at all as she inserted the wire in the keyhole and began wiggling it against the tumblers.

The lock was nothing special, but Kim took her time with it. After her experience with Mairelon's magic trunk, she was not inclined to take chances, particularly since this lodge also belonged to a bunch of frog-makers. Then, too, she didn't much want to flaunt her skill in front of Dan. It'd only give him another reason for wanting to get his dabbers on her.

"Losing your touch, dear boy?" Dan said. "I hope not."

The threat below the words was plain. Kim gave her wrist a final turn, wondering as she did whether Dan had forgotten that she was supposed to be acting under his command or whether he just enjoyed threatening people. "It's open," she said, rising.

"Good. Mr. Merrill?" Dan nodded toward the door. Mairelon gave him an ironic bow, shoved the door open, and went in. Jack followed, at Dan's direction, then Jonathan and Kim. Dan himself came last.

The interior of the lodge was dark and smelled of smoke and old wine. "Who's pulled the shutters to?" Jonathan demanded. "Blast it, can't anyone do anything right?"

"I fail to see—" Dan began, when a voice from the far corner of the room interrupted him in mid-sentence.

"Jon? That you? Well, of course it is. Nobody else would be so put about by a little thing like shutters. It's all right, Marianne, it's only Jon."

"Freddy!" said an agonized female voice in a piercing whisper. "Sshhh!"

"But it's only Jon," the first voice said, and a shadowy male figure rose from behind a clump of high-backed wing chairs. He stepped forward, peering through the gloom, then stopped short and said with considerable indignation, "I say, Jon, who are all these people you've brought along? Not the thing, old boy, not at all the thing. This lodge is supposed to be private, y'know."

"Meredith! I might have guessed," Jonathan said in tones of loathing. "What are you doing here?"

"Might ask you the same thing," Freddy pointed out. "*I* ain't the one who came barging through a locked door with a country fair's worth of people."

"That door isn't supposed to be locked! The Sons of the New Dawn should be free to come and go as they please; we agreed on that at the very beginning!"

"This is all very interesting," Dan said in a bored voice, "but I do have a few things to do here, and time presses. If you—and your no doubt charming companion—will just join the others here, Mr. Meredith, we can begin."

"Who's this?" Freddy said without moving. "Some jumped-up Cit? Really, Jon—"

"Freddy!" The female whisper was, if possible, more agonized than before. "Make them go away!"

Freddy turned his head back toward the corner. "I'm try-ing, Marianne. But it ain't an easy sort of thing. Jon's a stubborn fellow. Maybe he would if you asked him," he added hopefully. "I mean, favor to a lady and all that. Jon's a gentleman, after all."

"But I can't! Oh, I can't!"

"The lady doth protest too much," Mairelon murmured.

"It doesn't matter," Dan Laverham said, ignoring Mai-relon. He seemed a little put out by Freddy's determined thickheadedness. "Mr. Aberford isn't the one you have to convince. Do as I tell you."

Freddy looked at Dan with an expression of polite hau-teur that changed quickly to incredulity. "Jonathan! That fellow has—" He broke off and glanced back over his shoulder, then lowered his voice and continued, "I think that fellow has a gun."

"He certainly does," Jonathan said, disgusted. "And only a sapskull like you would take ten minutes to notice it."

"Enough of this nonsense," Dan said. "Kim, find some-thing to tie them with, and open the shutters while you're about it. We can't hunt for the platter in this light. Jack, get that blithering fool and his doxy over with the rest of them."

"Right," Jack said with an evil smirk, while Freddy spluttered a halfhearted protest. He sidled between a settee and a low, solid-looking table toward the darkened corner from which Freddy had emerged. Kim threw back the first pair of shutters, letting the dusty grey sunlight light up an-other cluster of chairs and a side table stacked with cards and mother-of-pearl marker chips.

A moment later, there was a quavering feminine shriek

from the far corner. "A pistol! Oh, it isn't loaded, is it?"

"Be a lot of use that way, wouldn't it?" Jack sneered. "Move it."

Kim glanced back as she opened a second set of shutters, and her eyes widened in surprise. The distraught and somewhat disheveled young woman whom Jack was pulling, with evident relish, from her hiding place was the lovely blonde who had been with Lady Granleigh in the carriage at the inn, that first day in Ranton Hill. Kim cudgeled her brain and summoned up the girl's name: Marianne Thornley. She blinked as a few other bits of information came together in her head, and almost smiled. So this was the heiress Lady Granleigh intended for her scapegrace brother! From the look of things, Jasper wouldn't have much luck, no matter how persuasive his sister was. Miss Thornley seemed to have her own plans.

"My, my," Dan said. "Gently, Jack; it's not a doxy, it's a lady."

"Miss Thornley!" Jonathan gasped. "Freddy, have you run mad?"

"Freddy! Oh, Freddy, do something!" Marianne cried. With a sudden spurt of strength, she jerked her arm from Jack's grasp and ran to Freddy, where she wrapped her arms around his neck and buried her head in his shoulder, effectively preventing him from doing anything even if he had wanted to.

"Now see what you've done," Freddy said reproachfully to Dan. He patted Marianne's shoulder in awkward and meaningless reassurance.

"Kim, where's that rope?" Dan called.

"There ain't none," Kim said, throwing open a third set

of shutters. Even with three windows uncovered, the room was not well lit, but at least it was now possible to move around without tripping over a footstool or a bench. From where she stood, she could even make out the wreaths carved into the mantel above the big fireplace, if she squinted.

"Well, find something! And hurry it up." Dan's temper was beginning to fray.

"Are you quite sure you want to keep on with this?" Mairelon asked with an air of polite concern. "You're accumulating rather a lot of witnesses, you know, and these three—" he indicated Jonathan, Freddy, and the shrinking Marianne with a theatrical wave of his bound hands, "—will be missed before long."

Marianne looked up, as if she were about to say something, but before she could speak, the door behind Dan swung open. "Good day," said Gregory St. Clair. "I hope I'm not interrupting, but I was getting tired of waiting."

In the momentary silence, St. Clair stepped into the lodge and pushed the door closed with his silver-headed walking stick. He was dressed for all the world as if he were paying a morning call at the height of the Season in London: Wellington coat, striped pantaloons, and Hussar buskins. His cravat was a snowy expanse of starched linen, and his gloves were grey kid. Looking at him made Kim's fingers twitch acquisitively.

Both Mairelon and Dan Laverham were staring at St. Clair with unconcealed dislike. Jack didn't seem to know whether to aim his pistol at the new arrival or continue pointing it at Jonathan and Freddy, who wore identical blank expressions. Marianne, on the other hand, clung more closely to her puzzled escort and said in faltering tones, "Oh, Freddy, it's Lord St. Clair!"

"Good," said Freddy, relaxing. "For a minute, I thought it was another Cit."

"St. Clair," Mairelon said in a flat voice. "I should have expected you."

"Gregory has a habit of turning up where he is not wanted," Dan said. He spoke as if responding to Mairelon's comment, but his eyes stayed on Lord St. Clair and his voice was cold.

"You have a great many unappealing habits of your own, Daniel, but I don't regard them." St. Clair's expression made Kim want to crawl behind one of the wing chairs; he looked exactly like Dan in his worst and most unpredictable moods. He glanced around the interior of the lodge, then added, "This time you seem to have outdone yourself, however. I expected Merrill, but who are all these other people?"

"Lord St. Clair!" Marianne shrieked as his gaze reached her. "You must do something, or we shall all be killed!"

"I doubt it," St. Clair replied. "Even Daniel isn't that foolish."

"But he wants to bind us!" Marianne said dramatically.

"Typical." St. Clair looked at Dan. "You should have gagged her. I begin to see why you're still standing here waving a pistol about instead of collecting the Saltash Set."

"The Sacred Dish is not for the likes of you!" Jonathan cried. St. Clair raised his eyebrows in polite incredulity. "That is, if we still had it," Jonathan added in a resentful tone, glaring at Freddy, "which thanks to him, we don't."

"You ain't still harping on that, are you?" Freddy said.

"Burn it, Jonathan, I told you what happened!"

"You had no right—" Jonathan began hotly.

"Quiet," Dan commanded without turning. "How did you get past Ben?" he asked St. Clair.

"I employed my talents to good effect," the Baron answered. "Which is to say, I put him to sleep."

"I took precautions against that sort of thing."

"Not very good ones; at least, not by my standards."

Kim could almost hear Dan's teeth grinding. "What do you want?" he demanded.

"The same thing you do, more or less," St. Clair said. "The Saltash Set." He looked around again with an air of languid disappointment, and Kim hoped she was only imagining that his eyes lingered on her. "I had hoped you'd have found the rest of it by this time, but then I hadn't expected you to have so much . . . assistance."

"However reluctant," said Mairelon, who had been observing this exchange with interest. "You have some unusual associates, St. Clair."

"No more unusual than yours," the Baron responded with a significant look at Kim.

"But definitely more long-standing," Mairelon shot back. "Or am I mistaken in thinking you and Mr. Laverham here are well acquainted?"

"This isn't getting us anywhere," Dan put in. "Jack, put them all in the corner and then start looking. Not him," he added as Jack started warily toward Lord St. Clair. "I'll deal with him myself."

"Will you, indeed." St. Clair sounded both bored and skeptical, but Kim thought she heard darker undercurrents in his voice. "Not the way you did before, I hope? You owe me for that, Daniel, and I intend to collect. In full."

"I owe *you*?" For an instant, Dan let his rage show; then he had himself under control again. "It doesn't matter. As soon as I have the platter, we'll leave. You won't be able to stop us."

"The platter?" St. Clair said sharply. "Is that all? What about the bowl?"

"I'll have no trouble finding the bowl once the platter is in my hands," Dan said with renewed confidence.

"Finding it? You mean you weren't aware that Merrill has the bowl?" St. Clair shook his head. "And you seemed so well informed."

Laverham frowned. "Is this true?" he demanded of Mairelon.

"Yes," Mairelon said. "Though it's not the sort of thing one carries around in one's pockets, you realize."

"Why didn't you tell me this before?" Laverham said, and his eyes narrowed as he spoke.

Mairelon shrugged. "You didn't ask."

"We'll get it when we're finished here," Laverham said.

"That would be foolish," St. Clair commented.

"Why?"

"Merrill's got a man at his wagon."

"That's the turnip-pated cove I told you about, Mr. Laverham," Jack Stower put in. "He ain't no problem."

"And even if no one was waiting, it is generally considered . . . inadvisable to assault a wizard on his home ground," St. Clair finished.

Jack's enthusiasm waned visibly. Laverham stared at Lord St. Clair, his face expressionless. "What would you suggest?"

"Send the girl with a message," St. Clair replied. "She can tell Merrill's man that Merrill wants the bowl brought here to help locate the platter. He'll believe that."

"Not if she's the one telling him," Dan responded with a contemptuous glance at the quivering Marianne. "Besides, I wouldn't trust her to keep her story straight."

"Not that girl," St. Clair said. "The one you've cast the control spell on." He gestured at Kim.

Kim swallowed hard, half terrified that Dan knew her secret at last and half hoping against hope that he would adopt Lord St. Clair's suggestion. If she could get away and warn Hunch . . .

"Ah," said Dan on a long, slow breath, staring at Kim. "Yes, perhaps that would be a good idea."

"Hunch won't believe Kim," Mairelon said a little too quickly. "He doesn't trust her."

"No?" Dan said. "Kim, tell the truth: could you make Merrill's man believe you?"

"Yes," Kim said, trying to sound sullen and reluctant. "He'll believe me."

"Good." Dan gave her a slow smile that chilled her to the bone. "We'll discuss the other business later. You know what I mean. Meanwhile, we'll wait here while you go—"

"No!" Marianne cried.

Everyone turned to look at her. She cringed back against Freddy and said, "We can't stay any longer; we can't! It's nearly teatime, and Lady Granleigh will look for me and find . . ." She faltered to a stop under the circle of astonished stares and buried her face against Freddy's coat once more, her shoulders shaking with sobs.

"Find what?" St. Clair asked. "Find you gone? Embarrassing and unfortunate, to be sure, but it's too late to do anything about it now."

"Even if we would let you," Dan added.

Marianne turned a damp face to the group once more and said defiantly, "Freddy and I are going to be married!"

"Oh, Lord," said Jonathan. "Freddy, you fool! Your uncle will cut you off with a shilling!"

"It don't matter," Freddy said. "Rather have Marianne than a whole mountain of shillings."

"Congratulations," St. Clair said politely. "I fear you'll have to postpone your arrangements a little, however. We can't just let you go, you know."

"But you must!" Marianne cried. "I—oh, you must! You must!"

"Are you trying to say that you left a note for your guardian?" Mairelon asked.

"Oh!" Marianne turned back to Freddy's comforting shoulder and hid her face against his by now damp and wrinkled coat. Safely hidden from hostile eyes, she nodded. In the silence that followed, the noise of an approaching horse came clearly from the drive outside.

TWENTY-TWO

No one spoke as the hoofbeats grew louder and slowed to a walk. "Hi, you there, wake up," someone shouted. "Who's here?"

"Putting Ben to sleep may not have been one of your best ideas," Mairelon said to Lord St. Clair. "Is he the sort that wakes up cross, do you suppose?"

"He won't wake up at all until I let him," St. Clair said. "Be quiet, Merrill."

"You take a deal of liberty with my men," Dan Laverham observed.

"I am only following your example," Lord St. Clair replied sweetly. "Your handling of my former footman, James Fenton, for instance, left much to be—"

"Austen! Edward! George!" the voice outside shouted, coming nearer with every name. "Out and about, you're needed. Jon's gone and been thrown by that fire-breathing nag of his, and—Jonathan!"

The lodge door had been flung open during the latter

part of this speech, revealing the speaker as Robert Choiniet. He stopped short when he saw Jonathan, then said in a more moderate tone, "I'm glad to see you weren't hurt, but you might have sent a message home. Your mother was frantic when your horse turned up without you."

"She's always frantic," Jonathan said callously. "She should know better, and so should you. How did she talk you into haring off after me?"

"Well, what was I supposed to do?" Robert asked. "There was the horse, all over lather and frightened out of its wits, with an empty saddle. The obvious assumption was that you'd been thrown. For all we knew, you were lying under a hedge somewhere with a broken leg."

"You didn't tell me you'd taken a toss, Jon," Freddy put in with interest. "That'll teach you not to call names. I've told you and told you, it's the sort of thing that can happen to anyone."

"I didn't take a toss," Jonathan snarled. "And even if I had, I'd still say you're cow-handed, because you are."

"Don't you say that about Freddy!" Marianne said, raising her head and looking daggers at Jonathan.

"Can't you keep them under control?" Lord St. Clair asked Dan, while Jonathan, Freddy, and Marianne embarked on a noisy quarrel that relieved their feelings even if it accomplished nothing else. "None of us will ever get anything done at this rate."

Dan gave St. Clair a glare that should have melted steel. "If you think you can do better, you're welcomed to try."

"Here, you lot!" Jack shouted, waving his pistol. "Stow your gob and listen to Mr. Laverham!"

This command did not produce the desired result. Instead, Freddy and Jonathan turned on Jack, demanding an apology for the interruption. Dan was obliged to intervene to keep Jack from shooting Freddy out of hand, while Robert did his best to distract the other combatants. Unfortunately, Jack's threats were all too clear to Marianne, who immediately went into strong hysterics.

Lord St. Clair stood calmly watching, as if he were observing a raree show that did not please him above half, though he made a point of keeping an eye on Mairelon as well as the row in the middle of the room. Kim realized suddenly that, for the time being, no one was watching *her*. She slid quietly behind a tall chair and crouched down, eyeing the path to the door. Two more chairs and a card table provided some concealment, but she would have to cross an open stretch of floor to reach the exit itself. Kim shrugged and began moving.

She was not even halfway to her goal when the door swung open yet again. "Villain! Unhand that girl!" cried Jasper Marston as he strode into the room. He stopped short, looking completely nonplussed, as he took in the scene in front of him.

The noise died as the adversaries became aware of their new audience and turned to stare at him. "Ah, Mr. Marston!" Mairelon said cheerfully. "I'm afraid you'll have to be more specific about whom you were addressing. There are several persons present who admirably fit the description 'villain.' Which of them did you have in mind?"

"Really?" Robert Choiniet said. "You mean this isn't all one of Jon's queer starts?"

"My queer starts? What do you mean, my queer starts? Are you saying you think I *arranged* all this?"

"It has all the earmarks. I mean, just look at those two—waving pistols all over the lodge and threatening Freddy, of all people. How do you expect me to take it seriously?"

"You'd better," Dan said. He sounded a little wild, and Kim was glad to be out of sight behind the card table. "Get over in the corner there, all of you, and *be quiet*. You, too, Marston, or whatever your name is."

"Ah, I don't want any trouble," Jasper said, eyeing Dan's pistol with misgiving. "I'll just leave quietly. It's no problem, really."

"Yes, it is," Dan said, recovering himself somewhat. "Into the corner."

" 'Ere, now, what's all this, then?" a deep, slow voice said from the doorway.

"I should think it was perfectly plain, even to someone of your limited understanding, Stuggs," a female voice answered acidly. "My brother has bungled things again."

"Lady Granleigh!" gasped Marianne. She turned as white as St. Clair's cravat and fainted into Freddy's arms. Unfortunately, Freddy was as dumbfounded as she by the new arrivals, and he failed to catch her in time. He overbalanced, and the two of them toppled backward into a chair and crashed to the floor in a shower of splinters.

Mairelon sank onto a nearby footstool, propped his head on his bound hands, and began to laugh. Lady Granleigh gave him a look of displeasure and marched into the room, followed by Stuggs. Her gaze swept imperiously around the assembly, barely checking at the sight of the pistols Dan and Jack still held. She passed over the struggling Freddy and the unconscious Marianne, dismissed Jonathan and

Robert as inconsequential, and fixed at last on Lord St. Clair.

"Good day, St. Clair," Lady Granleigh said with a dignity that did not conceal her annoyance.

"Lady Granleigh," Lord St. Clair responded, nodding a cordial greeting.

Below the table, Kim ground her teeth and made a rude gesture with her left hand. Lady Granleigh had left the door wide open, but tempting as the sight was, Kim still could not reach it. Lady Granleigh had stopped too close to the door, and what little space she had left was taken up by the overly large Stuggs.

"I confess I had not expected to find you here, but I thank you for your efforts on behalf of my ward," Lady Granleigh went on, smiling insincerely at Lord St. Clair.

"Efforts!" Freddy said, outraged. He extracted himself from the tangle at last, with some help from Jonathan, and climbed to his feet, staring at St. Clair the whole time. "What efforts? He ain't done anything but stand there and annoy people."

"Your conduct hardly bears examination, Mr. Meredith," Lady Granleigh responded. "I should be careful about casting aspersions, if I were you." She looked pointedly down at Marianne.

Robert, who had knelt beside the unconscious girl and begun chafing her wrists, glanced up and said to no one in particular, "Could one of you get a glass of wine?"

"No, but there's brandy," Jonathan answered. He started toward a small cabinet near the fireplace, but came face-to-face with Jack Stower before he had taken two steps. Jack's pistols and threatening glare were eloquent. Jonathan shrugged and went back to his original position.

"Aspersions! Well, I like that!" Freddy said to Lady Granleigh, undaunted by her arrogance. "I didn't barge in through a locked door without so much as a by-your-leave. I didn't wave any pistols about or make any threats. I didn't frighten any ladies into a fit of the vapors, and I didn't scare her straight into a faint!"

"You lured Miss Thornley here," Jasper charged.

Robert looked up, visibly impressed. "Did you really, Freddy? I hadn't thought you had it in you."

"I didn't lure anybody," Freddy protested.

"You made Miss Thornley extravagant promises you had no intention of fulfilling!" Jasper said.

"I dunno," Stuggs put in. " 'E don't look like the type, if you take my meaning."

Jasper gave his henchman a withering look. "Why else did you bring Miss Thornley here, to this lonely place?" he demanded, turning back to Freddy.

"Hardly lonely," Mairelon said in a low but clearly audible tone.

"Had to meet her somewhere," Freddy said reasonably. "It would have looked dashed odd for me to pick the girl up off the side of the road."

"No doubt," Jasper sneered with an ironic glance at Jack Stower's gun. "You and your ruffians would have looked odd anywhere."

Freddy frowned. "Here, now! What are you insinuating?"

"I think it is perfectly plain," Lady Granleigh said. "If Lord St. Clair and his friends had not arrived in time to stop you and your kidnappers, who knows what might have happened?"

"Marianne and I would have gotten married, that's what would have happened!" Freddy retorted, too angry to continue trying to be polite. "What's more, we're going to tie the knot as soon as we get out of here, no matter what you say."

"Freddy, you're crazed!" Jonathan said.

"No, I ain't, and I ain't as foolish as you think, either. Got the special license right here in my pocket."

"What!" Jasper's eyes widened; then he whirled to face his sister. "Now see what you've done, Amelia! If you hadn't set the girl on to this buffoon, we wouldn't be in this pickle!"

"Be quiet, Jasper!" Lady Granleigh commanded. "There is no need for you to worry. Lord St. Clair, be so good as to have your men assist Miss Thornley into our coach. After we have gone, you may deal with these felons as you see fit."

Before St. Clair could reply, there was a loud crash. Everyone jumped and turned. Dan Laverham was standing beside one of the long windows, which he had just broken, his pistols leveled at the assembly.

"I am afraid you have mistaken the situation, Lady Granleigh," he said. He stepped forward, and shards of glass crunched under his feet. His face was a cold, expressionless mask. "I am not in St. Clair's employ, nor have I the slightest interest in you, your ward, or any of your companions. I am here for one thing, and only one thing. Once I've got it, you may sort yourselves out in any manner that suits you. Until then, I have heard too much of your brainless chatter. I shall shoot the next person who speaks out of turn."

St. Clair nodded. "Crude, but generally effective."

"That includes you, St. Clair," Laverham said, glaring.

Lady Granleigh drew in her breath at this breach of manners, which seemed to disturb her more than Dan's pistols. St. Clair smiled, but said nothing.

"Much better," Laverham went on. "Now, you, the highwayman. Is there somewhere in this pile to lock up this lot of lunatics while we search the rest of it?"

"Highwayman?" Freddy said with interest. "I say, Jon, you never told us anything about—" He broke off as one of Dan's pistols swung in his direction.

"There are private rooms upstairs," said Jonathan sullenly. "I think one of them has a lock."

"The one on the end," Freddy put in. "But it's broken. The lock, I mean."

"This is an outrage!" Lady Granleigh said, finding her voice. "Who is this person? Lord St. Clair—"

"I told you to be quiet," Dan said. "Get over there with the others."

"Better do as 'e says, mum," Stuggs warned. " 'E looks the sort as 'ud do you without blinkin'."

Kim held her breath as Lady Granleigh, stiff with disapproval, moved away from the door at last. Now, if they would all stay busy at the other end of the room for a few minutes longer . . .

A shadow fell across the doorsill. Kim frowned and sank back into her uncomfortable half-crouch. Had Lady Granleigh brought a coachman, or had Ben awakened in spite of Lord St. Clair's precautionary spell? Either way, she would be running into trouble. Not that she wasn't in a proper mess already, of course, but Dan's temper looked to be deteriorating rapidly, and she didn't like to think what he might do if she didn't get away on her first try. It would be better to wait for a more certain chance.

The motley company was slowly assembling in the corner, with occasional low-voiced grumbling that Dan pretended not to hear. Robert and Freddy between them supported the slowly recovering Marianne, while Jonathan stalked past and Lady Granleigh glowered impartially at everyone. For a moment or two, it looked as if Dan had gotten things under control at last; then Jasper said in a cross, too-loud voice, "But what is it the fellow *wants*?"

"The Sacred Dish!" Jonathan answered. He gave Dan and Jack a dark look. "But he shall not get it, however he tries."

"The what?" said Jasper.

"The sacred dish," Lady Granleigh said, giving her brother a sidelong glance full of meaning. "The platter that we gave to Mr. de Mare this morning." She nodded in Mairelon's direction.

"What?" several voices said at once. Lord St. Clair examined Mairelon with angry speculation, and both of Dan's pistols swung to point at the magician. Kim cursed mentally and swiveled her head from side to side, trying to watch Dan and the door at the same time.

"I told you not to try any tricks with me, Merrill," Dan said. "Where's the platter? And this time, tell me the truth!"

The shadow on the doorsill shifted and withdrew, but Kim stayed where she was. With Dan so jumpy, she'd be shot before she was out the door if she made a run for it.

She edged toward the front of the table with a vague idea of doing something, she wasn't sure what, if Dan looked like shooting Mairelon.

"Merrill?" said William Stuggs, giving Mairelon a swift, sharp look. "Well, well."

"What does that mean, 'well, well'?" Jasper demanded, rounding on his servant.

Stuggs's expression instantly resumed its usual appearance of placid stupidity. "Ain't 'e the cove you was lookin' for in London?"

"Answer me!" Dan said to Mairelon. "Where is the platter?"

"Which one?" Mairelon asked. "The one your man Stower left by my campfire, or the one Lady Granleigh was so anxious to get rid of? Or one of the other fakes Fenton seems to have been peddling?"

"The Saltash Platter, you buffoon!" Laverham shouted.

"Infidel! What have you done with the Sacred Dish?" Jonathan cried at the same moment.

"Fenton?" said Freddy, frowning. "I've got a footman by that name. What's he got to do with Jon's dish?"

Mairelon lifted his bound hands and scratched his ear. "I don't have any better idea where the Saltash Platter is than you do, Laverham."

"Do you expect me to believe that?"

"Why not?" Mairelon shrugged. "It's true."

"I gave you the Saltash Platter this morning," Lady Granleigh insisted in her most superior manner. "How dare you suggest otherwise!"

"Oh, you gave me a platter, all right, but it was a forgery and you knew it," Mairelon said. He gave her a charming smile that expanded to include the entire ring of surprised, confused, and skeptical faces. "By the by, how do *you* happen to know anything about the Saltash Platter, hmmm?"

"Never mind!" Dan said. "I don't care about her, and I don't believe you." He raised his pistol and slowly and deliberately cocked it. "For the last time, *where is the Saltash Platter*?"

"I don't have it," Mairelon said.

"But of a certainty you do not," said a new voice. Dan whirled, and everyone else's head flicked toward the door. Kim bumped her head on a table leg, cursed, and turned to see Renée D'Auber standing in the doorway. Her auburn hair was dressed in ringlets and threaded with a peach-colored ribbon that exactly matched the delicate muslin of her walking dress, and she smiled brightly when she saw the faces turned toward her. "I have it."

"Renée!" Mairelon said. "What are you doing here?" Then his face went blank as a stocky, sandy-haired man stepped into the doorway beside her, and he added in a thunderstruck tone, *"Andrew?"*

TWENTY-THREE

"Hello, Richard," said the sandy-haired man. He sounded nervous and uncertain, which Kim thought was understandable under the circumstances, but his attention was fixed on Mairelon rather than on Dan or Jack Stower. "I, um, it's been a while."

"Well, well," said St. Clair. "This is becoming quite the family gathering."

Dan Laverham glared at St. Clair. Mairelon did not move; he seemed as oblivious to the crowd around him as the man he had called Andrew. Kim frowned, puzzled both by St. Clair's comment and the unusual strength of Mairelon's reaction. Then her head jerked and almost hit the underside of the table again as several fragments condensed into the memory of Mairelon's voice saying in a flat tone, "The evidence was overwhelming. Even my brother Andrew believed it."

"What are you doing here?" Mairelon said in the same tight voice Kim remembered.

"Trying to keep your head out of a noose," Andrew replied. Now that Kim had remembered who he must be, she could see how much he resembled Mairelon in his middling height, neat build, and rounded face. Andrew glanced at Renée D'Auber and added, "At least, that was the original idea."

"What do you mean by—"

"Then you *do* have the Saltash Platter?" St. Clair interrupted, looking fixedly at Mademoiselle D'Auber.

"Nonsense," Lady Granleigh said. She made an urgent motion at her brother, but Jasper, who did not appear to have the slightest idea what she wanted of him, remained where he was.

"But, yes, I have it," Renée D'Auber told Lord St. Clair. "Though I do not at all see why it is you who ask, when it is this person with the pistols who was so very curious before."

"Where is it?" Dan demanded.

"Don't tell him," Freddy advised. "Fellow ain't the thing at all, that's my opinion."

"For once, I agree with you, Freddy," Robert murmured.

"Freddy!" Marianne had recovered enough to pull away from Robert and clutch at Freddy's arm in protest. "Oh, be careful! That man might shoot you!"

"It would be a singular service to humanity if he did," St. Clair said. "I have seldom met a more tiresome group, or one more foolish. Mademoiselle D'Auber—"

"Quiet!" Dan commanded. "Or I'll shoot *you*, Gregory! I'm tired of your interference."

"You seemed in need of some assistance," Lord St. Clair said with unruffled calm. "I was only trying to help."

"I don't want your help, you insufferable—"

"But you know each other!" Renée D'Auber said in tones of pleased surprise. "It is a thing remarkable, I think."

Mairelon shook himself and tore his eyes away from the man in the doorway. "Yes, St. Clair, how *do* you come to know Laverham? And how long have you been, er, acquainted? At least five years, I think?"

"Oh, much longer than that," St. Clair replied. "I expect you would be vastly interested in the details, but unfortunately I don't intend to give them to you."

"Perhaps Laverham can be persuaded?" Mairelon said.

"Not by you," Dan snarled. He turned back to Renée. "Give me the platter."

Behind Renée, Andrew made a gesture of protest, but he had enough sense not to say anything. Renée D'Auber tilted her head and considered Dan Laverham with an air that suggested something unsatisfactory about the object of her scrutiny. "It is not at all possible for me to give you the platter now," she said at last, as if granting a great concession in answering at all.

"Renée," Mairelon said warningly.

A muscle in Dan's jaw jumped. "Don't lie to me," he said in a tone that made Kim shrink back from the edge of the table, just in case he turned in her direction.

"I tell the truth," the Frenchwoman said, affronted. "And it is quite true that I cannot give you the platter now. I am not a fool, me, and I do not wish to lose it. So I do not carry it about with me, especially when there are housebreakers and highwaymen and persons with pistols everywhere. If you were not yourself without sense, you would have comprehended that and not bothered me with silly questions."

Mairelon made a muffled, choking noise. Dan lowered his pistols slightly and studied Renée through narrowed eyes.

"She ain't no dull mort," Jack Stower offered. "I bet she done it like she says."

"I have no doubt of it," St. Clair said. "If, that is, she has done anything at all."

"Ain't no knowing," Stuggs said with an air of deep gloom. "She's French."

"It's easy enough to tell whether she's lying," Dan said. He walked over to the card table and set something heavy down just over Kim's head. She flinched and backed away slowly, hoping he would not drop anything. If he bent over, he could hardly miss seeing her. At the rear of the table, she stopped and curled into a lumpy, motionless ball, waiting for Dan to move away again.

"What do you think you're doing, Laverham?" St. Clair said sharply, and Kim had to suppress an urge to peer over the edge of the table to see what he was referring to.

"I'm going to find out which of them is telling the truth," Dan answered. "If it's Merrill, the Saltash Platter is in this building somewhere. That's close enough for me to find, even with only two of the indicator balls to use as a base for the location spell."

"Freddy!" Marianne said in a carrying whisper. "Is he going to cast a *spell*?"

"You know not what you do," Jonathan said in his best master-druid voice. "Beware the consequences of defiling the hall of the Sons of the New Dawn!"

"Quiet," said Dan. "I've had as much of your posturing as I can stomach. Jack, keep an eye on them."

This last instruction seemed unnecessary to Kim, since, from the way his pistols had been waving about, Jack had been trying to watch everyone at once for some time. She could just see him out the side of the table and through the latticed back of a wooden chair, his jaw clenched and his eyes compressed to slits of grim concentration. Stuggs was creeping around the outside of the group toward him, craning his neck to get a look at Dan. Did the great looby think this was some kind of show, or was he fool enough to try a trick on a real magician in the middle of a spell? Then Dan began to speak diamond-sharp words Kim could not understand, and every other thought left her mind instantly.

She knew at once that something was wrong. Always before when she had heard magicians at work, the too-solid words had settled quickly into an orderly arrangement, full of dangerous corners and edges but as firm and stable as the words themselves. Dan's words were floating free, jostling against each other like a market-day crowd, fighting the structure the magician sought to impose on them.

The magicians in the room were also quick to realize that Dan was in trouble. Renée D'Auber stepped backward into Andrew, her eyes widening, and brought up her left hand in a contorted gesture.

"Renée, don't!" Mairelon cried. "You'll only cut what's left of the basic binding!"

"Break off, you fool!" St. Clair said to Dan at the same moment. "You'll have the house down in another minute."

"He can't break off," Jonathan said with bitter satisfaction. "If he does, he'll lose what control he has. He'll lose it soon, in any case. His obstinacy has doomed us all."

Jasper Marston made a gobbling noise and collided with his sister as he tried to leap for the door. Marianne gave a ladylike shriek and fainted again. This time, Freddy caught her without mishap. Dan's voice droned on. Robert stared at Jonathan and demanded, "What do you mean by that, Jon?"

"He has fallen afoul of the protections of the Sons of the New Dawn," Jonathan answered. "I warned him not to meddle!"

"You might have tried warning him you had a protective spell up, you young idiot!" Mairelon said acidly as, with two swift motions, he undid the special knot Kim had used and stripped the binding cords from his wrists. "What did you use? Quick now!"

Jonathan mumbled something, and Kim stopped listening. No matter what he said, no matter what Mairelon thought he could do, there wasn't time. She could hear the note of desperation in Dan's voice; she could feel his words twisting like oiled eels. The very air inside the lodge was beginning to shine with reflections from the invisible, impossible crystal words, and with every syllable Dan spoke, the glow grew stronger. He had to be stopped *now*, before he put so much power into his distorted spell that it really would destroy them all when he finally lost control of it.

Kim took a deep breath, swallowed hard, and stood up with a surge, pushing the heavy wooden card table up and forward with all her strength. Cards and markers slid off and scattered across the floor; the pistol Dan had set on top of them followed with a metallic scraping noise. The table hit Dan hard, knocking him sideways. He staggered briefly, then regained his feet, but his concentration had been shattered and the spell broke free.

There was a brilliant flare of light, and sharp-edged words flew in all directions. Mairelon, Renée D'Auber, and Lord St. Clair flung their arms up in identical gestures of repudiation and simultaneously shouted the same unintelligible phrase. Kim ducked behind the upturned table as the unseen words bounced back toward her. Something hit the floor with a metallic ping, and something else with a clear ringing noise. Dan cried out and fell heavily against the table. Kim heard a peculiar muffled noise that sounded like Jack Stower's voice; then the remnants of the spell swirled and settled around her like dust. They lay in shimmering silver drifts on the wooden floor for a long moment before they melted into nothing.

"Well done," St. Clair's voice said to someone.

"Thank you," Renée D'Auber responded.

"Kim!" Mairelon called. He sounded very close; an instant later, he appeared, bending anxiously over the end of the table. "Kim?"

"I ain't hurt," Kim assured him. "Is that spell done with?"

"For the most part," Mairelon answered.

Judging this to be as near a "yes" as she was likely to get from him, Kim climbed cautiously to her feet and looked around. Freddy, his arms locked around the unconscious Marianne, was trading icy stares with Lady Granleigh and Jasper Marston. Jonathan alternated between baleful muttering and attempts to untie his hands with his teeth. Meanwhile, Jasper's man, Stuggs, had a firm and very professional-looking armlock on Jack Stower.

Stower's pistols had vanished, and his clothes were even more rumpled and disreputable than usual. Kim was sorry she had missed seeing their encounter. Robert Choiniet and Mairelon's brother, Andrew, were standing over Dan Laverham, who looked and smelled somewhat singed but seemed otherwise unhurt. Renée D'Auber stood next to the door, her face composed, her eyes bright and alert; on the opposite side of the room, Lord St. Clair watched the others with a cold, speculative expression.

" 'Ere, now," Stuggs said to Jack, who was struggling in vain. "None o' that."

"Get your hands off me!" Dan said to Robert and Andrew. They had considerately helped him to his feet and then neglected to let go of his arms.

"And give you a chance to grab one of those pistols again, or start some more magic?" Robert said. "Not likely."

"Someone should find those guns and get them out of the way," Andrew added.

"Did you say something about brandy a bit ago, Jon?" Freddy asked. "Like to get some for Marianne."

"Get me out of this first," Jonathan said crossly, holding out his hands and the tangle he had made of Kim's knots.

Mairelon was studying Kim with an abstracted air, as if she were wearing her coat inside out and he couldn't puzzle out why she should do such a thing. "Now what?" Kim asked him in a low voice. "We ain't much better off than when we started."

"Aren't," Mairelon said without thinking. He blinked. "Aren't we?"

"Well, Dan don't—doesn't have his guns any more,"

Kim admitted. "That's something. But we still haven't found that platter. The real one, I mean. And we ain't—aren't going to with this lot of Bedlamites muddling everything up proper."

"Ah, yes; thank you for reminding me," Mairelon said. He glanced around, then took two steps sideways and reached under a chair. He straightened and held up the vine-covered silver sphere that Dan had used to focus the spell he had cast on Kim. "You don't happen to see the other one, do you?"

"It's next to Mr. Aberford's foot," St. Clair said. Mairelon gave him a sharp, suspicious look, then retrieved the second sphere without comment. "I do hope you aren't planning to repeat Daniel's lunacy, Merrill," Lord St. Clair went on. "Not only was it an uncomfortable and dangerous bit of sorcery, it was pointless as well. I doubt that you could do any better."

Mairelon raised an eyebrow and smiled slightly. "You think not?"

"Richard, don't be a fool!" Andrew said.

"It matters not at all," Renée announced. "For that annoying person with the pistols was not so altogether unsuccessful as you think. Look!" She pointed toward the fireplace.

Kim blinked, not understanding; then she saw the silver shimmer on the hearthstone. Mairelon immediately lost all interest in St. Clair. "Well, well! Andrew—no, you'd better keep hold of Laverham. Aberford and Marston, then; come and lend a hand."

It was not quite as easy as that; Jonathan had first to be extracted from the rest of the cords on his wrists, and Jasper only stood and glowered until Lady Granleigh poked him and pointed eloquently. It took the three of them longer than Kim expected to find the notches in the edge of the stone and pry it out.

Mairelon reached down into the gaping hole and lifted out a familiar-shaped bundle. Kim held her breath as he pulled the canvas wrapping away and took hold of the silver handles.

"The Sacred Dish!" Jonathan breathed.

"Is it another fake?" Kim demanded, unable to bear the suspense.

"No," Mairelon said. He looked up with a broad smile. "This is the real Saltash Platter."

TWENTY-FOUR

There was a long silence while everyone stared at the heavy silver tray. Then Lady Granleigh swept forward.

"I believe that belongs to my dear friend, Mr. Charles Bramingham," she said. "It should be returned to him at once."

"By you?" Mairelon's tone was polite; too polite.

Lady Granleigh lifted her chin. "Certainly," she replied without blushing.

"No!" Jonathan Aberford leaped to his feet and planted himself between Mairelon and Lady Granleigh. "The Sacred Dish belongs to the Sons of the New Dawn! It will not leave this house!"

"No, no, really, Jon," Freddy protested. "I lost it to Henry at play; told you that ages ago. So it doesn't belong to the Sons. Doesn't belong to this Charles person, either, if it comes to that. It's Henry's."

" 'Ere," said Stuggs, "somebody give me a 'and with this

cove afore 'e breaks 'is arm accidental-like."

Kim grinned malevolently at Jack and crossed the room to retrieve the cord that had been used to tie Mairelon and Jonathan. She tossed it to Stuggs, who snatched it out of the air and had his grip back on Jack's arms before Jack realized he had missed a chance to get free. Kim grinned again to hide her unease and kicked a broken chair rung out of her way. Between the chair Freddy had smashed, the window Dan had broken, and the table Kim herself had overturned, walking across the room was becoming decidedly hazardous. Kim retreated to the back wall, where she could see everyone without getting in the way.

Lord St. Clair looked up from the platter at last and turned a cool, thoughtful gaze on Renée d'Auber. "So you were lying," he said.

"But of course," the Frenchwoman replied with a Gallic shrug. "I did not at all like that person with the pistols, whom I hope Monsieur Andrew is holding very hard. Why should I not lie to him?"

Dan lunged, almost breaking free of Andrew's hold. *"Salaude!"*

"What?" said Freddy. Lady Granleigh stiffened in outrage, from which Kim deduced that whatever Dan had said was disrespectful, if not actually shocking. Stuggs and Jack Stower wore identical expressions of bafflement, while Robert glanced warily at Renée. Andrew was plainly appalled, but Mairelon seemed to be holding back a smile. St. Clair was watching everyone with an expectant air, like a cat waiting for the right moment to pounce.

Renée D'Auber raised an eyebrow, looking faintly puzzled. "Pardon? Your accent is not at all good, monsieur. If you wish for me to understand, you should speak the English."

"I think not," said St. Clair. "It might distress the ladies."

"You!" Dan transferred his glare from Renée to the Baron. "You won't get away with this!"

"With what?" Lord St. Clair asked in a reasonable tone.

"You're not getting that platter! You've had everything else—the money, the title, everything—just because you were born on the right side of the blanket, but you're not getting this."

"That remains to be seen," St. Clair said calmly.

"Does it?" Mairelon said. "By whom?"

"The Sacred Dish is the property of the Sons of the New Dawn," Jonathan repeated stubbornly. No one paid him any more attention this time than they had the last.

"Richard," Andrew put in uneasily, "you're not going to keep that thing, are you? If you're found with it—"

"—there are at least thirteen people here who can say that I didn't have the smallest idea where it was until Laverham there did his locating spell," Mairelon interrupted. "I'm sure that at least one or two of them would be willing to say as much in court. Don't be a fool, Andrew."

"Ah, but you might have been acting," Lord St. Clair said with a cold smile. "I think Mr. Merrill's point is well taken."

"You would," Mairelon said.

"They don't like each other much, do they?" Freddy commented sagely to Robert.

"Freddy?" Marianne Thornley was coming around again, and the sound of her beloved's voice had caught her attention. "Oh, Freddy, what has happened?"

"You have behaved very badly," Lady Granleigh answered in a severe tone. "We shall, however, discuss it later, in private. Jasper! We have wasted enough time. Bring the platter out to the carriage at once. Come, Marianne."

"You aren't taking Marianne anywhere," Freddy said, stepping in front of the shrinking Marianne.

"Nor you the Saltash Platter," Mairelon said to Jasper.

"Amelia . . ." Jasper said, waffling visibly.

"Really, Jasper! You're larger than he is," said Lady Granleigh over her shoulder. "Just take it."

"Allow me to get out of the way first," said Lord St. Clair.

Kim frowned as St. Clair moved farther away from the hearth where Mairelon, Jonathan, and Jasper stood. She could understand a gentry cove not wanting to get involved in a turn-up, but St. Clair hadn't been close enough to be inconvenienced by a fight. She watched as he crossed the room to join Lady Granleigh, and saw him stumble as he passed a footstool. Her frown deepened. Had he scooped something from the floor? She couldn't be sure; he had turned away from her as he straightened.

The sound of a scuffle distracted her. She turned in time to see Mairelon shove the handle end of the Saltash Platter into Jasper Marston's stomach. Kim winced in sympathy as Jasper doubled over with a huff of exhaled breath. Mairelon yanked the platter back, grabbed the free handle, and brought it down on the back of Jasper's head. There was a satisfying clang, and Jasper collapsed without another sound.

"Very impressive," St. Clair said without enthusiasm.

Kim looked quickly back at him, but his hands were empty, if he had picked anything up, he had hidden it under his coat.

Mairelon turned and flourished the platter in an elegant stage bow. "Would you care to be the next to try to take it?"

"Richard!" Andrew said, sounding horrified. "You can't go around assaulting peers of the realm!"

"Oh, really, Andrew, he's only a Baron," Mairelon said irritably.

Renée D'Auber rolled her eyes. "It is not how it must be done," she declared.

"And giving St. Clair the Saltash Platter is?" Mairelon asked, his jaw tightening.

"I did not say such a thing at all," Renée said with dignity.

Lady Granleigh turned, her attention momentarily diverted from Freddy and Marianne. She raked Mairelon with a haughty look that had no apparent effect whatever, and sniffed loudly. "Lord St. Clair seems an infinitely more proper person to have charge of that object than you, Mr. de Mare, or whatever your name is."

"Just so," said St. Clair. "And after all, Mr. Merrill is a wanted man. I wonder what the Bow Street Runners would make of this little scene?"

Mairelon's lips thinned. Jack Stower lurched sideways, whimpering, in spite of William Stuggs's grip on his arms and the cord Stuggs had knotted around his wrists, dragging the two of them several feet nearer the door. Jonathan Aberford shifted uncomfortably and ran a hand through his hair as if in search of the stocking mask that had been taken from him in the carriage. Lady Granleigh turned a shade paler and raised her chin imperiously.

"Oh, no," Dan Laverham said softly. He was staring at Lord St. Clair with single-minded intensity, and Kim had never heard so much hatred in anyone's voice before. "Not this time, Gregory. This time, if I lose, you lose, too."

"You had better think what you are saying," St. Clair replied, frowning. "In any case, this is not a suitable place for that discussion."

"I have thought," Dan said. "You lied to me before and tried to use me; I won't make the same mistake again. You call the Runners in, Gregory, and I'll tell them whose idea it was to nick that bloody platter, yes, and exactly how it was arranged, too. Shall I tell this lot right now?"

"Please do," Mairelon said.

"Don't be absurd, Daniel," Lord St. Clair put in quickly. "No one will take your word for anything."

"St. Clair?" Andrew said. "You mean *St. Clair* stole the Saltash Set? I don't believe it."

"There, you see?" said the Baron.

"Not so fast," Mairelon said. "I want to hear him out."

Robert nodded. "Let him have his say."

"He's a gutter-bred criminal!" St. Clair snapped. "I give you my word as a peer of the realm—"

Dan's high, half-hysterical laughter cut off whatever Lord St. Clair had planned to say. "Peer of the realm! The only reason you're the peer and I'm the gutter brat is that our blueblooded father was too high in the instep to marry a kitchen maid, though he wasn't above giving her a tumble."

"Good Lord," breathed Mairelon, looking from Dan to St. Clair. "So that's it."

"This discussion is highly improper," Lady Granleigh announced. "Marianne, cover your ears. I recommend that you do the same, Miss D'Auber, though I am well aware that French persons do not have any real delicacy of mind."

Everyone, including Marianne, was too busy studying the two men to pay any attention to Lady Granleigh. The resemblance between them was marked. Kim remembered how shaken she had been by her first glimpse of Lord St. Clair, when she had thought for a moment that he *was* Dan Laverham, and cursed herself mentally for not guessing the truth before. But who would have pegged Dan for gentry blood, even on the wrong side of the blanket?

St. Clair looked a trifle pale, but seemed otherwise unmoved by the intense scrutiny. "This does not change matters at all," he said. "Your wild accusations are clearly the delusions of a mind deranged by jealousy. I am very sorry you have been subjected to this, Lady Granleigh, but I venture to hope that you will not hold my father's indiscretion against me."

Dan laughed again, bitterly. "Still wanting to have your cake and eat it, too, Gregory? You were pleased enough with me as long as you could make use of my services. You shouldn't have lied to me about the Saltash Set, though. If I'd known it was magical, I'd never have split it up to sell."

"You 'ad this 'ere dish as all the fuss is over?" William Stuggs put in unexpectedly. " 'Ow did that 'appen?"

"Fenton was my man," Dan said, speaking directly to St. Clair. "He wouldn't have dreamed of cracking a crib with-

out cutting me in. You didn't know that when you told him
to keep mum about it, did you?"

"Be quiet, Daniel," Lord St. Clair said.

"Why? I told you, this time you're going to lose, one
way or another."

"No." St. Clair sounded regretful, almost sad. "You may
make my life a little difficult for a time, but even if everyone here believes you, it won't make any real difference.
Bow Street won't take the word of a criminal against that
of a Baron, and without Fenton you have no proof of anything you say. There will be rumors, of course, and one or
two houses may shut their doors to me for a time, but
nothing more serious than that. It's one of the advantages
of my position, you see."

Dan Laverham growled and lunged again. St. Clair stood
quietly, smiling slightly as Andrew and Robert fought Dan
back under control.

"There, you," Robert panted. "Now, before you continue,
would one of you mind explaining why that—" he waved
a free hand at the Saltash Platter, then had to grab Dan's
arm again, "—is so all-fired important? I'm getting tired of
not knowing what, exactly, is going on."

"It's perfectly plain," Jonathan said. "The Sacred Dish—"

"Oh, stop nattering about the Sacred Dish," Robert
begged. "This is serious, Jon."

"Quite serious," Mairelon said over Jonathan's spluttered
protests. "This is—"

"—the Saltash Platter, part o' a set as was stolen from
the Royal College of Wizards upwards o' five years ago,
by a person or persons unknown," said William Stuggs. He

smiled seraphically over Jack Stower's shoulder at the circle of surprised faces, and before the surprise could turn to speculation he added, "I 'ate to disconvenience the Quality-like, but I 'ave to inform you that you, Lord Gregory St. Clair, and you, Mr. Daniel Laverham, and this cove 'ere, 'oose name I ain't 'ad the dubious pleasure of bein' told, are all under arrest in the name o' the Law, for the theft o' the Saltash Set, breakin' an' enterin', 'olding a lot o' respectable folk at gunpoint, an' one or two other things as are against the Law o' the Realm."

"He's a Runner!" Kim burst out before she thought.

"Jasper, you fool!" said Lady Granleigh, too angry to remember that her brother was still comatose on the hearthstone.

"Good Lord!" said Andrew. "Miss D'Auber, did you know?"

"It is to me a great surprise also," Renée D'Auber assured him. "It is entirely a good thing after all, however, since Monsieur St. Clair and that person with the pistols are arrested, so I shall not repine in the least."

"Well, well," Mairelon said. He stepped forward, holding out the Saltash Platter to Stuggs. "I expect you'll want this as evidence?"

"I fear not," St. Clair put in. Kim looked back at him and froze. He was holding one of Dan's pistols trained on Stuggs, who stood between him and the door, and his expression was grim. "Or rather, you may want it, but you won't have it."

"Don't shoot!" Jack Stower pleaded, twisting in Stuggs's grip in a vain effort to get out of Lord St. Clair's line of fire. "I ain't no nabbing cull! Don't shoot me!"

"You can't shoot all of us with only one pistol," Mairelon said gently to St. Clair, ignoring Jack's frantic cries.

"Quite true," Lord St. Clair agreed. His left arm shot out and grabbed Marianne, who shrieked loudly as he pulled her close and pointed the pistol at her head. "But I doubt that any of you will let the young lady be hurt just to keep me here. I shall let her go in Dover, when I board the packet for France—provided, of course, that no one does anything foolish."

"Here, now!" Freddy expostulated. "What d'you think you're doing?"

"Lord St. Clair!" Lady Granleigh exclaimed in tones of shock.

"You wouldn't dare," Andrew said to St. Clair.

"He certainly would," Mairelon said to Andrew. "I think you had better move away from the door, Stuggs. Your superiors will have to be content with half a haul this time."

St. Clair smiled and started forward, dragging Marianne along with him, as Stuggs reluctantly moved aside. "Don't forget the platter, Merrill," St. Clair said, turning his head slightly.

At that precise moment, Freddy Meredith stepped in front of Gregory St. Clair and astonished the entire company by knocking him down. His success was due only partially to his catching St. Clair completely off guard, Kim had to admit that the blow had been a regular wisty castor. Lord St. Clair fell backward, discharging his pistol into the ceiling above the hearth. A shower of plaster descended on Jonathan and the unfortunate Jasper, who coughed; choked, and sat up at last, holding his head and moaning.

"Well struck!" Robert said after a stunned moment.

"Dash it all, Freddy, that was a stupid trick to pull!" Jonathan complained, brushing at the plaster dust that covered his shoulders. "I might have been shot!"

"Oh, *Freddy*!" said Marianne, throwing her arms around him in ecstasy. "How *brave*!"

"Get up, you villain, and I'll do it again," Freddy said. "Dashed lot of nerve you've got, bullying ladies and frightening Marianne."

St. Clair did not reply. He lay sprawled on the floor, his top hat gone and his hair disarranged, staring at Freddy as if he could not believe what had happened.

"I knew he was a regular Captain Sharp," Kim said with considerable satisfaction to no one in particular.

To her surprise, Mairelon answered her. "Yes, you did, and very right you were, too. Just hand that other bit of cord to Andrew, will you, Kim? Then look around for something to tie St. Clair. I'll feel considerably happier when all three of them are, er, secure."

"That's good sense, gov'ner," Stuggs said approvingly. "An' pick up them other pops while you're at it. They 'adn't ought to be lyin' about for the likes o' 'im to get 'is 'ands on."

"There ain't no rope or string or anything," Kim said, picking up the second piece of cord and Dan's other pistol. "I already looked."

"Amelia?" Jasper's voice rose querulously from the hearth. "What's happening? Have you got the platter?"

"You imbecile!" Lady Granleigh stalked to her brother's side, the better to berate him. "Fool! That man of yours is a Bow Street Runner!"

"Stuggs? Don't be silly, Amelia. Monkton recommended

him; he'd hardly send me a Runner, now, would he?"

Mairelon glanced at the two of them, then took the cord and pistol from Kim and walked over to Laverham, Robert, and Andrew. He handed the cord to his brother and said, "Tie him up."

"Of course," Andrew answered. "Richard—"

"In a minute, Andrew. Mr., er, Stuggs, I believe you'll find this useful, at least until we've gotten things sorted out." Mairelon handed Stuggs the pistol, then tapped Freddy, who was still glaring pugnaciously at Lord St. Clair, on the shoulder.

"I think this would be a good moment for a discreet departure," he said when Freddy turned. He nodded his head in the direction of Lady Granleigh and her brother, quarreling in front of the fireplace.

"What?" said Freddy. "Oh, I see. Good of you to mention it. Come on, Marianne." He abandoned St. Clair to Stuggs and the pistol, and he and Marianne slipped out the open door.

"That was very kind," Renée D'Auber said to Mairelon. "But have you not perhaps made for yourself more trouble?"

"I'm sure of it," Mairelon said cheerfully. "But I believe I owe Lady Granleigh one, for setting her unspeakable brother on me, and I can't think of a better way of evening the score."

"It seems singularly appropriate," Robert said, stepping forward. "But I would like to point out that I still haven't had my explanation. Not in any way that is remotely satisfactory, that is. I don't suppose you'd care to try again?"

"Good luck," Kim said under her breath. She gave the

rest of the dropped pistols to Mairelon, then sat on a nearby footstool to watch. Andrew and Renée were both looking expectantly at Mairelon, Jonathan was scowling at him, and any minute now Lady Granleigh would realize that her wealthy ward had managed to escape again. It ought to be better than a Drury Lane comedy.

TWENTY-FIVE

Mairelon set the Saltash Platter on the seat of a high-backed chair and put the pistols Kim had given him on top of it. When he turned back to the group, he was no longer smiling. "Yes, there do seem to be a number of loose ends," he said. "For instance, what are you doing here, Renée?"

"It is as your brother has said," Mademoiselle D'Auber replied. She thought for a moment, then added scrupulously, "For the most part."

"We came because Miss D'Auber had heard there was a Runner on your trail," Andrew put in.

"And you wished to assist him?" Mairelon said politely.

"No!" Andrew looked hurt. "I—we came to warn you. And to help you, if we could, though I suppose you've no reason to believe that."

"Why didn't you just tell Kim the Bow Street Runners were about?" Mairelon asked Renée. "Why the meeting? And why weren't you there?"

"Meeting?" Andrew stared at Renée D'Auber in surprised speculation. "You didn't tell me anything about a meeting."

"But of course not," Renée said. She gave the brothers a brilliant smile. "You have both got the heads of pigs, and if I had told you—" she nodded at Mairelon, "—that Monsieur Merrill the elder was here, you would have said a great many things of no politeness and gone away without seeing him, because you thought he did not believe you. And if I had told you—" she glared at Andrew, "—that we were to meet with your brother, you would have made a great many excuses of no merit and not have come, because you did not want to face him and admit you made the mistake five years ago. That is why I was late," she added, turning to Mairelon. "He was being difficult."

"Difficult? *I* was being difficult?" Andrew was almost beyond speech.

"Do you mean to say that you dragged Andrew down here to force the two of us to make up with each other?" Mairelon demanded with equal incredulity.

Renée opened her eyes very wide. "But of course. This feud was all very well when you were in France and he was here, but it would be altogether tiresome if you were both in England, and me, I do not like the things tiresome. So I thought I would arrange it."

The brothers exchanged a look of complete accord, and Kim suppressed a grin. That served Mairelon a bit of his own sauce! Stuggs shook his head sadly. "French," he explained to the room at large.

"And you weren't looking for the Saltash Platter?" Mairelon asked Renée, though Kim could tell from his tone that he did not really have doubts any longer.

"It would have been a very good thing, I think, if I could have gotten it," Renée answered, unperturbed. "For then we should not have had all this confusion which you have still not explained in the least."

"But for yourself?"

"For me?" Renée looked at Mairelon with convincing horror. "But no! Only consider! The Saltash Platter makes persons speak the truth, and that would have been of all things the most inconvenient."

Kim laughed. Mairelon looked at her with an affronted expression, which only made her laugh harder. Slowly Mairelon began to smile. "Yes, under the circumstances, I can see where it would have been, er, inconvenient."

Lady Granleigh chose this moment to stop abusing her brother and turn back to the rest of the room. "Marianne, it is high time—where is Marianne?"

"Gone," Mairelon answered helpfully.

Jonathan snickered, and Lady Granleigh rounded on him. "It is not humorous, young man! Stand aside," she commanded Stuggs. "I must leave at once, to prevent my ward from throwing herself away on that lamentably foolish young man."

"I 'ave my duty," Stuggs said, not moving. "And I 'ave one or two questions as you ought to answer, beggin' your pardon for the inconvenience."

"Of course, you could always pay a call in Bow Street later," Mairelon put in as Lady Granleigh stared, unable to believe that Stuggs had not immediately followed her orders. "It would cause quite a sensation among the *ton*, you might even set a new fashion."

"Amelia!" Jasper had gone pale. "We can't! The duns would be after me the minute they got wind of it."

"What is it you wish to know?" Lady Granleigh said stiffly.

" 'Ow did you come to 'ave an interest in that there platter? An' what sort o' interest did you 'ave?"

"I am very much afraid that I can answer that," a new voice said from behind Stuggs.

Stuggs jumped back and whirled, so that he could cover both the doorway and the corner where Laverham, Stower, and St. Clair stood. Then he smiled and relaxed. "Sir!" he said, and stepped aside.

Four men entered behind him. Hunch was the only one Kim recognized; the other three were gentry toffs, middle-aged and dressed for riding, but she didn't recall seeing any of them before. She glanced around the room, sizing up the reactions of the rest of the group. Lady Granleigh was staring at the man who had spoken, and she had gone rather pale. Jonathan Aberford turned red when he saw the second toff, but Robert smiled in relief at the same man. Laverham and Stower wore blank expressions; St. Clair's eyes narrowed and his lips thinned as he stared at the newcomers, and Kim got the impression that he was not at all pleased. Stuggs was watching the third man with a respectful expression. Andrew, Renée, and Mairelon all looked startled to various degrees.

"What 'ave you been a-doing now, Master Richard?" Hunch demanded, ignoring the rest of the company entirely.

"An excellent question," Robert murmured. "Perhaps you'll do better at getting an answer than we have."

"Well, well," Mairelon said. He blinked, smiled, and swept a bow. "Your servant, Granleigh, Bramingham. I'm afraid you've missed most of the excitement, Edward."

"I am desolated," the third man replied. With a start, Kim recognized his voice: he was the Earl of Shoreham, who had sent Mairelon off to Ranton Hill in search of the Saltash Platter. "Richard, I hate to be overly particular, but I seem to recall telling you not to attract atten—*Andrew*? What the devil are you doing here?"

"No, no, we've already had that bit," Mairelon said. "I want to know what Granleigh here meant when he said he could account for Lady Granleigh's, er, actions. And how you all happen to be here," he added as an afterthought.

"I received some information last night, after Hunch left," the Earl replied. He glanced toward Laverham and St. Clair. "I thought it sufficiently urgent to post down, but it seems to have been an unnecessary effort."

"If you're talking about the irregular relationship between Mr. Laverham and St. Clair, yes, that's come out," Mairelon said. "But where did you pick up these others?"

"Hunch told me you'd gone to Bramingham Place," Shoreham said. "Naturally we went looking for you there. Mrs. Bramingham had just discovered that most of her house-guests had vanished, and Bramingham and Granleigh elected to come with me in hopes of hunting them up."

"And in hopes of getting away from the excellent Mrs. Bramingham's frenzy," Mairelon murmured. "Quite understandable. Now, what was that you were saying about Lady Granleigh?" he asked, turning to the tall, distinguished man who had been first through the door.

The first man sighed and glanced toward the Earl of Shoreham. "My wife has a tendency to meddle," he explained. Lady Granleigh stiffened and recovered her usual color, but her husband gave her a look that caused her to subside without saying anything. Kim was impressed, there must be more to this stuffy-looking cull than at first appeared.

"A tendency to meddle," Lord Granleigh repeated. "And considerably more ambition than I had realized. I believe she was trying to arrange for me to be the next Minister of Wizardry." He gave the Earl of Shoreham another sidelong look as he spoke, as though checking his reaction.

"Nonsense, Stephen," Lady Granleigh said unconvincingly. "You are perfectly capable of managing such matters yourself."

"True," Lord Granleigh replied. "A fact which you would be well advised to remember in the future, Amelia. Your interference this time could very easily have had unpleasant consequences."

"I don't know what you are talking about," Lady Granleigh said even more unconvincingly than before. "I am only here to keep Marianne from ruining herself with Freddy Meredith."

"I don't believe it," the last of the three toffs put in: "Freddy's a good lad. He wouldn't do anything, er, dishonorable."

"Freddy said something about a special license before he left, Mr. Bramingham," Robert said, ignoring Lady Granleigh's glare.

"Yes, I believe he has one with him," Mairelon said. "Amazingly sensible of him, too. Any number of things might have gone wrong between here and Gretna Green, if he'd chosen that route."

"Sensible?" Jonathan goggled at Mairelon. *"Freddy?"*

"There, you see?" Mr. Bramingham said to the room at large. His eye fell on St. Clair, and he frowned. "Shoreham, what's Baron St. Clair doing in the corner with this fellow pointing a pistol at him?"

" 'E's under arrest, in the name o' the Law," Stuggs informed him. "Along with these other two. I 'aven't got straight yet which o' 'em did what, but they 'as all done somethin', and I 'ave my duty."

"You ought to be arresting *that* man as well," Jonathan Aberford grumbled, pointing at Mairelon. "Whoever he is. Didn't someone say he was wanted?"

Andrew's face set in grim lines. Mairelon only smiled and looked at the Earl of Shoreham. Shoreham returned the smile, then said to Jonathan, "He is certainly wanted by the French, but though our relations with them have improved a good deal, I don't think our cooperation would stretch so far as to turn one of our people over to them. Particularly a man with such a distinguished record."

"You're too kind," Mairelon said.

"Probably," Shoreham agreed blandly.

Andrew's mouth had dropped open, as had Lady Granleigh's St. Claire had gone white; Renée D'Auber and Hunch looked smug. "What are you talking about?" Jonathan demanded.

The Earl of Shoreham sighed. "For the past five years, Richard Merrill has been one of the best agents the War Office has had the good fortune to employ. Is that clear enough for you?"

"But—but I thought he stole the Saltash Set," Jonathan said, frowning.

"Merrill?" the Earl of Shoreham said. "It's your turn to explain."

"In a minute. I don't think we were quite through with Lord Granleigh yet," Mairelon answered. "I still don't understand what Lady Granleigh's ambitions for her husband have to do with the Saltash Set, or how she found out about it in the first place."

"She listened at doors, that's how," Jasper Marston said waspishly, lifting his head for the first time since the Earl and his companions had arrived.

Lady Granleigh gasped. "Jasper, how dare you—"

"Oh, stop it, Amelia," Jasper said. "There's no use pretending to injured innocence. They already know most of it. They know *you*," he added spitefully.

"You are not thinking about what you are saying," Lady Granleigh said in a tone that could have frozen the Thames at mid-summer.

"I know exactly what I'm saying! This whole mess is your fault, Amelia, and I'm not going to take the blame for it."

"My fault? You are the one who brought along that Bow Street Runner! I suppose you are going to claim you knew nothing about it."

"As it 'appens, 'e didn't," Stuggs put in. "I know my business, and it ain't lettin' no buffle'eaded toff in on the nick, beggin' your pardon, sir."

"It was your idea to get hold of that blasted platter!" Jasper said, ignoring Stuggs. "The whole thing was your idea, start to finish!"

Mairelon cleared his throat, which recalled the presence of an audience to the combatants. Lady Granleigh closed her mouth on whatever she had planned to say, and Jasper subsided on the hearth once more, holding his head. Mairelon smiled blandly. "And how would Lady Granleigh's, er, acquiring the Saltash Platter advance you with the Ministry, Lord Granleigh?"

Lord Granleigh looked at Mairelon in surprise. "Good Lord, man, recovering the Saltash Set and catching the thief would give anyone a boost! One of those chaps down at the Royal College came up with a gadget that said so, and the whole Ministry has been buzzing ever since."

"A gadget?" Mairelon frowned, distracted. "Not one of fotherington's crystals? He's been trying to get them to make accurate predictions forever; do you mean to say he's finally succeeded?"

"As it happens, yes," the Earl of Shoreham said. "You can discuss it with him later."

"How did he get it to—"

"*Later*, Richard. Right now, we want your story, and you must admit we've been very patient."

"Too patient," Hunch said darkly.

"Oh, very well. I think I have enough of the pieces to put together a fairly good picture. It's a long tale, though, you'd best make yourselves comfortable."

The Earl suppressed another sigh and leaned against the door. Mr. Bramingham, looking mildly puzzled, held a chair for Renée D'Auber, while the rest of the company (with the exception of Stuggs and his prisoners) settled themselves around the room. Watching Lady Granleigh and Jonathan Aberford vie for a chair, Kim was glad she'd bagged the footstool before it had occurred to anyone else to sit down.

"The story begins about five years ago," Mairelon said, and Kim smiled, recognizing the familiar lecturing tone. "The Saltash Set, of which this is part, was being displayed in the antechamber of the Royal College of Wizards, to which I had recently been elected.

"Lord St. Clair—" Mairelon gave him an ironic half-bow, "—had for some time been attempting to obtain the Saltash Set from the College, but for one reason or another, the College refused to sell. So he decided to steal it. Having no experience with the finer points of theft, he approached his illegitimate half brother, Daniel Laverham, for assistance.

"Laverham sent St. Clair a young man named James Fenton, who I must suppose was both an accomplished housebreaker and extremely loyal to Laverham. Laverham, you see, disliked and distrusted St. Clair—"

"With reason!" Dan Laverham interrupted, glaring at Lord St. Clair.

"Quiet, you," Stuggs said. "You'll 'ave your chance to talk later."

"St. Clair arranged for Fenton to steal the Saltash Set," Mairelon continued. "St. Clair must have taken care of the Royal College's magical precautions against theft, and Fenton did the rest, including dropping one or two items he'd stolen from me in the antechamber to make it look as if I were the thief. He had even timed things so that I'd be on my way home alone from my club when the theft occurred, so he had no reason to worry about laying information at Bow Street against me.

"Unfortunately for St. Clair, things began going wrong at that point. I ran into Shoreham here outside the club, and we got to arguing about the use of invocations in wards and protective spells. We ended up at Renée's, experimenting with catnip and powdered pearls until the watchmen made their morning rounds."

"Then why didn't you say so?" Andrew burst out. "Why did you let everyone believe—"

"At first, because I didn't see the need," Mairelon said. "I didn't think anyone would take the accusation seriously. And there was Renée's reputation to consider."

"Which was a great foolishness," Renée D'Auber said emphatically. "I am the eccentric, me, and no one pays the least attention when I do odd things."

"Not *now*," Mairelon agreed. "But five years ago you were barely eighteen, and it would not have done."

"Bah!" said Renée, dismissing these imaginary terrors with a wave. "You are altogether English, and very silly besides. Papa and I would have contrived something."

"But once you knew the Runners intended to arrest you—" Andrew said and stopped, looking from Mairelon to Renée uncertainly.

"By then I had asked them not to say anything," the Earl of Shoreham said. "It was the perfect excuse for Richard to fly the country and take up residence on the Continent, and we needed someone like him to do just that. Someone who could deal with any level of society, someone who wouldn't look too suspicious, and above all, someone who knew magic. Richard was perfect."

"So Hunch and I fled to France," Mairelon resumed. "Meanwhile, Fenton took the Saltash Set to Laverham instead of St. Clair. Since Laverham didn't know the set had magical properties, he broke it up and sold it to spite his brother. By the time Fenton learned that the set was more useful together than apart, it was too late. The pieces were scattered, and practically impossible to trace."

Laverham and St. Clair were looking at Mairelon as if he had suddenly acquired two heads; the rest of the company was listening with rapt attention. Kim shook her head in admiration. Mairelon had put it together so neatly that he might have been eavesdropping on Laverham and St. Clair the whole time.

"One of the pieces of the set, the bowl, was purchased by a German Baron," Mairelon said. "I got wind of it, and after the war I stayed on the Continent to track it down. It took me nearly a year. Meanwhile, Laverham had recovered two of the four spheres, and the platter had fallen into the innocent hands of Mr. Aberford's little group."

Jonathan Aberford scowled, and Kim wondered whether he was more annoyed by Mairelon's reference to the druids as a "little group" or by his characterizing them as innocent.

"That was the situation some four weeks ago when I returned to England," Mairelon said, giving Jonathan a charming smile. "And things began to get complicated. Naturally I couldn't return as myself; the Runners were still after me, and I have a great deal of respect for their abilities." He and Stuggs exchanged nods. "So I chose the role of a market performer. No one expects a real magician to work for pennies and the occasional shilling in a market, so I didn't expect anyone to look for me there. But I did send word to Shoreham, and I presume he told you, Lord Granleigh."

Mairelon paused and looked at Lord Granleigh expectantly. Lord Granleigh nodded. "He did. We discussed the implications at some length." He glanced at his wife and added, "In my study."

"That will be how Lady Granleigh heard about it," Mairelon said with supreme lack of tact. "She, ah, persuaded her brother to help her find me, intending, I suppose, to collect me and as much of the Saltash Set as possible and present the lot to the Royal College on behalf of her husband."

"And a proper mull 'e made of it," Stuggs put in, looking scornfully at Jasper Marston. "Went around askin' this one an' that one, with no more sense nor a baby. Word was all over St. Giles before the day was out."

"How was I to know?" Jasper complained. " 'Find this Merrill person,' she said; well, how do you find one man in the whole of London without asking?"

"Which explains how Bow Street heard of my return," Mairelon said, "and undoubtedly how Mr. Laverham heard of it, as well." He glanced at Dan, who glared and said nothing. "Bow Street arranged for Mr. Stuggs here to keep an eye on Mr. Marston. At least, I presume it was Bow Street." He threw a sidelong look at the Earl of Shoreham.

The Earl laughed. "Right again, Richard. Stuggs has done a job or two for me before, though this wasn't one of them. How did you guess?"

"He recognized you when you arrived just now," Mairelon answered. "And only one of your people would call you 'sir' and not 'my lord.' "

Lady Granleigh sniffed, but a look from her husband kept her from saying anything.

"Once he found Mairelon the Magician, Mr. Marston hired Kim here to look through my wagon for the Saltash

Bowl. I, er, found her in process and persuaded her to come with me after she completed her commission from Mr. Marston."

"Cloth-head," Kim muttered, not entirely sure whether she meant Marston or Mairelon.

"I suspect it was Laverham's men we gave the slip to on our way out of London," Mairelon went on blandly. "It doesn't matter, though. Shoreham told us where the platter was, and we came here to recover it. I'm not sure how Renée found out where we were headed—"

"Lord Shoreham told me," Renée said. "And since Monsieur Andrew Merrill was of an unhappiness, and had besides heard some of the rumors, and since I also heard that the Bow Street Runners were of an interest, I thought, me, that it would be best to come here and arrange matters myself."

"Renée!" Shoreham looked horrified.

"Oh, I was very discreet," Renée assured him. "No one knew I was not in London, except of course Madame Bramingham and her guests, and Monsieur Andrew stayed at the inn in that town with the dreadful name I cannot remember."

"Swafflton?" Mairelon murmured.

"Yes, that is it," Renée said. "And it has all turned out well, so there is no reason for you to pull your mouth down, so, and make faces as if you have the stomachache."

"You should have left matters to me," Shoreham said, shaking his head.

Renée opened her eyes very wide. "Truly? But it does not seem to me that you have done very much."

"It wasn't necessary," Mairelon said. "Any more than it was necessary for you to come."

"Well, but it might have been," Renée replied, unperturbed. "And it is better to be too ready, is it not? Also, I do not see that you would explain anything at all to me if I had stayed in London, and I do not wish to perish of the curiosity. So I am glad I came, and I do not care if you look very sour about it."

Mairelon rolled his eyes, and Kim laughed. She was beginning to like Renée in spite of herself.

"I don't know whether Lady Granleigh knew that the Saltash Platter was in Ranton Hill when she came down to Mrs. Bramingham's house party," Mairelon went on after a moment, "but I rather think not. It didn't take her long to discover it and send for her brother, though, and the roads and weather being as they've been, both of them were settled in before we arrived.

"Laverham must have known the platter's whereabouts for several months, at least, but he was being very cautious. He arranged for James Fenton to take a job as footman to Freddy Meredith, intending to have Fenton steal the platter for him later. Fenton had other ideas."

Dan Laverham muttered something under his breath and glared at Mairelon. Mairelon smiled, and Kim shook her head. He was enjoying this altogether too much, she thought.

"Fenton's family was respectable, and his brother was a silversmith. Fenton persuaded him to copy the Saltash Platter exactly. Perhaps the original idea was to cover up the theft of the platter for as long as possible, but he must have realized fairly soon that he could make a tidy sum selling copies of the platter to each of the, er, interested parties. Since he wasn't a magician himself, he didn't know that the forgeries would be childishly easy to spot.

"When the copies were finished, Fenton replaced the real platter with a copy and hid it in the druid's lodge." Mairelon waved at the gaping hole in the floor in front of the hearth. "But he was stretching his luck; making the copies had taken a long time, and Laverham was beginning to worry, particularly since by then he'd heard that I was back. So Laverham sent Jack Stower there down to Ranton Hill to check on Fenton."

"Then he didn't follow me at all!" Kim exclaimed, remembering how frightened she had been by Jack's unexpected appearance at the inn in Ranton Hill.

"No, but it was as well that you kept out of sight," Mairelon said. "Think of the trouble we'd have had if Laverham had arrived a few days earlier than he did."

Kim shuddered.

"Richard," the Earl of Shoreham said. His tone was mild, but Mairelon sighed and returned to his story.

"Just to thoroughly confuse matters, at about this time Freddy Meredith lost the false platter to Henry Bramingham in a game of cards. Henry knew that his uncle," Mairelon nodded at Gregory St. Clair, "collected oddities of that sort and proposed to give it to him. That brought St. Clair down to Ranton Hill posthaste and set off an interesting round of burglaries at Bramingham Place. Kim and I were privileged to observe most of the parade."

"What, what?" said Mr. Bramingham.

"We hid in your priest's hole," Mairelon explained.

"Priest's hole!" Kim said, disappointed. "Is that what it was? I thought it was a spell."

"Bramingham showed it to me last time I visited," Mairelon said. "Next time your household is roused in the middle of the night, Bramingham, you should remember to check inside it."

"Yes, but what's this about burglaries?" Bramingham said. "Somebody broke into the library a couple of nights ago, but—"

"Several somebodies," Mairelon interrupted. "Actually, I believe Renée was the first, but she recognized the platter for a fake and left it where it was. She was long gone when Kim and I got there."

"I knew I 'adn't ought to 'ave gone to London and left you 'ere with 'er," Hunch said.

"It wasn't my idea!" Kim protested.

"I didn't figure as it was," Hunch said dryly, and Kim blinked in surprise. Then she grinned at him.

"We were interrupted by Mr. Stower's arrival," Mairelon said with a quelling look at Hunch. "Stower was interrupted in turn by Marston and Stuggs, who were interrupted by Jonathan Aberford."

"Jonathan?" Robert Choiniet said, startled. "Are you sure?"

"He has a turn of phrase that is unmistakable," Mairelon answered.

"Have you got maggots in your head?" Robert demanded, glaring at Jonathan. "Or have you suddenly gotten as bacon-brained as Freddy Meredith? Why in heaven's name would you try to burgle Bramingham Place?"

"I thought it would work," Jonathan said sullenly.

"He hadn't counted on the, er, competition," Mairelon said. "In the end, Lady Granleigh managed to obtain the platter by as neat a trick as I've seen. You might consider taking her on, Shoreham; she's got the nerves for it."

Lady Granleigh looked as if she did not know whether to be pleased or insulted by this remark, and Kim hid a smile.

"Lady Granleigh quickly discovered that her platter was a forgery, which left her in something of a dilemma. She couldn't return it to the Braminghams without awkward explanations, but she didn't want to keep it, either. And Jonathan Aberford was hanging about Bramingham Place and making a nuisance of himself; if Lady Granleigh and her brother made any attempts to locate the real platter, Jonathan was sure to notice. So she decided to give the forgery back to the druids and solve two problems at once.

"Miss D'Auber and I had agreed to meet this morning near here to compare what we had each learned. She was delayed—" Mairelon gave Andrew a quick look, and Andrew smiled wryly, "—so I was here alone when Lady Granleigh and her party arrived. I, ah, accepted the platter on Mr. Aberford's behalf."

"By what right?" Jonathan demanded.

Mairelon looked at him without answering. Stuggs made a peculiar noise that Kim realized, after a moment, was a smothered chuckle. Jonathan turned very red and subsided, muttering, and Mairelon turned back to the Earl of Shoreham and continued his tale.

"Meanwhile, Fenton was proceeding with his own plans. He gave or sold the second of his fakes to Jack Stower and presumably made arrangements to meet with a couple of other prospective customers." Mairelon glanced toward St. Clair, who did not react. Jonathan Aberford, however, scowled and shifted uneasily. Mairelon smiled. "Yes, I thought so."

"Get on with it, Richard," the Earl said. He sounded amused but determined.

"You have no sense of the dramatic, Shoreham," Mairelon complained.

"I have as much as I need," the Earl replied in a dry voice. "Though I will readily admit that I have not spent the last few years on a stage. No doubt it's a grave failing in my education."

"No doubt," Mairelon said, looking somewhat disgruntled. "Well, Stower was on the point of returning to London with his platter when he spotted Hunch in Ranton Hill. He followed Hunch to our camp and attempted to take the false platter we had collected; instead, he lost his own and prompted me to head by Bramingham Place to find out what was going on.

"I found more than I expected." Mairelon paused, staring at the far wall, and something in his stance kept the others from commenting. Then he shook himself and looked at Mr. Bramingham. "When you get back, you'd best send someone down to the wood by the Long Avenue. There's a body and two more copies of the Saltash Platter hidden there."

"Richard!" said the Earl, his voice carrying clearly over the confused babble that broke out among the rest of the listeners. "Who? What happened?"

"The body was the unfortunate and ambitious James Fenton," Mairelon answered. "As to what happened, I can only speculate; Kim and I heard the shot, but we didn't get a look at the man who fired it."

"Speculate, then!"

"I think Fenton had arranged to meet someone in the Long Avenue. Two someones, actually; he couldn't very well have sold both fakes to the same person. I think he miscalculated badly—remember, he didn't know that a magician could easily tell the difference between his forgeries and the real platter. So when he tried to pass off one of the fakes, St. Clair shot him."

"Unlikely," Lord St. Clair said into the horrified silence that followed.

"Not at all," Mairelon said with exaggerated politeness. "You, Laverham, and Aberford there are the most logical people for Fenton to pick as possible customers for his remaining forgeries. Laverham, or rather, Laverham's man Stower, already had a platter. Aberford would clearly do a lot to get his hands on his, er, Sacred Dish, but I doubt he'd commit murder. Besides, if he'd killed Fenton, he wouldn't have held up Laverham's coach half an hour later, looking for the platter."

Jonathan jerked. "How did you know—"

"It's the only reason you've done anything for the past week," Mairelon said. "You were supposed to meet Fenton, too, weren't you? How did you find out that he was hoping to sell the platter to someone else?"

"I heard him bragging about it at the inn," Jonathan said sullenly. "I didn't kill anyone!"

"Yes, I know," Mairelon said. "You thought you'd save yourself some time and trouble, not to mention money, and hold up the coach instead of paying Fenton."

"This is all speculation," St. Clair said. He acted as if he were calm enough, but there were small lines of tension at the corners of his eyes, and a muscle in his jaw twitched now and again when he was not speaking.

"Not entirely," Mairelon told him. "A moment ago, you told Laverham and Stuggs that they couldn't prove anything against you without Fenton, but no one has mentioned Mr. Fenton's unfortunate demise until now. If you didn't kill him, how did you know?"

"I was not referring to this Fenton's death," Lord St. Clair said coldly. "I merely meant that no one knew where he was."

"Convince the Runners of that." Mairelon nodded at Stuggs.

"You were the man he was to meet!" Jonathan said suddenly, staring intently at St. Clair. "You were the one to whom he would have sold the Sacred Dish!"

Robert Choiniet rolled his eyes. Lady Granleigh looked shocked. The Earl of Shoreham frowned. "How do you know?" he demanded.

"He was at the inn; I saw him hanging about while I was . . . following Fenton."

"Hardly convincing," St. Clair said.

"I doubt that the Runners will have any trouble finding proof, one way or another," Mairelon said.

"Now that they're looking at the right man," Andrew muttered.

"In any case: St. Clair shot Fenton, but Kim and I interrupted him. Laverham and Stower interrupted us and brought us here. I presume St. Clair followed us. Fenton had hidden the platter under the hearth; we found it and had a small disagreement over its ownership. I expect Stuggs can tell you the rest; he was here for most of it. And that's all."

TWENTY-SIX

t wasn't all by a long shot. Everyone wanted a chance to object, explain, or ask questions, and it took all the Earl's considerable force of character to keep them more or less under control. Mairelon was no help whatever; he took immediate advantage of the commotion to dodge past Hunch and corner Lord Granleigh, whom he began cross-questioning about recent magical developments at the Royal College of Wizards.

After a few minutes of chaos, Stuggs brought the confusion to a halt by pointing out that he ought to take his prisoners into town and make arrangements for them to be transported to London.

"There's another one asleep on the box of the coach outside," Mairelon said, turning his head. "I don't know what he's done, but I'm quite sure it's something nasty."

Stuggs frowned. " 'E ain't a wizard, too, is 'e?"

"What, driving a coach?" Jonathan said scornfully.

"No, he's just another of Laverham's crew," Mairelon

said. "Unpleasant enough, but quite ordinary so far as his skills are concerned."

"Still, that makes four of them," Shoreham said. "Which is a bit much to expect one man, however competent, to handle alone."

"Well, I could go along as far as the town," Mr. Bramingham offered. "It's not much out of my way, you know. I can't stop there, though, my wife will be waiting to hear what's happened."

"And to spread it over as much of the county as she can reach," Mairelon murmured. "I'm afraid St. Clair is going to be a social outcast no matter how the trial turns out."

"I should think so," Lady Granleigh sniffed. "His behavior to me, and to poor Marianne, has been simply unpardonable. If it hadn't been for him, Marianne would not have run off as she did."

Everyone looked at Lady Granleigh in patent disbelief, including Jasper. Lady Granleigh stared haughtily down her nose at the lot of them. "Pointing that pistol at poor Marianne clearly disordered her intellect. I am quite confident that, had you behaved as a gentleman ought, wiser counsels would have prevailed, and she would not have dashed off to be married in such a hole-in-the-corner fashion."

"I congratulate you, Lady Granleigh," Lord St. Clair said after a moment. "I have never before met anyone with so great a talent for seeing the world as she wishes it to be."

Lady Granleigh stared through the space occupied by Lord St. Clair as if he were not there, then turned to her brother. "Come, Jasper, it is time we were going."

"Time and past," Kim muttered. Mairelon glanced sharply in her direction, but no one else seemed to hear.

"I'll accompany you, my dear," Lord Granleigh said in a tone that brooked no argument. "Bramingham's right, we should be getting back."

Lady Granleigh did not look at all pleased by this development (nor did Jasper), but they had no choice but to go along. Kim wondered whether Lord Granleigh would give them both a dressing-down in the carriage. She hoped so, the bracket-faced mort deserved a tongue-lashing and then some for the way she'd been mucking about in everyone else's affairs, and Jasper was no better.

"Now, then, Stuggs," Lord Shoreham said when the Granleighs were safely out the door. "You'll want someone besides Bramingham to help with the prisoners, I think. No sense in taking chances."

"We'd be happy to help, sir," Robert Choiniet volunteered. "That is, if you think we'd be useful." He nudged Jonathan with his elbow.

"Happy?" Jonathan said bitterly. "Oh, yes, of course, certainly. The Sacred Dish is gone for good, the lodge is in ruins, and the Sons of the New Dawn will be a laughingstock. Naturally we're happy."

Mairelon looked at him. "I hardly think one broken window, a displaced hearthstone, and a couple of overturned chairs constitute being in ruins."

"Yes, we've done more damage ourselves on a good night," Robert agreed. "Do stop playacting, Jon."

"Playacting? Playacting? You don't seem to realize how serious this is! We *need* to consecrate the Sacred Dish before we can make any more progress in the Mysteries."

Robert rolled his eyes and Mairelon hid a smile. Kim felt sorry for Jonathan. She knew what it was like to lose something she'd depended on having, even if she didn't know anything about druids or magic. And after all, it wasn't *his* fault he'd gotten hold of the Saltash Platter instead of some ordinary silver tray that no one else would have cared about. A thought occurred to her, and she said suddenly, "Why'd you pick the Saltash Platter for your Sacred Dish? I mean, would any old wicher cheat do, or does it have to be this particular one?"

"It was perfect," Jonathan said sullenly. "It's exactly the right dimensions, and the pattern has the proper balance of natural form and abstract design. It took me two years of hunting to find it, and it had to be stolen!"

"Well, if all you need is something that size and shape, can't you use one of the fake platters? There's enough of 'em around."

Everyone looked at Kim, and she flushed. "It was just an idea."

"And a very good one," Mairelon said. "One of the false platters should suit you admirably, Aberford. Better than the real thing, in fact; you won't have to worry about your spells getting tangled up with the ones that are already in the Saltash Platter and exploding, or doing something equally unexpected."

Jonathan, who had opened his mouth, closed it again, looking suddenly very thoughtful. The Earl of Shoreham's lips twitched, and Renée D'Auber put up a hand to hide a smile. Andrew only looked bewildered, and St. Clair and the other prisoners studiously ignored the exchange.

"I doubt that there will be any fuss over ownership of one of the duplicates, either," Mairelon added.

"I think I can guarantee that no official questions will be

asked," Shoreham put in. "Provided there is no fuss made at this end, of course. I should warn you, though, that I can't do a thing about gossip." He glanced in the direction of the door, where Lady Granleigh and her party had long since vanished.

"Gossip won't do anything but increase our membership," Robert commented. "We might even get a couple of fellows who'll pay their subscription fees. That would please Austen no end."

"Yes, wouldn't it?" Jonathan said, failing to sound anything like as offhanded as he plainly wanted to. "Very well, we'll do it."

"Good. I have two at my wagon; you can come by this evening and pick one up," Mairelon said. "It's just down the road, on the left-hand side as you head toward the village."

"This evening? But I thought—"

"I have a few things still to do here," Mairelon interrupted, "and it won't be convenient for you to wait. Trust me."

"Yes, and your mother was in an awful taking when I left, Jon," Robert put in. "God knows what she's like by now. She'll have half the county out hunting for you if you don't get home soon, depend on it."

"Oh, very well," Jonathan said ungraciously. He swirled his cloak unnecessarily and stalked to the door of the lodge. "I shall wait upon you this evening," he told Mairelon in portentous tones, and left.

"Silly young chub," Mairelon said, but not loudly enough to be heard outside.

Andrew frowned. "Wait a minute. Didn't somebody say

his horse ran off? How is he planning to get home, wherever home is?"

"Oh, Jon never plans anything," Robert said in a resigned tone. "Except ceremonies. He'll probably take my horse. I think I had better come along with you and Bramingham, after all, Mr. Stuggs. I can stop in the village for as long as you need help with that lot, and then borrow a horse to get home on."

Stuggs nodded and handed him a pistol. "Right, then. Move along, now, you lot."

"I think I'd best go with them, at least as far as the coach," the Earl of Shoreham said to Mairelon as St. Clair, Jack Stower, and Dan Laverham started toward the door, flanked by Robert and Mr. Bramingham. "Two of them are wizards, after all, and it wouldn't do for them to take advantage, so to speak."

"You always were a cautious one," Mairelon told him. "Shall I come and help?"

"No, no, you've done enough already," Shoreham replied quickly. "And it'll only take a moment. You stay here." He followed Bramingham, who was bringing up the end of Stuggs's little procession, out the door.

Mairelon gazed after him with an abstracted air. "Now, do you suppose he was being subtle, tactful, or merely cowardly?" he asked the window Laverham had broken.

" 'E's a-doing of 'is job," Hunch said. "Which you ought to 'ave been, too, instead of breaking into 'ouses and things while I was gone."

"That *was* my job," Mairelon pointed out. "Or part of doing it, anyway, which comes to the same thing."

"You might 'ave got shot," Hunch said doggedly.

"Yes, well, I didn't, so there's no need to go on about it, especially since the main reason you're so nattered about it is that you missed out on the fun."

"Nattered about it?" said Andrew in a puzzled tone.

"It's one of Kim's expressions," Mairelon said. "Very descriptive." He paused, looking at Andrew, and Hunch closed his mouth on whatever further comment he had been about to make. "It's good to see you again, Andrew," Mairelon said after what seemed a very long time.

"It's good to see you, too, Richard," Andrew answered in a low voice. "For a while I . . . wasn't sure I was going to."

"What? You haven't been listening to Hunch, have you? That business on the Peninsula wasn't anything like as serious as he claims."

"I can see that Hunch and I are going to have to have a long talk," Andrew said with a crooked smile. "But that wasn't what I meant."

"Yes, well, actually I know that, but it doesn't matter," Mairelon said quickly.

"It matters to me," Andrew persisted. He took a deep breath and went on, "I misjudged you very badly five years ago, and I want to tell you that I know it now, and I'm sorry."

Renée D'Auber gave a small nod of satisfaction, and a slow grin began to spread across Hunch's face. Kim felt like cheering, but she didn't dare. She was almost afraid to breathe, for fear someone would notice, and remember she was there, and make her leave.

"All right," Mairelon said gently, his eyes on Andrew's

face. "You've told me. Apology accepted. Can we leave it at that?"

"You mean I—you'll—that's all?"

"Really, Andrew, were you expecting me to demand satisfaction?" Mairelon said in the mildly exasperated tone he used with Hunch and Kim. "A pretty thing that would be; you are my brother, after all, not to mention that dueling's illegal. Or did you think I'd throw a fit of temper? I could turn you into a frog for a few minutes, if it would make you feel better, but I'd really rather not. It's the devil of a nuisance to measure out all the ingredients for the powder, and I can never remember the proper endings for the verbs."

Andrew laughed. "I—well, thank you, Richard. Will you be coming home now?"

The words were a question, but his tone made it clear that he expected Mairelon to answer yes. Kim's heart lurched as she realized just how inevitable that yes was, and how much it would mean. The Mairelon she knew was an act, a trick to fool the Runners, and the trick was no longer necessary. He would become Richard Merrill again, and go back to a gentry life she could hardly imagine. She tried to be glad, but all she could think was that there would be no place in that life for her. She wrapped her arms around herself and hugged hard. At least she had the five pounds Jasper Marston had paid her, and the clothes Mairelon had bought. Maybe Mairelon or Shoreham would give her a few guineas more for her help with Laverham. It was as much as she had wanted when she got into this; she couldn't help it if her wants had changed somehow since then.

"Home," Mairelon said, rolling the word as if he were checking its taste. "Not just yet, I think. Until the word gets out, I prefer to lie low. We'll stay here for a few days, then start back to London. Is the old stable still there?"

"In London?" Andrew asked, bewildered.

"No, in Kent. The one we used to climb on the roof of, when we were boys."

"Oh. Yes, it's there. Why?"

"It would be a good place to leave my wagon. I'll send Hunch down with it once I'm settled in London."

"And not before," Hunch put in darkly. "You ain't fobbing me off with no tale this time, Master Richard."

"You're going to stay in London for the Season, then?" Andrew said with an uncertain look in Hunch's direction.

"It is an excellent plan," Renée D'Auber said. "You will be the nine days' wonder, and it will be entirely plain to everyone that you had nothing to do with the robbery."

"I expect I'll have more to do than attend social events," Mairelon said with a hint of sarcasm. "Shoreham is bound to want me for all sorts of things. Which reminds me, there was one other thing I wanted to attend to. Kim!"

Kim jumped and nearly fell off her footstool. "What?" Her throat felt scratchy, and she experienced a sudden desire to run. She knew what he was going to say, and she didn't want to hear it.

"Why did you tip that table over on Laverham when he was in the middle of that spell a few minutes ago?" Mairelon asked.

"The *table*?" Kim said blankly. The question was so completely different from what she had expected that she couldn't quite grasp it.

"Yes, the table." Mairelon looked at her sternly. "I've told you more than once that interrupting a wizard is dangerous, and if you claim you forgot, I won't believe you. So why did you interrupt Laverham?"

"Because his spell was queer as Dick's hatband anyway," Kim said. "You know that."

"Yes, *I* knew it," Mairelon said. "But how did *you* know?"

"It was the words," Kim said. She frowned, trying to think how best to describe what she had sensed when Laverham's spell began to go wrong.

"You speak the Latin, then?" Renée D'Auber said, raising her eyebrows in polite incredulity. "Or the Greek, perhaps?"

"I ain't got no need to speak it," Kim snapped, wondering why they were staring at her like that. "Laverham's words weren't . . . They weren't lined up neat and proper like they should of been."

"Should *have*," Mairelon murmured. "And I did warn you, Kim, about reverting under stress."

"Do not be hard with her," Renée reproved him. "It is not at all wonderful that she should have the difficulties after all that has happened."

"No, the wonderful part was the bit about the words," Mairelon said. "Kim, do you mean that you can feel when someone is casting a spell?"

"I don't know about that, but I can tell when somebody says some of them—of *those* shiny, sharp words you use for spells," Kim replied carefully.

"You mean like *apheteon*? Or perhaps—" Mairelon rattled off a long, bumpy sentence and raised his eyebrows at Kim.

"No," Kim said, happy to be sure of something. "Those sound right, but they don't have no edges. They're just nonsense."

"And these?" He said a short phrase that crackled and glittered.

Kim flinched and nodded. Mairelon stared at her. "My Lord," he said in a low voice. "No wonder you weren't hurt when the spell shattered."

"There ain't nothin' wonderful about *that*," Kim said, staring in turn. "I ducked, that's all."

Renée and Mairelon exchanged glances. "Nothing wonderful about it at all," Mairelon agreed. "For a wizard."

"What?" Hunch gasped. "That Kim, a wizard? She ain't no such thing!"

"Not yet," Mairelon said, smiling. "But with proper training she will be."

"Me?" Kim said, stunned. "Me, a wizard? Me?"

"Ah, bah!" said Renée to Mairelon. "You do not explain at all well, I find, and so you are frightening her." She stepped forward and put a comforting arm around Kim's shoulders. "It is because you can feel the magic, which is a thing very difficult for most people to learn and for some quite impossible. So you have the talent for magic, and now, if you wish, you will come to London and get the training."

"Of course she wishes," Mairelon broke in. "Kim likes London. We'll start the lessons as soon as we've found a house to hire for a few months, and—"

"Richard!" Andrew sounded horrified. "Are you mad?

You can't live with this . . . girl in the middle of London!"

"Really, Andrew, you're as bad as Hunch," Mairelon said. He gave Kim an uncertain, sidelong look that Kim, in her confusion, found impossible to interpret. "I'll make Kim my ward; that will satisfy the proprieties."

"But, yes!" Renée said before Andrew could object again. "That will do entirely well. And you and Mademoiselle Kim will stay with me to begin, and there will be no foolish gossip such as Monsieur Andrew Merrill fears, because I will be there and everything will be proper." She tilted her head to study Kim, ignoring the brothers Merrill.

"It is a great pity we cannot take you to France," Renée went on. "But there is a dressmaker I know who will do well enough, although she is entirely English. You will be quite charming in a gown, I think." Her eyes flickered from Kim to Mairelon and back, and she smiled to herself, as if contemplating a private joke.

"Hold on a minute, Renée," Mairelon interrupted. "I'm not spending hours at some dressmaker's. I refuse. Positively."

"But of course you will not," Renée said gently. "You will be spending hours with Milord Shoreham. He will want the details of all your work, and he is very persistent."

Mairelon looked at her with a blank expression that changed slowly to chagrin. "Oh, Lord, you're right again. It'll take hours. Days."

"Naturally," Renée said. "And while you and Milord Shoreham talk, Mademoiselle Kim and I shall shop for the kind of clothes that will be proper for your ward to wear in London." She turned back to Kim and leaned forward conspiratorially. "But we will save the boy's clothing for other times, because, all the same, Monsieur Richard Merrill is not at all proper and of a certainty you will need them."

"It ain't fitting, Master Richard," Hunch grumbled, but he was not chewing on his mustache at all, and Kim decided he was only complaining for the form of the thing.

"Well, Kim?" Mairelon said. "You do want to come, don't you?"

"Come?" Kim shook herself, thinking *Me, a wizard*!, and gave Mairelon a look full of scorn. "Do I look like a looby? Of course I want to come!"

"Good," Mairelon said, relieved. "That's one thing settled. Now, Hunch, about the wagon—"

He half turned, to include his henchman and his brother in his conversation, and Kim stopped listening. She was going back to London. She'd never have to sleep on the streets again as long as she lived, or bear the cold and the nagging hunger. She had escaped Dan Laverham and the looming shadow of the stews for good. She was going to learn real magic, and not just tricks, but proper wizard's training. She was going to stay with the notorious Mademoiselle Renée D'Auber, who might be willing to teach her a thing or two of a different kind. And she was going to be Mairelon's ward. She wasn't quite sure what that would mean, but it was certain to be interesting. She looked at Mairelon, who was arguing with Hunch and Andrew about the passability of some obscure road in Kent, and shook her head. Interesting wouldn't be the half of it. Slowly she began to smile. After this, anything might happen.

Anything at all.